Poisoned Saints

Ben Coulter

Copyright © 2012 Ben Coulter

All rights reserved.

ISBN:1481099426
ISBN-13: 978-1481099424

FOR BODHI…

ACKNOWLEDGMENTS

Thanks to everyone for their help in getting
Poisoned Saints finished. Lisbet for her patient ear.
My Mother and Father for their time. Susie, for her
time. Anthony Hewson for his editing skills.
Spiffing Covers for their cover design.
And last but not least, all my friends over the years
for the inspiration. You know who you are.

CHAPTER 1

11th November 2011 10:11pm.

Charlie pulled out from between the slender thighs of the gorgeous young woman beneath him rolling over and collapsing his five and a half-foot frame into the space beside her, the sweat from his short black hair saturating the pillow of the oversized bed. He let out a long satisfied moan, and then unashamedly went straight for his still-erect penis. The elasticated snap of rubber, and a smiling glance in its direction, indicated his sperm being safely locked away in their ballooned prison. He then tied a slippery knot and slung it down gracelessly on the floor next to him. He was 28, lean and had the kind of olive tone to his skin that gave away a Mediterranean lineage. He cheekily grinned at the unveiled beauty lying beside him. She gazed up at the ceiling, totally lost in her own thoughts of orgasmic adoration. Her pale skin, wrapped tightly around her petite bones, sparkled with tiny beads of sweat, caught in the moonlight that drizzled through the top floor window of the high rise. His dark brown eyes worked their way up, lustfully, from her delicate red toenails, along the thin veins in her small feet, up her skinny toned legs, to the perfectly trimmed hair above her vagina, where they paused, before admiring her taut stomach muscles and then her impeccably shaped breasts. The 25 year old hairdresser suddenly snapped out of her daydream, noticed his wandering eyes and then flew for the thin duvet, shyly pulling it up over her body to leave only blushing red cheeks, wide eyes and clenched fingers on view. He smiled coolly, fixing his gaze firmly upon her glistening hazel eyes now, impulsively reaching up and running his fingers through her long dark hair in the kind of thoughtless invasion of another's space that only a situation such as this could allow. And allow it she did, with a forgiving, ice-melting smile. That wondrous smile shone in Charlie's otherwise wonderless room.

"Wow; that was definitely worth leaving the boozer early for," he blurted out in his chirpy, Hertfordshire-cum-Mockney accent.

"I should think so too, cheeky git!" Alice replied, in her easy feminine form of the same Cockney counterfeit.

He grinned back like a cheeky schoolboy caught swearing, and then pursed his lips ready to explain.

"Don't worry, I know what you meant, and you're right, it was worth leaving for," she reassured him, with the confidence of that night's alcohol reassuring her too. "My girlfriends probably won't agree though, they'll have the right 'ump with me for leaving them in a Crowley pub, with loads of leering old Crowley men!"

"Oh yeah, what's wrong with Crowley then?" Charlie asked, with a sharp, mock frown.

"Us Aleister girls aren't supposed to be in Crowley pubs, you know that, right?"

"Oh Christ, you're an Aleister girl! Right, get ya things and out ya get," he joked, pointing to the closed bedroom door.

They were referring to the two largest estates in Stambro, the broken-down Hertfordshire town 20 miles north of London. The estates were like two small towns themselves, each on opposite sides of the main centre, and each with their own schools, shops, public houses and an ongoing, bitter rivalry between the respective younger residents.

"You didn't care where I was from a few minutes ago?"

"You could be from Mars with a body like that, and still be allowed in this bed any time, don't you worry," he beamed in response. "In fact, I'd fly to Mars just to get to you."

"No, women are from Venus, men are from Mars, stupid." She replied mockingly, trying to shrug off his compliment with a defensive squint of her eyes.

"Oh yeah, of course they are." He frowned in confusion and reached to the bedside dresser for cigarettes.

He took a tightly rolled, disease-giving stick from a half-empty pack and lit it up, then seized with his other hand a can of lager he'd only managed a few sips from before being dragged into bed. He took a long drag and even longer swig before offering one of each to Alice, both of which she shunned, cringing.

"What's up, you not feeling good?"

"Nah, got work in the morning, that's all," she responded meekly.

"Yeah, what'd you do then?" he fired back,

genuinely interested.

"I'm a hairdresser at Apple Salon in town, I take it you don't have work then?"

"Me?" Charlie smirked. "I don't."

"Don't what?"

"Don't work, especially on a Saturday!" he exclaimed.

"Oh really, how do you afford this place then?" She stared around the expensively decorated room in puzzlement. "Scratching on like all the rest of 'em in this town I'd bet, while all us decent lot work 'ard. Either that or you won the lottery," she added, bitterly.

Charlie pulled himself up angrily and sat with his back to her, then took a big, hard swig of his warm beer before replying, "Listen Alice, I ain't some Stambro chav ya know, I was one of the best footballers this town ever produced. 'Till I fucked my knee up!"

She winced at his mild aggression, noticing she had struck a painful chord, then immediately attempted an apology. "Sorry Charlie, I didn't mean it like that, it was a joke, that's all, just 'cos you said you don't work. But you got this lovely flat with all these lovely things, and that lovely car we came here in." She punctuated her apology by pointing around the room at the flashy electronic entertainment and designer clothes strewn about.

He calmed down and smiled at her, recognising her genuine submission. He gently placed one hand down on her duvet-covered leg, which was now bent up at the knee defensively.

"I do work, just not nine to five like all the other mugs, that's all, and I'm on a good earner too."

"Oh yeah? Well, doing what?"

"Bit of this and that, ya know, nothing special. It's not all above board, but it don't harm anyone either, I'm not a crack-head burglar or anything like that." He turned away again, making it quite clear he didn't want to carry the conversation on any further.

Alice said nothing, and Charlie reached down and grabbed his trousers up off the bedroom floor, pulling out a wallet from the back pocket. He fished out a small clear bag containing some fine white powder. He then proceeded to tip some of the powder onto the dresser next to the half-empty can of beer and overflowing ashtray.

"You wanna nose?"

She looked at him in shocked curiosity as he whipped out a card from the same wallet and started chopping the white powder up.

"Some bag, do you want some bag?"

"Oh no, not for me Charlie, I don't do it." she replied, cautiously.

"Bloody 'ell, I'm starting to think you're in training for a nunnery."

He smiled at her and then quickly thrust his nose towards the dresser and noisily sniffed up a foot-long line.

He paused for a minute, welcoming his high with a sigh and a backward flick of his head, then eased himself back down onto the bed next to her.

"I got my reasons for not doing that crap, why do you do it?" she asked.

"Feels good, don't it? A buzz, but nowhere near as good as the buzz I just 'ad with you."

He lifted himself up on one elbow and in a bid to change the subject, grabbed the back of her head with his free hand, pulled her swiftly towards him, and kissed her soft pink lips firmly and passionately. He held the embrace for a few silent moments, and then drew back, holding her gaze.

"You're fucking beautiful Alice, why have I never seen you before?"

She smiled bashfully in return, and then looked away.

"Dunno, we don't really come over here much I 'spose," she began to explain. "My friend Shell, she's with Freddy Dunn ya see, and if he knew we were over here, she'd know about it, if ya know what I mean... Do you know who he is?"

"I know all the Dunns, and they're all complete and utter wankers." He frowned in hatred, and then quickly grinned at her. "And they're even bigger wankers now, for keeping you from me for so long!"

"I wouldn't let them hear you call 'em that."

He sniggered cockily in return.

"Don't worry about me Alice, they know what I think about 'em all right."

She looked innocently impressed with the open show of bravado towards men she'd been taught to fear. When he noticed this he took the fleeting moment by the horns, quickly swinging in for another fervent kiss, but was interrupted by the aggressive sound of his mobile phone ringing away on the side. He looked at it, annoyed. 'Harry W calling'.

"Shit, I gotta take that. Sorry Alice."

He slid his finger across the touch screen to answer, dropping back on the bed as he did.

"Harry, what's up mate? Better be important." His tone was openly impatient.

"Chill out Charlie, course it's important son, I

don't call you for a fucking chinwag at this time of night, do I!" The response from the other end of the line was cocky and wired.

Alice, curious, listened in. Harry's voice loud enough to be easily heard half way across the room.

"I need a wizard pal, ASAP."

Charlie let out a long, tired sigh, but knew all too well a 'wizard' meant good money, so answered reluctantly.

"All right you fiend, where are ya? And I hope you got the rest of the money with ya."

"I ain't the fiend mate, it's these fucking bag heads. My blower's going off the hook tonight, must be the full moon or something. And don't worry about the money geezer, it's all in hand, yeah."

"Yeah, whatever Harry. So where are you?" Charlie replied sarcastically, knowing all too well Harry was in fact a major league cokehead. A dealer himself, he worked under Charlie, and because of this, had a spiralling debt which had been raging out of control.

"Right, you know London Road, just off the dual carriage way leading to the A1?" Harry explained excitedly, impatiently.

"Sort of, I think so…"

"Right. Go down the dual carriageway and there's a left-hand turn just before you get to the A1, there's one of those little stone markers on the corner, London 20 miles or some'ing. Take that left, that's London Road, then go down it a bit, 'bout a minute, go left again down Drivers End Lane. It's the only turning, you can't miss it, proper little country track," he explained, with the tongue-twisting speed of twelve hurricanes.

"Right, I'm with ya," Charlie lied, confused.

"Okay then, as soon as you turn, turn left again down a little farmer's track that runs alongside London Road behind the hedgerow, and I'll be waiting there."

"Jesus 'arry! Bit covert, ain't it?"

"What, you wanna get pinched Charlie? I fucking don't mate."

"Fair point. Okay I'll be there in about half-hour."

"'Alf-hour, can't you do it any quicker?"

The desperation leaked through the smart phone, and irritated Charlie's ear. They always wanted it quicker.

"No Harry, half-hour, take it or leave it."

"Oh yeah, bet you got some tart round yours, ain't ya?" he mocked in reply.

Charlie looked to Alice, who was still listening in, to make sure she wasn't. But she didn't let it show and smiled back obliviously as she secretly wondered, a little insecurely, if 'tarts' were a regular feature at his glitzy bachelor pad.

"Right, half an hour 'arry, you bell end, and you better bastard be there."

He ended the call, and turned sheepishly back to Alice.

"Did you hear any of that?"

"No, who was it?" she lied perfectly.

"Oh, just a pal I gotta go pick up from the pub, he's drunk and don't wanna drive home." His lie was natural and practised.

"So are you!" She retorted.

"What?"

"Drunk."

"Me? Nah, don't be daft, that line's just sorted my

nut right out, I'm as sober as a judge, I only 'ad a few tonight anyway."

She shook her head in disbelief, but couldn't resist his cheeky charm.

"You can stay here if you want. I won't be long, half-hour tops."

"No, I'd better go, work tomorrow and that," she replied, regretfully.

"Really, I cook a mean fry up and I can take you to work first thing," he half begged, not wanting to lose his newfound goddess to the clutches of the cold November night.

"Nah, I need my clothes and make-up ya know. Gotta get home really, but I can come back round tomorrow," she paused, realising she might have sounded too keen.

"Yeah, yeah, deffo. I wouldn't miss it for all the coke in Columbia!" he instantly agreed, displaying a cool grin on the outside, but feeling a childlike excitement within.

"It's a date then." She beamed back, then leant over and delivered a long, promising kiss.

He lost himself entirely right there and then while committing to her gentle lips, the darkened top floor flat becoming a solitary, flashing beacon of warmth to the haggard town of Stambro below. He pulled away to examine her soul as it shone out a thousand sunrises from behind her glinting hazel eyes; neither spoke a word as eyes filled the tongues' void entirely.

The harmony was suddenly shattered, but not lost, as a buzzing text message from Harry W infiltrated the air.

'c u soon m8'

Charlie winced at reality and reluctantly managed

to pull himself up out of the warm bed and fumble his way back into his casual Friday night clothing. He then walked across the room and switched on the huge flat screen television hanging from the wall, partly to entertain Alice and partly to keep her from following him, or listening in on, what he had to go and take care of in the kitchen.

"Back in a minute, put on what you like," he offered, tossing the remote down gently onto her side of the bed, trying his best to not chase the soothing tranquillity they had just amassed out into the cold winter air. She smiled back locking the tranquillity firmly in place, as she hopped channels lying contentedly in his bed.

Charlie pulled a plastic carrier bag out from the cupboard under the sink of his sparklingly clean, modern black and walnut kitchen, and then emptied its contents onto the side. One set of jeweller's style digital scales, one teaspoon, one piece of folded card, one box of self-seal sandwich bags, and one click-shut food storage container. The tools of his illicit trade. He hooked his head around the kitchen door inquisitively upon hearing MTV, and then quietly continued on with his work, reassured that Alice was happily entertained. He flipped the lid up on the scales, placed the piece of card upon them, and hit the tare button. He then snapped open the food container revealing a rather large boulder of Stambro's finest repressed cocaine. He dug into the boulder with the teaspoon and took a chunk to the scales whose blue digital display read 28.00gms exactly.

"Spot on!" Whispered Charlie jubilantly, pleased that he had successfully and in one well-learned manoeuvre, weighed out Harry's encoded 'wizard', referring to the Wizard of Oz because of an ounce's shorthand form. Code was supposedly used so anyone listening in on the call wouldn't understand what was being discussed, but it was hardly MI6 or CIA level mathematical code. There was a 'Henry' for an eighth of an ounce, as in Henry the Eighth, the less inventive 'daughter', for a quarter of an ounce, and the plain stupid 'dirty bath' for a half ounce. There were plenty of other rudimentary rhymes for drug weights, but these were Charlie's personal favourites. He also didn't ever move anything above a wizard; he made more money that way and any more wasn't worth the risk or time. Also people who bought any more than that in Stambro would then probably end up selling it to the same people he was, and that wasn't any good either. The cocaine, other drugs and the tools used were normally kept at a secret, and well paid for safe house elsewhere in the town. He'd only picked up tonight's brick that morning and got rid of most of it that day, and was being lazy with getting the rest to the intended safe house, breaking one of his own most important rules, which he was doing increasingly often.

He popped the jagged lump into one of the sandwich bags, then into his jean pocket. He then threw all the other pieces of incriminating evidence back in their bag and back under the kitchen sink. He glanced at the Spanish postcard on the wall, and stopped to read the back.

'Dear Charlie, hope all is well, can't wait to see you

at Christmas, if you can get over here (hopefully). Love Mum and Dad xxx'

He smiled, switched off the kitchen light and headed for the bathroom, rolled on deodorant and reorganised his short, messy hair and then sprayed on some cologne before giving himself a highly egotistical grin in the mirror. He then looked down at the basin, with a fanatical glare and complete switch in personality. He turned on the hot tap, and with some water in his hands, proceeded to lather them up with soap, as the steam rose from the water he grabbed a nail brush from the side and begun to scrub. His already sore looking hands becoming bright red, he scrubbed, and scrubbed some more, before he was suddenly startled by another face looking back at him in the mirror, Alice, who was now fully clothed.

"All right pretty boy?" she laughed. "Been in here long enough ain't ya? Don't 'spose I could have a quick wee before we go?"

She looked down to her watch.

"It's quarter to eleven."

"Shit, really? Yeah go on then, but only if I can watch!"

"Oi! You cheeky bugger, out you get!" she joked back, punching him gently on the arm while pointing to the door.

He grabbed a towel from the side and began to dry his red raw hands.

"They look sore, why do you scrub them so hard?"

"I dunno. I'm a bit of a weirdo like that I 'spose."

He hastily threw the towel back down on the side and left her to it, stopping the conversation before it could go any further.

As soon as they left the main entrance of the high rise block, and not a second after, the rain came.

"Bloody typical," Charlie swore as they raced towards his black Mercedes Benz, parked in a disabled-only space.

"Do you like living up there then?" Alice asked as she slammed the car door shut, wiping the rain from her forehead and looking up at the tall, tatty block looming above them.

"Yeah I love it; I can see the whole shitty town from up there." He turned the key and the engine happily purred into life.

"I don't mean to be rude, but I always thought Ambrose Court was a bit of a dump..."

She giggled innocently,

"You're right, most of it is: smack heads, prossies, you name it, all the lowlifes. But they're decent sized flats you know, and if you do 'em up like I have, they're a proper little gaff."

"Proper little bachelor's pad you mean."

"Well, I ain't found the right woman yet have I?" He answered with a sudden seriousness, looking directly into her eyes, as she looked back, spellbound. Charlie's olive cheeks turned a light crimson as he put the car into reverse with a quick change of subject. "He was a saint you know?"

"Who was?" she asked, shaking her head and pulling herself violently out of adulatory daydreaming.

"St. Ambrose, who the block's named after."

"Oh, really? I never knew that," she replied slightly uninterested, preferring the previous subject matter.

"Yeah some Catholic Saint, the whole town's named after him."

"Stambro? How?"

She was a little more intrigued now, and looked left and right for Charlie as he pulled out onto the main road.

"Well, Stambro is just St. Ambrose shortened down. Out there towards the back of your area where the old church is, that used to be the village of St. Ambrose, then the London overspill hit in the sixties, and all this crap went up."

He motioned his head to the cold grey concrete, of the prefabricated houses lining the street, old mattresses and overflowing wheelie bins littered their front gardens.

"Crazy ain't it, to think this place is named after a Saint? He invented the saying when in Rome, do as the Romans do."

"Ironic to say the least. I feel sorry for the original residents of St. Ambrose to be fair, happily living their peaceful little country lives, then our parents turn up, all apples and pears, how's ya father and jellied eels!" she joked, lightening the mood.

Charlie gazed over at her slowly, so she wouldn't notice. She smiled, studying the rundown streets around them. He squinted his eyes with an intense conviction; the kind of conviction a man feels upon finding his ideal catch.

As the blacked-out Mercedes pulled up outside Alice's small two-bedroom house, Charlie checked up and down the empty streets, alert and on edge, as the rain gradually stopped its heavy pounding.

"Don't worry Charlie, this ain't the Bronx, and it's no worse than the Crowley estate, trust me."

"I ain't worried, just don't get on too well with a few boys round here, especially after dark, know what I mean?"

"Who?"

"Well, your mate Shell's other half for one."

"Oh he don't get on with anyone Charlie. None of 'em do; people treat them like the bloody Krays around here."

"Yeah well, if they're the Krays, me and my firm are the Richardsons, Alice." Charlie smirked, oozing male bravado.

"Leave it out will ya? This is Stambro, not the East End," she mocked in return, clearly unimpressed.

"Well, the Richardsons were South London, technically, but I'm only pulling ya leg anyway. I ain't into all that plastic gangster shit, doesn't interest me in the slightest, I just need enough money to retire."

"Well, I've seen them do some horrible things Charlie, especially that Tommy Dunn, he's a loose cannon that one, I wouldn't wanna be on the wrong side of any of 'em, just saying."

Charlie's only reply was a knowing, confident smile. He moved into his beautiful passenger's space for a farewell kiss, she gladly accepted, and they forgot all the talk of violent men and their violent deeds as their passion for one another took over.

"So we still on for tomorrow?" she asked, while fumbling around for the door handle, eyes still locked on his.

Charlie noticed the small, black symbol tattooed

on the inside of her wrist as she finally found the walnut handle. It was a wooden-looking wheel, with spokes, like the wheel of an old steamboat.

"I like that, what is it?" he asked, pointing to the artwork.

"It's the dharma wheel. I had it done it Thailand when I was out there, with bamboo."

"Cool, an actual piece of bamboo?"

"Well no, they don't do that anymore; it's a real needle, sterilised and that, but they do it by hand and hold the needle in a tube of bamboo while they're doing it."

She attempted a demonstration with her hands, poking and prodding his arm.

"Yeah, I see what you mean. So what's the dharma wheel?"

"It's a Buddhist symbol; dharma is the Buddha's teaching."

"So you're a Buddhist?" Charlie asked, bemused. His sarcasm revealed itself on his slightly upturned lips.

"Well, I like the idea of it, yeah. I got into when I was over there, Thailand, on holiday. Went to a temple, read a book, and it just sort of made sense to me, you know?"

"Nah, not really. Buddhism sounds like a weird cult from what I've 'eard, everyone all cross-legged, in robes and that. Weird," he replied, shaking his head as he revealed his ignorance on the subject.

"No, it's not a cult. Loads of people follow it, more over there and that part of the world, but it's not a cult, no way."

"So, what, do you have to pray and that, go to

church?"

"No, it's not like Christianity or Islam, like religion; it's just a way of life, like trying to live a certain way, a better way."

"Like not drinking, smoking and doing bag you mean?" Charlie sniggered, referring back to Alice's earlier rejection of his usually alluring substances.

"Yeah, I guess that would be a start," she laughed back. "But it's your thoughts too, and how you treat others, that kind of thing."

"Okay, fair enough, but what happens if you don't? Do you still go to hell and knock about with Satan, all hot and that?" Charlie asked, a little less sarcastically now, and a lot more selfishly, thinking on his own wrongdoing and how this Buddhism thing could affect him.

"No, there's no god, so there's no devil; you are your own god. If you don't live your life right, you get bad karma, but do good, you get good," she explained, still smiling. Alice was used to people in England, especially in Stambro, being ignorant of the facts of her favourite philosophy. "I see that written on a little wooden boat over there actually, and it kind of summed it all up for me: do good, get good."

"So you must do good things to get good things; I get it, it's nice, but you weren't that good earlier, were ya? That was a bad girl in my bed!" Charlie mocked, pushing her shoulder playfully.

"Well, a girl's allowed a bit of fun, ain't she?" she replied, looking down timidly as she did.

"Of course she is, but seriously, that's a cool thing. If it works for you, then it's cool."

"You don't believe in karma then, Charlie?" she asked, suddenly deadly serious.

He paused while he thought a while. "Well, maybe, but you can't always be nice to everyone can ya? Some people, well, some people are just cunts!"

He burst out laughing, breaking the stern silence, clearly not ready or at a place in his life where he could answer a question like that. She popped open the car door and stuck one leg out, little speckles of rain water running from the door frame and hitting her beautifully firm calf muscle and her black plimsoll shoe. "And on that note," she joked back.

"Yeah, fair point, I better get going, Poor old 'arry will be 'alf frozen by now. I'll probably turn up to see his corpse gripping the steering wheel."

"Steering wheel? Thought he weren't driving?"

Charlie paused to think, to lie. "Yeah, but he'll wait in his motor 'cos the pub's closed, ain't it."

He pointed to the car's digital clock: 11:01.

"Listen Charlie, I heard the conversation and I don't care what you do. It's your life, and I know a good bloke when I meet one, but please don't lie to me anymore if we're going to see each other again and that. It hurts, and I've been in those kinds of relationships before."

"Okay, fair play Alice, I like you, you're a good girl; no more lies from me. I'm only doing this temporary, so I can make enough money to move to Spain and open up a restaurant with my old man. I don't wanna live in this shit hole when I'm sixty years old," he tried to explain desperately.

She smiled at his honesty, nodding in recognition of his desire to get out of Stambro, and then climbed still slightly drunkenly, out of the car.

"So what time you gonna come and get me tomorrow?" she asked, leaning back in and feeling the blood rush to her head in response.

"Dunno, give us your number. I'll call you in the morning, and we'll sort something out." He reached for his phone, and started tapping away. "Shit, I don't even know your second name," he announced, feeling slightly embarrassed of the fact.

She paused, then answered, "It's Liddell, Alice Liddell."

He saved the number and then rang it, so she had his too.

"Well, guess what, I don't know your second name either!" she laughed, pulling her phone out and cancelling the call.

"Mine's Paccadillo."

"Pacca what? What's that, Italian or something? I like it, my Italian stallion!"

Charlie laughed back, the laugh he'd laughed a thousand times before when asked the same question.

"No, it's Spanish. My grandparents came over from Spain in the fifties and my parents actually live back over there now."

"Oh nice, my Spanish stallion it is then!"

"Couldn't you tell from my lovely skin tone?" he joked.

"Nah, I just thought you were one of those sun bed types."

"Sun beds? Do me a favour! I ain't one of those The Only Way Is Essex twats, I'm a proper geezer!" he jibed her, slightly offended.

"Well I'm sorry; I like that programme anyway, so don't worry."

"I ain't worried, 'cos I don't use sunbeds! And they're all two-bob poofs, proper wet bastards!" He shook his head with disgust.

"Okay, calm down! Anyway, maybe you can take me to Spain one day, but for now, I gotta get in. I'm bloody freezing. Look at these!"

She opened her tight leather jacket, alcohol still fuelling her confidence, to reveal her small erect nipples bursting through her thin yellow top.

"I could look at those all day girl!" Charlie cried.

"Well, you'll just have to wait 'till tomorrow, won't ya!"

She winked at him and then slammed the door shut and walked off up the path. Charlie laughed at her boldness, and gently hit his horn to get her attention. She quickly turned around and motioned him with a finger to her pursed lips to be quiet, then pointed to the upstairs window of the house. He put his hands up in surrender and then marvelled at her perfect buttocks as they rose up and down through her tight jeans. She walked with the finesse of a catwalk model. He was smitten and he knew it, but another text from Harry reminded him that he had work to do.

'am hre now m8, drivers end lane, dnt b long, frzing, brrrr.'

Charlie slowly pulled off down the street, still smiling until he recognised the white Range Rover with private plates coming up the other side of the road towards him. 'T0M5Y' was Tommy Dunn's car. Charlie hooked a quick left and sped off at full throttle, checking in his rear view that he wasn't being followed. The cocaine in his system and a glut of Hollywood movies fuelled his not completely misplaced paranoia.

He finally pulled into Drivers End lane and looked at his car clock.

11:13

He pulled off the small country lane and onto what Harry had described as a farmer's dirt track. He drove down a few hundred yards until he could see Harry's car. The Merc's full beams lit the white Honda Civic up as though it was caught in a search light, but he couldn't see inside.

"Where is this pain in my tits?" Charlie murmured to himself aggressively. He pulled his phone out and on seeing a missed call from Harry, immediately called it back. It rang,and rang, and rang.

"Fuck's sake."

He stopped the car from its gentle roll and switched the engine off before slowly stepping out, trying his best to keep the thick mud from ruining his bright white trainers. He headed over to Harry's car, but still couldn't see him inside, or standing anywhere around it.

"Harry! It's Charlie, where are ya, ya fucker? I'm getting shitting frostbite, come on!"

He scanned a quick 360, but saw nothing.

He squelched his way around to the other side of the car, and then saw – and felt, like a stinging slap to the face - Harry's body lying on the floor by the hedgerow; flat on its back, completely motionless.

"Fuck!"

He ran over and knelt down in the sopping wet mud next to Harry. Then he saw the blood. There was a huge, crimson, sticky puddle of it, seeping into the mud around Harry's torso.

"Shit, shit, shit! What the fuck? Harry!"

He reached down and lifted Harry's head from the mud with both hands, staring long and hard into his cold, wet face. But there was nothing, no life, not a murmur.

"Harry, talk to me mate, what? How? What's going on mate? Please fucking wake up!"

Reality kicked in with a wave of lighting white shock. Harry was dead. He scanned the body, searching for an answer, a clue as to what had happened. He could see the blood was coming from the centre of his chest, a wound of some sort, but then he noticed his own hands and jacket were also covered in the blood, and his OCD didn't like that one iota. He attempted to wipe his hands clean, hard on his jean legs, trying his best to get it off. His heart began to race and his head began to sprint in a thousand directions at once. As he continued frantically trying to rub his sore hands clean, he felt the mini-boulder of cocaine still sitting in his pocket, and then gulped in a huge lungful of the freezing November air with sudden panic, thoughts of blue flashing lights and busy policemen flooding his fragile, eggshell mind. He got up and ran, the opposite way he had come, around the back of Harry's car this time, then paused and looked back with a sudden, overwhelming sense of responsibility soaking his soul. Harry wasn't what he'd call a friend, he didn't even really care for him that much - in truth, he had disliked him - but he was a human being with a mother and father all the same. He slowly walked back to the body, and then studied it carefully from above. This time though he noticed Harry's exposed genitals and that was the final nail in the coffin; he ran full speed, miraculously not landing face first in the mud as he did, back to the warm sanctuary of his car. He jumped in, started it up, reversed it back and around slowly, and then quickly stuck it into first gear and hit the accelerator. But the rear wheels, with all their supercharged horsepower, just span like Catherine wheels in the wet dirt.

"Fuck, come on you bastard, not now!"

He hit the accelerator again and again the wheels just span, smoking slightly this time, as the rubber heated the water below. He took his foot off the pedal and breathed in, deeply, slowly, gathering his scattered thoughts. He slid the gearstick into second, and then slowly put the weight of his now shaking foot back down on the accelerator, and with that, the Mercedes played ball, and slowly, but surely, pulled off and away.

"Thank Christ!"

He kissed the steering wheel with grateful elation and drove slowly back down the track, taking one last glance in his rear view at Harry's abandoned car. His elation was immediately replaced with desperation again as reality tightened its cold, sobering grip.

He sped the car up London Road and launched it dangerously back onto the dual carriageway towards Stambro, 120mph clocked on the Mercedes warm red dial. He skidded a left back into town, almost losing the rear end of the car. Noticing an old smashed up phone box to his right hand side, he slammed down hard on the breaks, swerving dangerously onto the other side of the road as he did. He then hammered it into reverse with a damaging clunk, pulled a skilful - turn, and screeched back up the darkened road to the phone box.

"Hello, who am I speaking with please?"

"Err, Jim, Jim Smith."

"What number are you calling from Mr Smith?"

"This number, I dunno, it's a payphone," he replied, panting with panic.

"Okay I have that number sir, which emergency service do you require?"

"Police, ambulance, both."

CHAPTER 2

12th November 12:30am.

Detective Inspector Jack Cloud rolled past the London 20 Miles white stone marker, lazily following his satellite navigation. Suddenly he saw the pulses of flashing blue lights in the distance, like electric angels in the night, and switched off his digital map. He yawned, elongated and dramatically, rubbed his itching eyes and making them water, and then lit up a cigarette. It had been a long and tiresome week already at Beds and Herts Major Crime Unit, one he had hoped was over when he had got into his warm bed that evening, but then he got the murder call to tell him otherwise. He drove gently onto the muddy farmer's track, and slotted himself in next to a flashing patrol car. He reluctantly pulled himself up out of the silver Astra into the chilly dark night. He then studied the scene around him as he stretched his aching bones and focused his tired mind. There were five patrol cars, two ambulances, one paramedic's vehicle, three forensic vans, and lots of busy bodies. One of the bored-looking uniformed male officers, apparently protecting the scene, approached Jack.

"Morning, Jack, couldn't steal a ciggy could I?"

"In the car on the dash, Cooper. Take a couple; it'll be a long night, feller," Jack instructed him generously in his naturally gruff voice.

He was an imposing man at 6ft 2, the sort that silences a room upon entry. People instantly knew what he was about: serious business, no time for jokes. His square jaw line and dark blue eyes screamed authority before his toned arms and wide shoulders needed to. His short, sweeping dark blonde hair added to his handsome good looks. As always when on duty, he was in a dark suit, white shirt and coloured tie, old-school CID uniform.

As he walked closer to the scene, he stubbed his cigarette out on the sole of his shoe and slipped it back in the box. He then ducked under the yellow tape and was greeted by a smartly dressed, petite female: Detective Constable Jenny Pearce.

"Evening Jack. One victim, single gunshot wound to the chest."

"Gunshot?" he responded, suddenly alert and eyebrows rising in anticipation.

"Yep, I know, crazy ain't it? He was dead when the paramedics arrived though, we got a tip-off from a phone box nearby."

Jack watched as much as listened to her explanation: her pretty pink lips sought his approval, her eyelids fluttered over dazzling blue eyes.

"You got enough of that fake tan on? You're glowing brighter than those flood lights. It's even outshining your hair tonight! Jen, you're 29 and a detective now, time to leave the tan out?"

He glared at her as he spat out the uncalled-for rant.

She in turn looked slightly wounded and tried to explain, smoothing down her shoulder-length, bleached blonde hair self-consciously. "I've been out sir, it's a Friday night, and one of my best friends just got engaged."

"Don't tell me you're drunk too, Jen?" he snapped back, just as viciously as before.

"No, of course not sir! I was on call tonight, I'm not bloody stupid!" She raised her voice, clearly and understandably offended.

Jack backed down and smiled uneasily, as if it didn't come naturally to him; his insult had been issued on impulse rather than actual thought.

"Okay, sorry, I'm tired, it's late… So what have we got on the victim then?"

Jenny knew him well, and accepted this as more than enough of an apology and went back to her bubbly self.

"His name is Harry M Whittington."

"Sounds posh?" Jack butted in, with a confused expression.

"No, not at all, guv. Local lad, from Crowley, 28, few previous charges for drunk and disorderly, but nothing major. Nothing that would lead to this."

By the time she had finished explaining, the two had reached the site of the bloodied corpse. Men in white paper, hooded suits and face masks where searching the area methodically for evidence. There were small numbered markers, spread out, marking footprints, blood locations, and a mobile phone. Jack inspected the body from where he stood. Jenny was trying to avoid looking at it, without revealing her nausea. Jack though, was completely unfazed by the gory scene, even as he noticed the coagulating blood that had settled in the thick pubic region around Harry's exposed genitals. As he continued to study the gruesome sight, one of the men in white suits, who had been previously taking photographs, stepped towards and greeted him in an excited, childlike tone.

"Hello Jack. Shooting in Stambro, eh, what next?"

"Evening Barry, doesn't surprise me one bit to be honest," Jack lied, trying to keep his celebrated cool among his peers from breaking into an excited mess. "The amount of stabbings I've dealt with the last couple of years, it was only a matter of time until guns got involved," he finished, shaking his head with an upturned lip and cocky squint of one eye.

Detective Constable Barry Trump nodded back, impressed as always at Jack's calm exterior in the face of hideous criminal acts. He pulled down his paper hood to unveil a bald, round head, and then removed his face mask to reveal a kind, gentle smile, eyes crinkling slightly with the beginnings of middle age. His features and demeanour were a perfect accompaniment to his short, plump stature.

"No, I 'spose you're right Jack, I shouldn't be surprised really, not with the way it is nowadays."

He dropped the smile and glanced back down to the body, shaking his head sadly.

"So what's the situation anyhow, Barry, what happened to the poor sod?" Jack was stern again, getting back to business and sidestepping a long social debate with DC Trump.

"Well, it would appear that he was parked up, here, got out of the vehicle to urinate - that's why he's exposed like that - and someone's come up and shot him in the chest. There's two sets of footwear impressions, only a couple of which are his. Here and here,"

He pointed to some prints in front of the body.

"It looks like he may have stumbled back a couple of steps before falling, probably died fairly instantly though, as there the mud around his body hasn't been disturbed, apart from those prints."

He motioned with his hands excitedly around the scene as he went on, "The shooter knew what he was doing though, that's for sure: straight through the heart by the looks of things."

They both looked back down to the small, apparent entry point in Harry's clothes and the main source of all the messy blood; it was in just left of dead centre.

"You get any shell casings yet?" Jack asked.

"Nope, not a thing. It was either a revolver, or again, he knew exactly what he was doing and retrieved it before he left. I got my guys searching the hedgerow and field for the gun, but I very much doubt we'll find it, Jack."

Jack nodded acknowledgement, then dug some more. "Okay, so what are the footwear impressions giving us?"

"Well, the shooter came from behind. His prints are clearly visible, hardly any of the victim's though, as I say; rain maybe hadn't soaked the ground enough before he got to this spot. The shooter must have got away with creeping up close while the victim was probably on the phone, and, you know, doing his business," Barry paused and pointed to the phone just out of the reach of Harry's outstretched arm.

"Is it soaked? The phone? I need it working," Jack interrupted.

"Not sure about that. It has been rained on obviously, but not a great deal."

"Okay, get one of your guys to get any prints off it, dry it out, bag it up, then get it to my office ASAP, Barry."

"Okay, consider it done," Barry replied dutifully, then continued back with his assessment of the scene, "so to finish up, the shooter somehow managed to get in front of him, maybe they had a quick exchange of words, maybe he knew the shooter. - Your guess is as good as mine on that one at present - Anyway, that's when I think he shot him, once in the chest, and ran off that way."

He pointed at the footprints leading away behind Harry's car. "But then the shooter stopped for some reason, came back, and then off again, in the direction he'd originally come."

"So where did he go then?" Jack asked, impatiently.

"Well, that's where we have a problem. The prints over that side of the car are no good; have a look round you Jack, we have got about forty bodies here, obviously the ambulance guys were careful, but they couldn't see the body straight away, so there was some fumbling about, of course."

"Okay Barry, good work here. I'm gonna take a look around. Make sure I get that phone on my desk though as soon as, please, and as dry as possible, I need it working."

Jack reiterated his request with wide eyes and a pinched forefinger and thumb. He turned and walked away from the body and over towards the other side of Harry's car, beckoning the unusually quiet Jenny, who was still trying to look the other way discreetly.

"DC Pearce, wake up!" he barked.

She immediately snapped to attention and followed her superior.

"What's the matter Jen? You're not squeamish are you?" he pried, mockingly.

"No, not at all, guv," she lied.

He quickly scanned the spread of muddy footprints, soon realising what DC Trump had already told him: it was hopeless. He then spread his search out a bit further and found his way, led by his keen detective nose, around the back of one of the parked ambulances, where its two man crew sat drinking from steaming flasks. He noticed the skid marks immediately and screamed out for DC Trump, who dashed over as fast as he could and stood, as upright and to attention as he could, panting and slightly out of breath from the short run.

"What is it Jack?"

"Here, these skid marks," Jack pointed down to the edge of the ploughed field where the ground had been chewed up by the spinning tyres. "They lead off that way, towards the entrance and I'll bet my life on them being the shooters, get a copy of them straight away, and seal off this area too."

"No problem Jack, right away." Barry lowered his head, clearly embarrassed for not finding the crucial evidence himself. He then jogged off at a sluggish pace, trying not to slip in the mud, back over to the body, where he barked out orders at some of his men.

"Right, we're getting back to the office then Jen, see you there in ten," Jack ordered, heading back towards his car without another word.

"We're going back to the office now guv?" she questioned. Her surprise showing, if not her annoyance at heading to the station at one in the morning on the only day off she was due that week.

"Yes, Jen, this is a shooting, not a bag of smack behind the bike sheds."

He marched off towards his car, without giving her the slightest glance. He was like a dog with a scent, and it would have been wasted breath to try to argue.

Jack leant back in his well-worn black leather chair, feet up on the desk, fingers joined across his stomach, his face a frowning mass of thought. A knock at the door of his small office broke his concentration in an instant; it was Jenny, holding a bag with the phone from the crime scene inside. He looked to his watch: 4:15am. She closed the door, with the name plate Major Crime Unit, and stepped inside.

"Bloody hell, took them long enough, didn't it?" he moaned, as Jenny sat herself down gracefully in the seat in front of him, her slim legs crossed and revealing their perfectly toned lines. Jack pretended not to notice.

"Does it work?"

"Don't know, they just handed it to me and I wanted to bring it straight to you," she replied, nervously.

Jack reached across and took the bag, unzipped the top and took a deep breath. He pulled the phone out, and then paused, looking all around it for an on button. Jenny noticed the embarrassed frown, his face blazing red, and gently took it back from him. She held the on button, discreetly flush with the top of the phone frame, and the phone flashed and buzzed into life. Jack beamed a very rare and very wide smile from ear to ear, but managed to hide it just as Jenny looked back up at him with an even bigger grin.

"Well, that's a result isn't it? It bloody works!"

"You're not wrong, well done Jen," he mumbled, with genuine yet uncomfortable appreciation.

She passed the durable little piece of evidence back over to him, with which he fumbled around some more, toying with its tiny buttons like a baby with its first toy.

"Right, I've got no idea how to work this sodding gooseberry!" he blurted, going even more cherry-red in the cheeks now. He immediately passed it back to her and she did her very best to hold in the building fit of laughter.

"Gooseberry, sir?"

Then she let it burst out, showering Jack in a quick hail of humility, and then immediately reined it back in.

"Whatever it's called… Why can't a phone just be a phone anymore? It's ridiculous. Just go through the call list and text messages, if you can find them, and see who he was speaking to before he got shot."

Jenny flicked through the phone as instructed, knowing exactly where to look.

"Right there's a call from a Charlie at eleven

fourteen pm; that's the last call he received, it never connected. And then a call to Charlie, at nine minutes past eleven; again that didn't connect. Err, a few other names calling him, all missed, then, another call to Charlie at ten thirty-one pm; that did connect, for one minute and nineteen seconds."

"Right go into the texts, look for anything from Charlie." Jack instructed, excited but as ever trying not to let it show.

Jenny pushed buttons and scrolled about. "Okay, here, the last two text messages he sent, both to Charlie, first one at ten thirty-one pm saying 'see you soon mate', next one at ten fifty-nine pm, 'am here now mate, Drivers End Lane, don't be long, freezing', then he's written a 'brrrr'."

Mistaking Jack's silence for confusion, she explained, "As in he's cold, guv."

"Yes, I get it Jen." He frowned back at her, shaking his head. "Okay, Charlie's our prime suspect as of now and until he can tell us different. Go get his number checked out with the phone company and get all the details you can."

She smiled, then repressed a yawn. "Right, will do, sir."

She got up out of the seat and pulled her dress down with an unintentional but highly sexual wiggle of her tiny hips, revealing her tight, firm behind to Jack as she turned around to leave, who now had free rein to stare. And being a red blooded male, stare he did.

Jack started from his semi-doze as his desk phone rang irritatingly loudly. "Hello?" he growled into the receiver.

"Jack, it's your mother," the firm, faux-posh voice explained impatiently.

"Yes, Mum?" he replied, a sigh revealing his opinion of her call.

"Where are you darling? It's six-thirty in the morning! You've been out all night!"

"I'm at work; where else would I be at six-thirty on a Saturday morning?"

"But, all night, sweetie? What are they trying to do to you down there?"

"We've had a big case come in, a murder just outside Stambro," he explained, exhausted and in no mood for the conversation.

"A murder!" she shrieked, at an ear-piercing pitch. "My god, are you okay?"

"Of course I'm okay, Mum, I'm the bloody detective investigating the murder."

"I know, but, are you sure you're all right?"

Jack gazed across his desk to the picture of his mother, happily posing away with his father as they sipped champagne on the deck of a cruise ship, both having the time of their lives in their mid-fifties. His face – and voice - immediately softened as he replied,

"Mum, listen, when Dad died last year, and I agreed to move back in with you for a bit, we set ground rules, didn't we? Do you remember those ground rules?"

"You're my son Jacobe, am I not supposed to worry? What sort of heartless mule do you take me for?"

He could hear the crack in her voice, but lost his

patience. "I'm 36 years old, Mum, this is ridiculous, and I'm very busy, I've got to go, I'll see you when I'm home."

"Fine, fine, I'll see you when you decide to show up then. I'm going to your father's grave today, so if I'm not in you'll know where I am."

He softened once more, and just as he was about to speak, the door opened and in walked Jenny, looking as radiant as she would with a full night's sleep behind her,

"Bad news sir: pay as you go."

"Jack, Jack?"

"Yes Mum?"

"Who the hell's that, Jack? Where are you?" The desperation in her voice, almost gripped at and pulled his ear through the phone, and back to their house now, like a naughty boy caught scrumping in the neighbour's garden.

"I told you, I'm at work. Gotta go, bye Mum." He slammed the phone onto its base and composed himself. Jenny looked uncomfortable. "It's taken you over two hours to bring me that, DC Pearce. Is this a joke or something?"

"No sir, it's not, and quite frankly… " She stopped, bit her tongue and continued, "the offices of the phone company aren't open at this time; I really had to pull out all the stops just to get this."

"Shit, well didn't he register it when he bought the sim card?"

"No, you don't have to. You just walk on in and buy it, simple as that."

Jack looked down at his desk, opened the drawer and pulled out an electronic cigarette, on which he started to puff furiously.

"Okay, get a warrant for a tap on that line now. Text messages, phone calls in and out, voicemail, everything. Also, ask the phone company how the sim card was paid for, if he used a credit card, or if he's ever bought credit for it with a card. I want details, Jen. Oh, and get one of those lot out there to check the system for Charlies with known history in Stambro."

"Okay guv, I'm on it."

"I know you're tired Jen, but this is what we do. This case could get you up to sergeant if you play it right." Motivational speeches weren't Jack's strong point, but he knew all too well how a persuasive point could make all the difference.

"Thanks sir, and I'm not tired now, I got my second wind I think." She smiled at him, trying her best to impress.

"Well done, Jen. Let's catch this bastard."

She nodded her acknowledgment and ducked out the door, poking her head back round again almost before she'd disappeared from sight.

"By the way, guv, DCI Brent just came in and asked for you."

"Great, tell him where I am then, Jen."

She went to answer, but stopped in shock as the door was pushed open out of her grasp.

"Morning, Jack."

In walked Detective Chief Inspector Malcolm Brent, his long thin body striding towards the chair, where he ran his fingers through his grey side parting and took a seat.

"Morning, sir," Jack replied.

"I'll leave you to it," Jenny announced and she closed the door behind her.

Malcolm Brent was the head of Stambro's Major Crime Unit, and Jack's boss. He had an air of royalty about him, and half believed he was, from his days as a young man back at Eton College. He had a long pointed nose, which stuck up in the air when he talked; it seemed a ludicrous mockery of the stereotype of this kind of man, but it did it all the same.

"So, a blasted shooting eh? The animals have evolved another step, or regressed, as the case may be, but whichever way you look at it Jack, it's no ruddy good, and it's the last thing this department needs." He stared at Jack, awaiting a pleasing response.

"I know sir, but rest assured we're on the case, and we will find the shooter."

"What leads do you have so far?"

"Well, we've got a name and a phone number of the possible shooter from the victim's phone, and I'm waiting on the pathology department with autopsy results for the bullet, and also forensics with some footwear impressions, blood samples, and tyre tracks."

"Oh, jolly good. Well, I've got the main details of the incident on my desk for the family death call, and coming press report, so I'll include the fact we're currently pursuing a suspect, see if we can't flush the little bugger out," he laughed, as if he were hunting a fox, dressed in a red jacket on the back of a galloping country horse.

"Sounds good to me sir. I'll let you know of any updates as they happen," Jack replied submissively, and then with an honest but boastful declaration, assured him, "we will find him. It's just a matter of time, and some good old-fashioned police work."

CHAPTER 3

12th November 12:20pm.

Charlie sat bolt upright on the edge of his pristine black leather corner couch, a cup of steaming tea clenched in his hands, dressing gown on, curtains drawn, awaiting the local news. Anxious for it to broadcast its way into his front room via his 50-inch plasma screen and the huge black speakers standing repulsively beside it.

'This is BBC Look East, and now for today's top headlines.'

He tensed up, rested the cup down on the black wood, glass-topped table in front of him, and reached for a pocket-sized hand sanitizer instead, a look of unnatural dread chiselled into his handsome young face.

'A man was found shot to death in the early hours

of this morning, in a field located on the outskirts of Stambro. The victim has been identified as Harry M. Whittington of Sollershot East, also in Stambro. DCI Brent of Herts and Beds Major Crime Unit said they were following up on a number of leads, and are pursuing a suspect. He also expressed his condolences to the victim's loved ones, with a stern promise they will be working around the clock until the suspect is brought to justice. More news on this as it comes.'

Charlie rubbed the bacteria-eliminating alcohol through his fingers and palms with a manic ferocity. His eyes remained glued to the screen, but the sound had gone, his mind being taken over with the violent crashes of feverish, paranoid thoughts, until his phone resonated louder than they could and startled him back into the real world... Che calling.

"Charl," the slow, sedated voice mumbled down the line, "I swear I just heard them say Harry's been shot and killed on the news? Now either it really is time to give up smoking or, well, or I actually saw it, the thing I just said... are you with me?"

"Yeah, Che, I'm with you. Believe me, for once I'm fucking with you."

Che was one of Charlie's four-man crew and an expert in all things drug related.

"What's up Charl? You sound... unusually panicked."

"He is fucking dead, Che. I was there... Get round mine now mate, can't say too much over the blower." Charlie panted away, rubbing his free hand dry of sanitizer on his jean leg.

"Riiiight, with you Charl... say no more man. I'll be up in a bit, gotta take Jonny to the vets first, scratching his ass all over the carpet again, Mum's going nuts," he replied, blasé as ever.

"Che, are you fucking winding me up mate? Fuck your mum's dog and his poxy worms, get round here now!"

The phone beeped abruptly in his ear and he pulled it away to read Billy Marine Calling.

"Che, I gotta go, just get round here mate, now!"

He tapped his finger on the screen, answering the incoming call and cancelling the genuinely bemused Che.

"Billy."

"Charlie, you heard the news mate?" the stern, bass-ridden voice demanded.

"Where are ya' Billy? Need ya' round here pal."

"Just got out the gym. So have you heard the news? Everybody's talking about it, Harry's been shot, last night. It's fucking mental son, did he still owe that money?"

Billy's pitch rose to a slight baritone now in excitement, but still too heavily affected by long-term steroid abuse for there to be any real difference.

"I was there Billy. No more over the phones though, eh? Just get round 'ere and I'll tell you everything."

"Fuck me, right. On the way, Snow, ten minutes tops," he paused, "You didn't fucking do 'im did ya, with that thing from London?"

"Not over the phone Billy!" Charlie demanded, putting more authority into his voice.

"Understood mate, understood." Billy replied, backing down to his benefactor.

"I need you to pick up Knighty too," Charlie instructed, still panting and now wiping his other hand clean on his jeans.

"Is the lazy cunt up though? I ain't hanging round, I know what he's fucking like."

"I dunno Billy, just sort it would you please mate? I'll see you in a bit, yeah?"

Charlie ended the call and threw the phone, along with all its irritating questions, down on the couch next to him. He then swiftly made his way to the kitchen where he cracked open an ice-cold can of lager, taking one mammoth guzzle and simultaneously chopping out an oversized line from his cocaine boulder, the beer bubbles finding their dizzying way to his rickety brain. And then whoosh, the white powder scorched up his nose, as he threw his head back like a forgotten child movie star, more for the dramatics of his own constantly rolling personal movie than an actual high. He then noticed his desperate reflection looming back at him from the reflective surface of his American style chrome refrigerator, as he opened it up, reaching for another unnecessary lager.

"Fuck, I got to sort me nut out," he declared to himself anxiously.

He grabbed another cold beer all the same, drained the other one and tossed it into the shiny chrome bin, and then ritualistically washed his hands in the steaming water of the shiny chrome kitchen sink, rubbing them red raw with a tough nail brush. He dried them even more obsessively with a fresh black hand towel, which he then dropped on the floor next to the glistening black washing machine before making his way back to the living room, grabbing the fresh can of lager in one clean hand and the ominous materials for a serious cocaine binge in the other.

After a twenty-minute, weak attempt to clear his

head which consisted of getting out of his dressing gown and changing into his expensive designer clothes, and which didn't work, he opted for some music, and some more drugs. Flicking through the row of compact discs on the black shelf above his gaudy entertainment system, his attention was nostalgically grabbed by football trophies which sat above them: *Stambro FC* under 15s player of the year, *Stambro FC* under 18s player of the year, *Stambro FC* player of the year, then the framed letter for acceptance into West Ham United's reserve team, then a long empty space, with only a handful of *Tottenham Hotspur* home game tickets to fill the void. He chugged back a fresh lager with the abandonment of an alcoholic, forcefully withdrawing his dejected gaze from the once-proud trophies. He pulled out a pre-made trip-hop mix from the messy music collection, hit the eject button on the CD player, the whole system lighting up in a cosmic explosion of blue lights as he did, then slid the disc into the drive. He turned the volume up five notches more as the droning melodies kicked in, engulfing the room in a sultry blanket of heavy bass lines. He took to the couch once again, where he crushed a lump of the hard cocaine ball into a neat pile of powder. With the aid of a tea spoon and credit card he shaped the powder, with skilful speed, into a line across the glass-topped table, and then hunched himself over it, rolling up a £20 note. The ambient trip-hop bounced off the darkly painted walls as he stuck the note into his left nostril, aiming it with a careful and exact 45 degree slant, to the beginning of the lengthy white line. Then boom, the powder disappeared in an instant, and he whipped his head back, Hollywood style again, closing his eyes and falling back into the soft embrace of the black leather couch. His mind soared way above the 17th storey flat and up into the grey November clouds. Then higher still, into the blue stratosphere beyond. He hovered there, weightless and free, as an ideal flashback of a football pitch entered his eggshell mind: Stambro FC, he shoots, he scores, goal! The whole team run as one to lift him up in the air, as the crowd cheer. Then bang. He crashed back down with a violent thud, as he opened his eyes and glared at the ugly Artex ceiling. Looking for the pre-imagined blue skies he realised painfully, that reality was right there in his front room: the drugs, the drink, the murder.

"Bollocks!" he snarled through gritted teeth, as he reached for his cigarettes.

His phone unexpectedly lit up with a text message, launching him to another reality all together: one that included other people, and not just him and his shattered ego. Alice. He quickly snapped out of his coke-fuelled angst, as her dazzling hazel eyes smashed their way into his grey, freezing heart, he opened the message.

'Hey Charlie, hope we're still on 4 2night?.. Quite excited ;)'

He hit the call back option without a moment's hesitation, and clicked the stereo remote to hush the pounding trip-hop tune.

"Hi Charlie!" Alice exploded eagerly down the line. "I'm just on my lunch, what you up to my Spanish Stallion?"

"Alice," he asked, the panic seeping back into soul, and so his voice.

"Yeah, who else, dummy?"

"Have you heard the news?"

"What," she paused to think, "the shooting? Yeah, everyone who's been in has been on about it. It's the talk of the town, why?"

"Remember I was going to meet my mate Harry after you?" he explained hurriedly.

"Yeah, sort of, I was a bit tipsy, but yeah," she replied, curiosity raising the pitch of her voice.

"It's the same Harry who got shot last night, Alice."

"Oh my god!" she cried, then paused, "let me go in the toilet, I'm with my work mates."

Charlie proceeded to chop out another line as he waited for her to find privacy.

"Okay, I'm in, please don't tell me it was you, Charlie?"

"Of course not Alice! Fucking hell, who do you think I am?"

"Well, I don't really know, do I? I only met you last night."

"Yeah, but we had something special Alice, something I've never had before. You know I wouldn't do that, don't you?"

"I guess so," she replied, the polar-opposite mixture of trust and paranoia lowering her tone.

"Good, I'm glad."

He lit the waiting cigarette he'd pulled before the phone call, and took a soothing drag.

"So, what happened? Did you see anything?"

"Yeah, I was there, but I can't talk about it over the phone."

"Why not?" she asked, naively.

"In case anyone listens to this conversation."

"But you didn't do anything wrong. Why would it matter, and why would anyone be listening to our conversation?"

"Listen, I'll explain everything when I can, but not over the phone. You just gotta trust me," he insisted.

"So you still gonna come get me tonight?" The excitement quivered back into her voice, and he paused to answer.

"I doubt it, got a lot of shit to sort out. Talk to my pals and that. But believe me it's not out of choice; I really, really wanna see you."

"That's fine Charlie, I completely understand," she replied, as the excitement took a running jump down the toilet on which she sat.

"Honestly, Alice, you gotta believe me. I really like you. I'm not messing around here, but this thing, it's just come out of nowhere you know, messed my head up a bit," he explained with complete sincerity, hearing her dejection. "You're not working tomorrow, are you?"

"Sunday, nah, they're not that bad here, but I got a family thing I gotta do," she explained regretfully.

"You gotta go?"

"Yeah, 'fraid so, Charlie, wish I could see you but this is family."

There was a sudden and insistent thudding coming from the flat door.

"Shit, I gotta go Alice, someone's at the door. Listen, Monday then, yeah?"

He panicked, hoping it was Billy and not the police hammering at the front door.

"Okay Monday, yeah cool, it's my day off," she agreed without hesitation. "Please be careful until then Charlie, I don't wanna lose my Spanish Stallion already."

"And I don't wanna lose you, Alice; you're the

only thing that's felt real in a long time."

He hung up the line and stubbed out the cigarette.

He opened up the door as Knighty's long arm went to knock again. Knighty stopped mid-flow and strolled on in as he would have done at the home of a close family member, no need for invitations. His grin exposed freshly whitened teeth shining like stars in the night against his cinnamon mixed race complexion.

"Wassup bruv, the fuck you been up to? Last I saw, you was off with that sket, now big bad Billy Marine tells me you merked someone, da fuck?" Knighty screeched in his usual high-pitched, excitable tone. As his long thin frame waltzed through the entrance it revealed the short but muscular explosion that was Billy Marine behind him.

"I said shot, not merked, now get inside before the whole fucking floor 'ears ya. Cunt."

Knighty swung his lanky body around, his large diamond earring glistening in the light and began delivering joke body shots to Billy, his oversized, flashy silver wrist watch sliding back and forth with each jab. Billy angrily launched one of his tree trunk arms into the air, and grabbed Knighty around the neck, pulling him down into his waist and into a headlock position, the muscles bulging through the black tattoos which laced his forearm and biceps as he did. No matter how cold it was outside, Billy had a Lacoste polo top on, cum rain, sleet or snow.

"Don't make me snap your scrawny little neck Knighty!" he threatened, smiling wider with each squeeze.

"Right, sort it out you two - the neighbours!" Charlie panicked, pushing past them and closing the front door.

Billy released Knighty, who immediately began to worryingly scruff at his short afro hair. It hadn't moved an inch from its original neat styling, but he was a vain, self-proclaimed ladies' man who kept a constant eye on his appearance, wherever he was and whoever he was with.

Billy had no such problem. His short black hair, was cut in a military style cut, which complemented by the large scar under his eye and his thousand-yard stare, gave him the ex-Royal Marine look he was most definitely after. He strode on through to the living room, almost shaking the pictures off the wall as he did.

"Fuck's sake Charlie, bit early, ain't it bruv?" Knighty bellowed upon seeing the cocaine-dusted table and empty beer cans.

"Not after the fucking shit that happened to me last night." Charlie chirped back in his usually mockney tone, the banter, and sheer presence of two of his best friends lifting the weight from his shoulders.

"Right, what 'appened?" Billy growled while helping himself to a line of the cocaine.

"Well if everyone's getting on it, rack me up one too, big boy." Knighty instructed Billy.

"This ain't party time, lads. Harry was shot dead, and something's gone seriously wrong," said Charlie, becoming slightly edgy again.

"Stop being prang, bruv, we're all in this together yeah? One for all and all dat business."

Knighty reassured him, putting his long arm around him and squeezing tight with loyalty.

Charlie eased up as Knighty sat down for his line.

"Who wants a beer then?"

"That's the spirit, blad," Knighty replied in his mock street accent.

"Right I'll get 'em in, then tell you all about it."

Charlie leapt off to the kitchen, happy to have his friends and their support close at hand, where he needed them most.

Billy crushed his third empty beer can as if it were a human skull. "It's those fucking mugs the Dunns, I'm telling ya. Two-bob Aleister cunts, we gotta hit 'em back, tonight!" he boomed, as if the small room's subwoofers were connected directly to his vocal chords.

"I'm going with Billy, bruv, who else could it be?" Knighty agreed.

"Yeah, but why shoot Harry and not me? Why do it before I got there, and how the fuck did they know we were meeting there? We've never met there before" Charlie aired all his bottled-up concerns.

"They did it as a message." Billy pushed knowingly, sitting up on the black leather couch, "They took out one of our top earners, to try and show us who's boss, and I for one ain't having a slice of that 'umble pie. I'm cracking skulls tonight!"

"But why not wait and shoot me Billy? Why take Harry when they could have me?"

"Maybe they wanted you though init, fam" Knighty joined in, "but got him first, then shit it and done the off, get me?"

Charlie paused, rubbed his temples, drank some more beer, then answered, "Okay, so say all this is the case, it was them, they done Harry and left, fair enough… how did they know we were meeting there?"

Charlie's puzzled colleagues both paused to think, drinking, frowning, and then Knighty spoke up first.

"Well, either 'e told someone where 'e was going, that then told dem, or you did. Did you?"

Charlie froze for a moment, thinking of Alice, but there was no way… why would she? No way. He didn't bother to even mention it, until,

"What about that slut you took home last night, the Aleister gal?" Knighty asked, suspiciously.

"No way, and she ain't a slut. How did you know she was from Aleister?"

"'Cos of that sket with her; Shell or smell or some shit. She's Frankie the fool Dunn's woman," he explained.

"Hold on, what you two yapping on about?" Billy interjected, bemused.

"If you would have been out last night, you would have known, Billy," Charlie replied, bitterly.

"Yeah, well, I had a bit of business, like I said."

"What business?" Knighty quizzed him.

"My fucking business shit cunt! Now, what bird are you on about?"

"Aleister girls in the pub last night. Charlie took one 'ome, didn't he? Proper sort too."

"Yeah, I did, but I took her home before I met Harry, shit, tried to meet Harry. Fuck, I dunno," he blurted out as he lined up some more white powder, his thoughts becoming jumbled with confusion again.

"Did you tell her where you were going?" Billy asked, as he started to get up,

"Where's she live, this 'sort'? We need to go and

have a little word in her shell-like."

"Listen, just leave her out of it. She's a nice girl and I really like her, and she didn't have a clue where I was going, or who I was before last night," he lied, before sniffing his 10th line of the day.

"Are you for real bruv? You reeeealy like her?" Knighty mocked him in a soft, feminine voice. "You gone soft or some'int?"

Charlie shot up from the couch, the cocaine speeding his motions to a double pace, and launched himself over to Knighty. He grabbed the scruff of his black button-down shirt.

"I ain't gonna fucking tell you again, leave 'er out of it!" he screamed as he stuck his finger forcefully into the shocked Knighty's face.

Billy jumped across and pulled him back, then forcefully sat him down in his seat again.

"That's enough, you pair 'a wankers, that's all we need, to start scrapping each other. Save it for the fucking Dunns; they're the enemy. If we ain't got each other as a unit, we've got nothing." Billy informed them, his Royal Marine training ever-present.

Charlie relaxed and then nodded his head at Billy in agreement.

"Sorry Knighty. I'm just well stressed pal; this whole thing, it's twisting my nut up, mate, you know?"

"I'm sorry too, bruv. I shouldn't take the piss, init. You seen a man dead at your feet last night for fuck's sake."

He got up and walked over to Charlie, straightening out his shirt, then lent down and gave his friend a big, genuine hug. Charlie hugged back, the cocaine and alcohol making them embrace closer than they would sober, by a long mile.

Billy looked on, unimpressed. "Easy, I didn't say start sucking each other's cocks, let's plan the counter-attack!"

He split them up and shoved Knighty back down in his seat, before standing bolt upright to begin hatching his military-style plan. "I say, we get camo'ed up, head to toe…"

"Hold on, where the fuck is Che?" Charlie interrupted him, sniffing the runny snot caused by the burning powder at the back of his nose as he checked the clock on his phone.

"It's four 'a fucking clock!"

"He's taken the dog to the vets or some shit; spoke to 'im earlier. He said he told ya," Knighty replied.

"Jesus Christ, that fucking geezer, sometimes I could…" Charlie motioned a throttling effect with his hands as he picked up the phone and dialled Che.

"Where are ya, Che?"

"Just left the vets, dude, on the way to yours now. Chill out man, you sound all tense and that. You'll never guess who I saw in there."

Someone tapped the front door to the familiar rhythm of Kumbaya My Lord.

"Get that will ya, Knighty, it'll be Che. He always does that fucking annoying tap, right up until I answer it, he won't stop." Charlie shook his head as he cut out three fresh lines.

Knighty got up as he was told, and headed for the door.

"Get a fresh round of beers too, son," Billy instructed him, then turned to Charlie to add humbly, "If that's all right, of course?"

"Fucking course it is, don't be stupid Billy."He replied, generously.

Kumbaya continued to be tapped into the front door, until Knighty jogged a bit to stop it.

"Hello Sir Lancelot, how goes thee, fair prince?" exclaimed Che as he breezed through the door, referring to Knighty's surname and nickname.

A strong cloud of marijuana smoke swept in with him from the joint blazing away in his fingers, his long, greasy, Jim Morrison-esque hair flowing with every step, catching slightly on his thick beard as it did. He passed the smouldering spliff to Knighty, who gladly accepted, then continued on to the lounge. He removed his leather jacket and tossed it onto the hallway floor, revealing a Neil Young gig T-shirt underneath. He kicked off his pointed black leather shoes, revealing white socks which clashed horribly with his skinny black jeans; jeans that fitted a tiny bit too tight due to a few too many late nights of stoned 'munchies'.

"Hello, hello, hello! Are they class 'A' drugs I can see, strewn across this fine looking kitchen table?" he asked coolly, in his slow, drawn out style, waving a hand in slow motion across the table while trying to find a seat next to the bulky Billy Marine.

"Oh, here he is," Billy growled up at him. He shifted over to make room on the sofa.

Charlie looked up from his drug-cutting duties, which he was taking a ridiculously long amount of time to perform. He was unimpressed.

"Che, you're in the lounge mate, not the kitchen. Now where the fuck you been? On the phone I told you..."

"I know what you said on the phone Charl, but

Jonny needed his ass sorting out. It was a matter of extreme urgency as I told you."

"Who's Jonny?" Billy bellowed into Che's cringing face.

"The dog," Charlie explained, shaking his head.

Billy continued to glare at Che, faces mere inches apart, the disappointment at this poor time-keeping made very clear.

"So my finding a dead body - Harry's dead body - wasn't a matter of extreme urgency?" Charlie interrogated him, still somehow chopping at the powder.

"Well, that had happened. He was dead. The sense in rushing was what?" Che quite fairly pointed out, while trying to pretend Billy wasn't still boring a hole in the side of his head with psychotic, bloodthirsty eyes.

He pulled out his joint-rolling equipment from his tight jeans pocket as Knighty came back in with the fresh lagers and handed them round. Knighty then headed over to the entertainment area, a change of music in mind, as the marijuana crept into his thoughts. Che tried, to no avail, to roll a fresh joint, Billy's continual glare setting his delicate nerves on edge.

"Billy, man," he slowly turned to him. "Enough with the marine sergeant shit. I can't skin up dude, you're fucking freaking me out!"

Billy squinted his eyes and shook his head in disgust, then looked away. "Filthy fucking 'abit, wouldn't last a minute on an 'op' smoking that shit."

Charlie belted out the previous night's horror story with cocaine-quickened speech, to Che's amazed and pleasantly stoned ears.

"Wooooh, that is fucking out there, Charl. I've always wanted to see a dead body," he replied, enviously.

"It ain't all that, mate, I can tell you. I'm not hoping to see one again in a hurry, 'specially not a someone I know, or knew."

"Harry was a cunt, let's be honest," Billy butted in. "I saw a dead body in nick once."

Everybody yawned mockingly, as they always did when Billy started another prison story. Charlie quickly interrupted him to quiz Che again, who had just lit up a fresh joint.

"So who did you see earlier, at the vets?"

"Oh, the Dunn brothers, up there with one of those horrible little staffs. I hate those things. And some new dude, not seen him before, bit of a big bastard man, fucking arms like this, man, bigger than Bill's," Che explained slowly through a cloud of smoke, while exaggerating a set of human arms with his hands. Billy looked furious at the muscle comparison.

"I was gonna call them all wankers, you know, fucking let 'em know what I thought, but the vet called me in."

Everyone rolled their eyes at this blatant fabrication. The Dunn brothers weren't the sort of men that men like Che call wankers. Not to their faces anyway.

The Dunn brothers were Tommy, Micky and

Freddy. All three complete and utter sociopaths, and each one fully committed to the Stambro criminal underbelly.

Tommy was knocking on the door to his thirties, the toughest and eldest of the Dunns. He had a face full of scars, each one telling a vicious tale, trademark curtain styled, curly black hair which looked permanently wet, and a muscular six-foot frame which was covered in badly designed ink work. You could argue he was old enough to know better, but there was no turning back, he was what he was. An animal. A vicious animal that got where he was by biting the head off any other animals that got in the way on his bloody rise to the top. He was also the king of the Stambro cocaine trade, until Charlie and his firm came along, of course.

Then there was Micky, hurtling his way through his mid-twenties with the aid of a serious drug habit which consisted of any drug he could get his grimy hands on, which could only have contributed to his undiagnosed but frighteningly self-evident psychosis. He was half a foot shorter than his elder brother, and carried a little pot belly. His stocky yet out of shape frame was illuminated from above by scruffy, bleached blonde hair. He was known for being fond of carrying a blade - not to stab, just to cut. He'd apparently cut up a lot of people in his short life, although though no one was too sure of the figures, or if they even believed all the rumours doing the rounds in Stambro. But one thing was for sure, nobody wanted to test him to find out.

Last but not least, and only just recently strutting boldly into his twenties was Freddy. More of a ladies man than his elder brothers, which could be attributed to the fact he was Tommy's height, made of pure lean muscle, and also the best looking of the trio by a long mile. Freddy based his style on the modern Essex fad: short side parting, espadrilles, chinos, tank tops, vests; the works. And the girls fell for it hook, line, and sinker. The pretty boy style or young age never got mistaken for softness by people who knew him though. Only his brothers dared to mock, but he was as game as either of them when it came to a confrontation, which had already gained him a fierce reputation about Stambro and the surrounding areas. To top it off, he had his finger on the pulse of the younger generation, a great advantage when it came to selling them drugs.

"So who's the new bloke with 'em then?" Charlie asked.

"Dunno man. Huge bastard, like I say, arms bigger than," he looked worriedly at the now red-faced Billy.

"Yeah, we heard that bit Che, anything else you can think of?" Charlie stopped him, before Billy could.

"Yeah, actually there was."

He rubbed his oily beard, as he took an epic-sized lug of his slowly smouldering joint, held the hot smoke deep within his lungs for what seemed like an inhuman amount of time, and then blew half of what he'd appeared to inhale, with a deeper grey to it now, back out, swamping the room with its potent aroma. Billy waved it away angrily from his own sacred area on the couch.

"He had a great big swastika tattoo on his forearm. I remember thinking, is he a Hindu, a Buddhist, or just a fucking Hitler worshipping fag, man."

Che laughed at his own 'joke', which prompted a tar ridden coughing fit.

"So you had time to check out da man's tatts, but not call him a wanker, Che, yeah?" Knighty mocked. He was turning up the stereo, pumping out his choice of 1960s northern soul, to which he then danced around like a Mod on a floor of talcum powder, singing along as he swigged back his beer.

"I would you call you a 'twat' Knighty, but you just redeemed yourself with this little number," Che informed him, nodding his head to beat, his long slippery locks dancing atop his shoulders.

Charlie cut up more cocaine, four lines now, and four big lines at that.

"Hold on!" Billy suddenly gasped, nearly choking on a mouthful of beer. He grabbed at Che's unsuspecting arm, causing Che to jump half out of his skin, like a scared fox as the hound caught his neck.

"This tattoo, was it on his left forearm?"

"Yeah man, how'd you know that?"

"It's Lee Frost, or Frosty as the complete and utter prick likes to be known. Frosty the fucking snowman I used to call him."

"Who is he, Billy?" Charlie asked, sniffing up a huge line and passing the note to Knighty, who was still wearing holes out of the carpet.

"I was in the nick with him. Him and that mug Tommy Dunn were celled up together, he must have just got out. He'd been in for fucking years, used to tell everyone it was for murder, but I had my doubts about that one to be honest with ya. Doing ya bird in a C Cat for murder, don't think so."

Billy explained disdainfully, his voice almost as low in tone as Knighty's bassy soul numbers thudding away in the background.

"Wait a minute!" said Charlie, putting the pieces together in his drug-fuelled mind. "Che, you're telling me the Dunns have a new geezer bowling about with 'em, and Billy you're telling me he's just got out of prison for murder?"

"Fuuuuuuck dude," Che cried out.

"You think it was 'im, last night, that done 'arry?" Billy asked, eagerly.

"That makes sense ya 'naa," Knighty joined in.

"Right, that's it, they're gone. Tonight. I'm gonna open 'em up like a can of fucking sardines!" Billy jumped up out of his seat and started shadow boxing, his school boy title, and naval wins shining through the years of heavy steroid abuse, as his arms popped back and forth as if they were dandelions in a summer's breeze.

"I'm gonna fucking eat 'em, tear 'em, rip 'em, shit 'em!"

He threw a different combination of punches for each violent threat. The room looked on in wide-eyed humour, mixed with a touch of well-placed fear, not saying a word, just letting Billy be Billy as he stormed over to the entertainment area,

"Out the way, Knighty!" he commanded, shoving the lanky dancer aside.

Knighty didn't put up any resistance; he knew better. Billy flicked his way destructively through the previously neat CD collection, as Charlie winced at the disrespect for all things chronological. He ripped out what he was looking for, and then shoved it into the CD deck, almost putting it through the wall and slinging Knighty's choice down on the floor as he did. The 80s synthesized keyboards and drums kicked in from Tina Turner's *The Best*. Everyone in the room giggled quietly, like naughty children, but keeping their eyes firmly on the madman that was Billy Marine. He shadowboxed away, each jab in time with the next synth beat, singing along, having the time of his life, the thoughts entertaining his irate mind. Not for the faint-hearted.

Billy Marine had earned his second name locally when he had joined the Royal Marines at the tender age of 16. He was the kind of man who was born to be a Royal Marine Commando, to wear the green beret; he was fit and in shape from his years of childhood boxing, and breezed through the basic training without a hitch. Much to the joy of his superiors he then also breezed through the infamous commando course. He should have had a promising career in the Royal Navy and his dream of becoming a member of the elite SBS was never in doubt, until one ill-fated night while away on a training exercise in Norway. He and a fellow marine, Eddie Vincent, who had been a solid friend to Billy throughout his naval career, just so happened to suffer minor frostbite to the fingers at the same time. They were sent back to the barracks for two days' sick leave. Billy's 20th birthday had been the week before, but as they had been stuck in an arctic igloo, urinating in a water bottle at night and using it to keep warm, he hadn't had the chance to celebrate the birthday. So, the pair decided to get drunk back at the barracks, and celebrate Billy's 20th a week late. One thing led to another, as it often would when the pair of young marines and alcohol mixed, and before they knew it they were stupidly taking a joyride in a battalion Land Rover. Billy took to the wheel as they thrashed it down the dark country roads, which were stricken with black ice. Being extremely drunk on cheap whiskey, and not his usual ultra-observant self, he'd taken to driving on the left side of the road, thinking he was back in England, and the incorrect side for Norway. One oncoming car, an icy swerve, and a huge pine tree later, the vehicle was upside down in a snowy ditch, Eddie Vincent dead, but miraculously, Billy somehow still alive. His chances at a glittering naval career, and a huge chunk of his soul, did die that dreadful night though, for good, and he never spoke of it again, to anyone.

As the song and Billy reached their crescendo, he jabbed away to each of Tina's powerful words until he was panting and slowing with each uppercut, before losing her timing completely, puffing for breath, his forehead dripping with sweat. The lack of cardio and overuse of steroids in the gym had taken their toll, his glory days of fighting twelve three-minute rounds in the ring were well and truly over. But the fire still burnt as strongly inside him as it had when he was 16, and in his mind, at least, he was still The Best.

"Sit down you fucking madman, before you do yourself an injury," Charlie instructed. He and the others were now cracking up with laughter. Billy nodded in agreement, gripping at his wide chest, and then turned Tina down a notch or two before coming back over to the couch, wheezing and coughing as he did.

"We gotta do 'em though, Charlie, in all seriousness. That's why we got the shooter from Leon, ain't it?" he puffed.

"No, Billy, that's for protection only."

"What? Where is it anyway? I wanna look it over,

make sure it does the job. I can field-strip any gun ever made in under five minutes mate. Go and get it."

Billy tried in vain to hide his childlike excitement about the gun.

"Billy, it's a serious thing, and we only have it so people who need to know we have, know we have it. Fear perceived is fear achieved," Charlie explained, calmly.

"Well, how they gonna know we have it, if we don't go and show it to them?" Billy replied, with a valid point.

Charlie gazed at him, with woozy eyes. He had no answer.

"Wo, wo, woooo," Che slurred. "The gun is here?"

Charlie looked at him, just as fuzzy eyed, and nodded.

"This place is in your name Charlie, you can't keep a fucking gun here, dude! Especially as you were at a fucking shooting last night, man, what are you thinking?"

"I know, I'm gonna get it to the safe house in a bit. I haven't had time," Charlie replied, trying to cover his lazy, drug-addled tracks to his rightly concerned friend. "Right, anyway, on this serious note, I almost forgot the point in getting you all round here." Charlie was suddenly awake and alert.. "We need to text all the punters and tell 'em we're shutting up shop for a few days, just until things quieten down."

"What, you mad, bruv?" Knighty screamed out in his high-pitched, excitable tone. "It's Saturday night, busiest bar Friday only!"

"We're shutting up shop, Knighty. End of, mate. Get texting," Charlie told him, sternly. "Come on, you two as well," he instructed Billy and Che, reaching for his phone to do the same. "Gotta be done."

Knighty went for his own phone, shaking his head in dramatic disapproval.

"Fine by me, I could do with a few days away from those fuckers," Billy exclaimed, happy enough.

Che on the other hand, still looked at Charlie in utter disbelief, as if he was on the brink of a heart-imploding panic attack.

"What's up with you, you don't normally mind a day off?" asked Charlie.

"You've still got your phone too?" Che asked.

"Yeah, and?" Charlie shook his head with impatience, looking back at his phone.

"Schoolboy fucking error dude! I'm guessing you used that phone to ring Harry last night and him ring you?"

"Yeah, it was all in code though, and it ain't registered in my name. So what?" Charlie still defended. He reached for his hand sanitizer in instinctive response to the sudden rush of dread that ripped through his guts.

"They'll be looking for anyone who was on his phone around the time of the murder, and you arranged to meet him there! It's a fucking iPhone, dude, Charl! American, CIA, people-tracking shit!" Che cried out, shaking his hands in the air wildly. .

"Not all dat Illuminati, New World Order shit again, bruv!" Knighty tried to stop him, thinking Che was about to go off on one of his internet-fed conspiracy theories.

"What the hell is wrong with you lot? Get the sim outta that now, Charl. I'm not kidding." Che instructed, widening his eyes.

Charlie stopped what he was doing - washing every

millimetre of his hands with sanitizer - reached for his cigarettes, and for the first time that day took Che seriously. For it was Che who had told the group to get pay as you go and not contract phones, and how not to pay with anything registered in your name when buying credit. Charlie had known Che since they were five years old; he was his oldest friend in the room, and as much as he knew he was massive pot head, he also knew he was highly intelligent when he could be bothered.

"So you're saying they can track this phone?" he asked, lighting up a cigarette.

"Yeah, man, totally. To this fucking address too. Take the sim out, now!"

Charlie did as he was told without another word. He placed the cigarette in the ashtray, reached inside a decorative box on the table to grab the iPhone's sim extractor, inserted it into the top of the phone, and popped out the deadly sim. Che reached across the table, with his quickest movement that day, grabbed it, then chucked straight it into his mouth and started chewing.

"Che, what the fuck are you doing?" Charlie shook his head in amazement, wondering if he was in fact listening to a sane man and not a paranoid schizophrenic after all.

Billy and Knighty watched on with the same disbelief. But before anyone had the chance to question the chewing stoner again, he'd grabbed the phone out of Charlie's hand, lunged across the lounge with his latest record in speed for that day, drawn back the curtains, opened the big swinging window and hurled the phone out of it, then stood happily watching it as it flew 17 floors to a horrible death.

Charlie jumped out of his seat.

"What ya doing? That's six hundred quid, you muppet!"

"Yeah, and a personal tracking device to the old bill, Charl. You should be okay though, I doubt they even went through Harry's phone yet, let alone had time to track you," Che tried to reassure Charlie and the rest of the room, instantly switching to his more familiar laid-back self. He headed hungrily for his still burning joint. "You know what the pigs are like, man, lazy fuckers, dude. Be cool."

He winked confidently in Charlie's direction.

CHAPTER 4

12th November 03.03pm.

Jack rolled up the gravel drive of his parent's Victorian four-bed house. The white wooden bay windows loomed down over him, ivy creeping neatly around their edges. He switched off the ignition and jumped out, noticing that his mother's car was not there. An instant wave of relief came over him and he grabbed his bag, slamming the Astra's door behind him.

After slipping his suit jacket and shoes off in the dimly lit hallway sparsely dressed with a wooden antique side and lamp, he went straight into the country style, higgledy-piggledy kitchen, where the sloppy construction of a cheese sandwich and glass of red wine raised a temporary smile. The plate and glass left messily on the wooden kitchen bench, he grabbed his bag and headed up the creaking old stairs, enjoying the warmth of the paisley carpet under his feet. Closing the tall, solid, white wooden door behind him, he pulled his laptop from its bag and went straight for his large welcoming bed. He booted up the laptop, resting it on his stomach, as he stretched out fully on the comforting white duvet, a huge breath out signalling his body unwinding in this well-known, well-loved sanctuary.

After being bombarded with several unwanted emails the moment he went online, he clicked on the Google Chrome bookmarks tab, and logged onto the Herts and Beds Major Crime Unit website. The murder came up straight away as the main story, credited as a DCI Brent investigation. He sighed as he lifted an electronic cigarette from the old mahogany unit next to him, but as he took a vaporised puff he saw his and Jenny's names at the end of the same report and smiled. He clicked impulsively onto Jenny's highlighted link, which brought up her profile, including a portrait shot of her attractive, smiling face. He clicked on the image, which opened in a new tab on the browser; larger now and more intense. He gazed lustfully at the screen and his facial muscles relaxed in awe. He held his thumb down on the Ctrl button and used his middle finger to zoom in by clicking the + button. Her perfectly formed cheekbones and radiant smile took over the 17-inch screen, causing an unholy tingling sensation in his groin. He slowly moved his right hand down past the laptop, towards his belted trousers. He fumbled around one handed with the belt, not taking his eyes off the screen.

Then, suddenly, and without warning, as his

bedroom door swung open, "Hello darling, you're home," his mother greeted him in her commanding tone.

He quickly withdrew his hand from his aroused genitals and pulled his leg up to hide any tell-tale clues.

"Get out!" he screamed, like a spotty teenager, ranting "Can't I get a moment's peace?" as his mother stood there open-mouthed. "Why the hell did I come back here? Why can't you leave me alone, woman?"

When the ranting had returned his penis to a sufficiently flaccid state, he ran to the heavy wooden door and slammed it shut in her face. He then stormed back over to his old bedside unit, reached in, grabbed his real cigarettes, and headed for the large bay window. Defiantly lighting one up before he had even had chance to open the window, he heard her solemn footsteps creak back off down the aging hall, then the stairs, and wondered why he hadn't heard them on the way up.

"Christ's sake," he whispered through gritted teeth as the smoke oozed out alongside the blasphemy.

Jack crept, slowly, ashamedly, down the creaking old stairs, guilt injuring his brain to the point of headache. As he nervously reached the bottom he peered through the open door of the lounge. She was sitting in her armchair staring quietly at the upright piano which sat boldly in the far corner of the room. He went through to the kitchen and continued to keep his eye on her through the service hatch in the wall. He ran the cold tap and filled himself a glass tumbler, which he emptied with three large gulps and refilled. He inserted two aspirin from a bottle left out on the side into his mouth, and then washed them down with another three large gulps, emptying the glass once more.

"I'm sorry, Mum," he announced, woefully.

"What's that, darling?" she replied, pretending that she was oblivious to his prior outburst.

"I said I'm sorry," he spoke a little louder now. "It's this case; first shooting I've had, making me unusually tense."

"I wouldn't say unusually, dear," she replied, in that faux posh tone, with a bitter drizzle of sarcasm.

"Come and play for me, would you, Jacobe?" she asked, warming her tone in a bipolar instant.

He half-filled the glass, with whiskey this time from another bottle conveniently left out on the side, and made his way through to the lounge. The large front room was like a snapshot from the mid-1900s, every piece of furniture featuring dark wood and thick patterned fabric. The television, a large old fashioned valve type, sat in the opposite corner to the piano, and was never used. The piano and an old record player were always the main source of entertainment for the cold, damp smelling room and his cold, damp mother. He hurried past her, en route to the piano, and noticed the usual gin and tonic on the side next to her single armchair, a lipstick mark staining the edge. The piano was illuminated by a green fabric shaded lamp, held up by a small porcelain woman dressed in 1940s dancing girl attire with a real feather in her black silk hat. This was the most upbeat area of the room, as either side of the lamp, were the happy, family photos.

Jack placed his drink down next to the lamp, careful not to disturb the photos, and then sat down graciously and professionally upon the piano's stool. He looked up knowingly, to the page of already open sheet music: *Chopin's Piano Sonata No.2 In B Flat Minor, Op. 35, "Funeral March" - 3. Marche Funèbre.*

He placed both hands, and their individual sets of well-trained fingers, slowly and methodically on the cold ivory keys, gently pressing with many hours of learnt skill. The opening notes' haunting resonance bounced around the icy room. He lifted his fingers and gently washed them back down, as waves lapping at a winter's shore. Up and down they flowed, elegantly and with faultless timing, as the strings played out Chopin's dark melodies. He sat bolt upright, face to the music, as his mother looked on with an evocative gaze, rubbing her frail fingers around the glass of gin, feeling every sultry note as they worked their way around her depressed, old body. He took his eyes from the music, continuing to play, and raised them to a picture of his father. The opening piece built in pressure and entered its louder phase. He closed his eyes with a dramatically tight squeeze, to visions of his father's slow, painful and untimely death, the cancer eating him alive with a vicious mercilessness. Then the funeral, then the depression, then his mother's depression, then last night's murder, then back, way back to his divorce at the tender age of 25. Then his years being bullied at school for being the son of a teacher, a teacher he had loved so dearly. Then his eyes flicked back open just as dramatically as they had closed, and reaffixed upon that very teacher, his beloved and eternally missed father. A tear rolled down his cheek, taking all his bottled up sadness with it, a tiny, rolling ball of salty desolation which eventually began to dry out on his strong jaw line. He then suddenly stopped playing, before the piece rose to its complementary uplifting section, just as he always did; For that posed no refuge for his tortured soul, or hers. He closed the lid over the keys, stood up, and took a mental bow. He walked back past his glooming mother, avoiding eye contact as she reached out and desperately grabbed at his passing hand.

"Oh, Jacobe," she sobbed.

He squeezed back warmly, and then left the room, without another word being spoken.

When Jack walked back through the station doors that same night, after a meagre 4 hours' sleep, he knew he was late. He hated being late; he saw it as a form of weakness and certainly didn't care to display weakness to the detectives below him. He looked at his watch: 08:11pm. He was supposed to be back at eight. He nodded to the custody sergeant and was buzzed through with a quick nod back. An early Saturday drunkard was already getting processed; Jack nodded to the arresting officers and worked his way through to the Major Crime Unit offices, leaving the sound of the complaining drunk behind him. He was immediately greeted by Jenny, who took his apology for being late with a big forgiving smile and followed him into his office, accompanied by DC Trump, who moaned about missing his Saturday night takeaway while rubbing his dangerously large belly and laughing.

"Okay, what we got?" Jack quizzed the pair as he leaned back on his chair and put his feet back up on the table.

They both took it upon themselves to be seated, as Jack wasn't known for his formalities.

"Well," began DC Trump with a long drawn-out sigh and a rub of his big, saggy chin with the back of his hand. "The coroner recovered the bullet, and we've got that bagged up in evidence. It's a nine millimetre, it definitely followed the trajectory we thought; entry wound in the chest, went straight through the heart, then deflected off the spine and into the right lung, where it stopped, causing instant death, he would guess. Which ties in with there not being much evidence of any struggle on the ground."

"Least that's something, poor bastard," Jack added mournfully.

"Yeah, that's what the coroner said actually. Anyway, that's about it for the post mortem. Obviously if we can find the gun we're onto a good thing, even without finding any shell casings. And on that note, as it was a nine millimetre, it was more than likely fired from a pistol, which means the shooter must have collected the casing after he fired."

"A pro," Jenny interjected, smiling at Jack for recognition. He rewarded her with a diluted smile.

"Okay, so next it's the tyre prints. They're low profile, sports type, and not cheap, so you're probably not looking for a souped-up Corsa, more likely a Mercedes or a BMW, something of that class. But that's just a guess, once you find the tyre you think it is, we'll run them and see if it's a match, obviously."

"Good work, Barry, but one thing I don't get: if he's such a professional, why did he leave the tyre marks and footprints behind?" Jack asked..

"I'm guessing the rain got the better of him, but who knows? And on the point of footprints, it was a pair of size nine Adidas training shoes."

Barry finished off his report with a wide spread of his plump lips across his plump face.

"Okay, brilliant work again, Barry. And thanks for coming back tonight."

"Not a problem, Jack, now would it be all right if I buggered off again?" he asked, laughing and rubbing his oversized, rumbling belly once more.

"Yes of course, Barry, but you're gonna have to be back first thing I'm afraid. I know it's a Sunday, but how many shootings do we get?"

"Understood guv, and hopefully this'll be the last. What is Stambro coming to?"

He got up from the tight-fitting chair with a bit of trouble which he laughed off with another tap of his giant belly, then bid the remaining pair goodbye.

Jenny looked to Jack and smiled as soon as they were alone, a radiant beam framed by freshly washed skin and hair. Jack managed to keep a straight face and immediately got back to the matter in hand.

"What we got, Pearce?"

"Okay, no Charlies on the system at all. Well, one old bloke of seventy-odd, but there's no way it could be him, right?" she joked.

"Well, never rule it out, but we'll put it to one side for now, yes." Jack stayed stern.

"Fair enough," she replied, weariness in her voice revealing that she was just as tired as him, having only managed to steal a few hours' sleep herself.

"Oh, and that phone? The account has never been paid for in any way with a card, always cash."

"Tell me something good, Jen," he pleaded.

"I'm saving the best 'till last, guv. He used the phone a lot this afternoon, didn't say much, but admitted to being there last night, which we got recorded. I know it's inadmissible in court, but we could scare him with it in the interview?"

Jack kept a poker face and waited for her to continue. She coughed, nervously, and carried on.

"Anyway, the best part is, he used the phone from one address all afternoon, and then it went offline at eleven minutes past five this evening. And the address is…" she looked down to the notes sitting delicately upon her sexually inviting lap, "seventy-eight Ambrose Court."

"Is that the high-rise?" Jack quizzed, immediately impressed.

"Yep, and guess who is registered at that address?"

Jack shrugged impatiently.

"One Charlie Paccadillo, guv. White male, twenty-eight years old, he's lived in Stambro all his life, parents moved to Spain a few years back. He did okay at school, played for Stambro FC for a few years where he actually had quite a promising career, even got signed for West Ham under 21s, then suffered a knee injury, and that put him out for life,"

"Tragic," Jack replied, genuinely. "But no previous?"

"Nope, nothing. Although he hasn't worked since he was twenty-five, on paper anyway. He had a job in the washing machine factory, then nothing for the last three years. His flat is paid for by benefits, all claimed under the knee injury."

"Oh, not so tragic then," Jack retorted.

"Well, I'm guessing he would rather have been on

twenty grand a week at West Ham, guv, but yeah, I see where you're coming from."

"Okay, well we hit him with a dawn raid tomorrow, see what we can find and bring him in."

Jenny smiled and got up from her seat. Jack followed to plan the attack in the main office, watching her figure from the rear as he did. Her hips moved with the elegance of a supermodel in her tight grey pencil skirt, and her tight buttocks followed suit.

DCI Brent gave the dawn raid the all-clear via mobile phone from his warm bed at home at 6:06 on the dot, Sunday morning.

"Okay, all units when they're ready, Jack. I'll leave it in your capable hands, my good man."

"Yes sir, I'll keep you posted."

Jack hung up the phone and led the raid team up the elevators to the 17th floor, leaving a man at each entrance to the building on the ground floor. The team of ten men exited the two elevators simultaneously. Other than Jack and Jenny, everyone else was in uniform. The breach team up front, consisting of two men, had the heavy metal battering ram, and then the six men behind them, had body armour, Kevlar helmets, and Heckler and Koch MP5 submachine guns, laser dots on, locked and loaded. The two detectives stayed at the back, unarmed. The breach team crept into place and the armed officers shuffled in behind them, a tight fit in the thin, high-rise hallway.

"Okay, everyone ready?" Jack whispered from the

back.

All eight men turned and gave the okay sign, each one poised to go and adrenalin surging, ready to put their long hours of training into practice. It wasn't very often an armed team carried out dawn raids in Stambro; the local council usually liked to keep the use of excessive force to a minimum in a public relations bid, but Jack had easily gained the right on this raid, as most members of the council tax-paying public wanted gun-toting murderers off of the streets as safely and quickly as possible.

"Go!"

The breach team smashed the ram hard into the front door with trained aggression. The door shook on its hinges, but remained defiant. Bang. They slammed it in once more and this time it flew open like they had a key. The breach team moved aside and the armed and armoured officers rushed past them, guns pointed from the shoulder, scanning from right to left, knees bent, attack mode.

"Armed police, armed police!" they roared as their perfect assault routine swung into play. Two men searched each room in lighting speed, screaming their deadly position of power as they did.

Then, as soon as it had started, it was over; shock and awe tactics at their very best.

"No one inside, sir." The sergeant of the small unit had returned to the hallway.

"What, no one?" Jack demanded, unimpressed with the result.

"Afraid not, sir. They're doing a quick sweep under beds and in cupboards, but at this hour it's unlikely we're going to find anyone."

"Damn it!" Jack roared past him as he stormed in

to look for himself, not waiting for the rest of the team to come out with the all-clear, as was the usual, safe practice.

Jenny followed close on his heels, giving the sergeant a gratifying nod and one of her jaw-dropping smiles as she did. He turned off his laser pointer and switched back to safety, as the rest of his team exited the flat.

"All clear, Sarge."

Jack walked around the flat, cringing at what he deemed a tacky use of money, violently opening drawers and doors with his gloved hands. Jenny radioed the rest of the search team up from the ground floor. Jack then instructed two officers to stay behind, and start running number plates in the car park against the DVLA database for registered owners.

"There's some expensive tastes in here, for a dole scrounger eh, guv?"

Jenny asked from the kitchen, as he searched the living room.

"You're not wrong, Jen, I just wish the little bastard was here. Got a lovely picture though."

He picked up a framed photo from the side, Charlie and his parents at their villa in Spain, all smiles, all sunshine.

"Look what I found, Jack." Jenny called out in excitement, jogging in from the kitchen.

She held, between gloved thumb and index finger, a black, semi-automatic pistol by the trigger guard. Jack smiled a broad grin back at her his mood rapidly lifting.

"Well done, Jen. Get the sergeant back in here."

Jenny did as she was told, and the armed sergeant came back from the hallway.

"Would you say that was a nine millimetre, sergeant?"

"I would guess, quite confidently, at a yes, sir," he replied, smiling. The team briefing had featured the weapon as chief among the evidence they'd be searching for.

The rest of the search team made their way back into the flat, and started ripping through cupboards and drawers. One of them quickly found the bloodstained jeans and jacket in the washing machine and brought them through to an increasingly elated Jack, then another with a small lump of cocaine, from a bedroom drawer. Jack beamed from ear to ear, a brightness to match that of the warm morning sun as it lit up the cold November day. The evidence was bagged up and taken down to the forensic vehicles below. Jack received a radio report from the team downstairs to tell him they had found a black Mercedes registered to a Charlie Paccadillo in the car park, sporting expensive low profile tyres

"Looks like we've identified our shooter, Jen. Just gotta find the bastard now."

CHAPTER 5

14th November 11:11am.

Charlie woke up with a giant's yawn and a phlegm-filled cough. He took a hazy look around, rubbing his sore, watering eyes. Billy's ground floor flat was small yet cosy, and there was enough space in the front room to sleep three men comfortably. Knighty was top and tailing on the biggest sofa with Che, both (of whom) were still quietly asleep. Charlie was crunched up on the other, smaller couch, which he vaguely remembered choosing at three o' clock that morning, the time he finally decided to call it a night. He scanned the room for evidence of their drug-fuelled decadence; there were crushed beer cans, a vodka bottle, a whiskey bottle, half-filled glasses, ashtrays filled with stinking butts, CD cases, money, cards, and the bag from under Charlie's sink. Next to it lay what was formerly the boulder of cocaine, now more of a pebble. They had moved on from Charlie's flat late Saturday night to a local pub, at his request as cabin fever had started to take a paranoid, mind-shattering hold. The landlord of the pub, and friend of the crew, had allowed them a lock-in until three o' clock Sunday morning. From there at Charlie's behest once again, they had retreated to Billy's flat, deep in the heart of the Crowley estate. Charlie always felt safe at Billy's. As much as he loved his own lofty apartment, it never felt completely safe to him: 'stuck up their like a sitting duck' his reasoning. The drug and alcohol bender had continued on throughout Sunday morning, promises and plans for the Dunns abounding They had finally taken a break in the afternoon, stopping the cocaine for an ordered-in greasy pizza and the FA cup first-round football match of that day. As soon as the match was over however, the cocaine rejoined the party with a vengeance and a disgusting explosion of endorphins and dance music, which didn't stop pumping until Charlie had essentially passed out at three am that morning.

"Jesus fuck," he shuddered, as he reached for his jacket, pulling out his hand sanitizer and giving his hands a thorough going over. He then pulled the dark green British Army sleeping bag back up over himself, cursing Billy and his ridiculous claims that 'central heating's for pussies'. He lay there shivering, partly from the cold, partly from the toxins leaving his body, gazing through squinted eyes around the Boy's Own style front room. Billy's green Royal Marine Commando beret proudly hung from the wall, accompanied by a commando dagger in its scabbard.

Then there were the boxing posters of all the greats surrounding the area where a duct-taped punch bag hung from the ceiling in the far corner of the room: Muhammad Ali, Joe Frazier and Mike Tyson. Billy admired these men with a great passion, and took any opportunity in his front room to tell stories of their best fights, illustrating the tales with jabs and blows whenever he could. Charlie suddenly had a humorous flashback to Sunday morning, when Billy had tuned in via his satellite dish to some random American boxing matches, taking to the floor with each one as if he were there in the ring himself and throwing clumsy, crazy, drunken jabs. Charlie smiled inside as the memory warmed his aching stomach. Billy was not an easy man by any stretch of the imagination, but a rather endearing one all the same, in his own special way.

Charlie reached for his phone and when he couldn't find it, the reason for the two-day binge crept swiftly back into his consciousness and struck him hard in the face, like a blow from one of the boxers on the wall. He tensed up and gritted his teeth, as images of murder and jail cells went through his brittle mind. It wasn't long before the thoughts made him feel terribly alone and he got up to wake the others. As he did, he saw the local newspaper on the large wooden living room table, left open on the classifieds section for female escorts. He immediately headed for Billy's room, and opened the door, quickly and without knocking. Sure enough, Billy was lying there snuggled up in bed with a bleached blonde lady of the night; her hair extensions and leopard print bra the most noticeable giveaways to her profession. They were both fast asleep and surrounded by the evidence of pure, unadulterated hedonism.

"One sick puppy," Charlie sniggered to himself before pulling the door shut quietly and going back to the lounge,. There he found Che now awake and rolling a fresh joint at the still sleeping Knighty's slightly smelly feet.

"Really, Che?" Charlie asked, amazed, but happy his oldest friend was now awake; to share the heavy burden he was carrying on young, unprepared shoulders.

"Fuck yeah, dude! Every goddamn morning; this is a way of life, man! Jah bless!" Che dribbled, as he continued rolling with yellow fingers and an obsessive level of concentration.

"Did you know he had a brass in there?" Charlie asked, pointing to Billy's bedroom and giggling to himself.

"Yeah, I was still up. I had one too." Che smiled.

"What?" In here, when we were out of it? With Knighty next to you?"

"Nah man, I was in the kitchen. I couldn't fucking get it up though, so we just talked and that, and then she left. Fucking bummer, dude."

"You lot are fucking mental. How comes this one has spent the bastard night?" Charlie started to laugh as his friend's seedy misadventures helped to ease his tender soul.

"Dunno, Charl. You know what he's like, probably tied the poor girl up or something."

"She's 'appy as Larry, mate! They're all cuddled up and that!"

Charlie roared uncontrollably with laughter now, waking an extremely hung-over Knighty, much to his annoyance. A trip to Billy's room with Che lifted his spirits again, and they both tried their hardest to contain the laughter. There was something utterly absurd about that huge bodybuilder, all toughness and scarcely restrained aggression, lying there cuddled up to a skinny escort.

Che's phone rang from his leather jacket pocket as he sat there squeezing the final pulls out of his first joint of the day. Billy was just closing the door after kissing his paid sex buddy for the night goodbye.

"Err, It's Jimmy Vole from your floor of Ambrose, Charl. You wanna speak to him?" Che mumbled through the joint butt, looking down at his ringing phone as a stoned paranoia of outsiders swept over him.

"Nah, you deal with him please, mate. Just tell him the same as the others: we've shut up shop."

Che reluctantly answered the call.

"That fucking joker's never got any money anyway, bruv," Knighty moaned, as he sipped a steaming mug of tea.

Billy strode into the lounge in a red silk dressing gown, and a wide smile spread across his flushed face.

"Did you see the fucking tits on that, lads?" he asked, cupping his own large chest with heavy exaggeration.

Che took the phone from his ear and held it to his chest, "Charl, he says it's not good mate," he explained, woefully.

Everyone stopped what they were doing and listened in.

"He said he wants a bag for the information?"

Billy shook his head in disapproval. "Liberty-taking cunt. Tell him to go fuck his mother!" he growled through gritted teeth.

"Okay, Che, tell him yes, whatever," Charlie replied, ignoring Billy.

Che gave the answer, and then looked more and more concerned as the information flowed through the phone and into his spaced-out mind. He quickly hung up and nervously repeated what he'd been told.

"He said your flat got raided yesterday morning, armed police and everything. Apparently there's a notice on the door for a number to call, if anybody knows of your whereabouts." Che puffed on the remnants of his spliff, burning his lips and letting out a small cry. "It's about Harry's murder," he finished, with a disheartened look.

"Ball bust," was Charlie's only reply as he stared at the ground, shocked to his core.

"They must have traced the phone calls then, raaaah!" Knighty groaned, stating the obvious.

"But you didn't have anything there did you Charlie, the gear's all here isn't it?" Billy asked, optimistically.

"Yes I did, Billy, the gun, the fucking gun, remember?"

"Oh shit, dude!" Che suddenly piped up, not the best at quelling another man's panic.

Charlie cursed himself for going on a binge with his friends and not doing what any sensible person would have done: kept a straight head, and got everything safely tucked away. He wasn't in a sensible man's game, but that was all the more reason to be careful.

"There was my clothes too, in the fucking washing machine, with Harry's blood on 'em. And about half ounce of gear in the bedroom drawer. I'm fucked."

Charlie chewed his lips with fear and rubbed his fingers through his short black hair.

Everyone looked around the room, deep in thought, as Billy went and crashed himself down on the sofa next to Charlie. He turned to him, still clearly upbeat from the night before, and in an effort to console spoke sternly, Marine sergeant style. "Well, the fact still remains, you didn't do 'im Charlie. There must have been other evidence, phone calls, footprints, whatever, at the murder. That Frosty is a dumb cunt, not the type to cover his tracks; they'll work out it was 'im, and not you. Worst you'll get is fleeing the scene mate, and possession of the gun and drugs of course."

Charlie looked to him, squinting one eye slightly, wanting to believe everything he said.

"You'll get five years tops, sunshine, and be out in half that with good behaviour. You'll be at a cat C nick; piece of piss, mate. Shower in your cell, telly, PlayStation. We'll look after everything out 'ere don't worry about it pal, honest." Billy wrapped his big arm supportively around Charlie's shoulder.

"Yeah, it's true, Charlie bruv. All of us 'ere got your back 'till the end, init," Knighty added, reassuringly.

Che was the only one who didn't say anything. He and Charlie had been friends a long time and Che wasn't stupid. He knew it didn't look good.

Charlie lit up a cigarette, taking long pulls, thoughts of telling his parents he was going to prison attacking his brain like thought-hungry mind mosquitoes.

"You reckon they might just wanna question me about that night then? Find out who might have done it?" he asked, wanting to believe what Billy was telling him and ignore his churning gut.

"Listen bruv, you give 'em the right info about who done it, they might even drop the gun charge, get me?" Knighty explained, grinning slyly out of the corner of his mouth, his whitened teeth shining through like polished china plates.

"I ain't a fucking grass, Knighty," Charlie answered.

"Nah, I didn't mean grass," Knighty tried to explain, then quickly shut his mouth and drank his tea.

"I need to get out, get a new phone and that. I wanna go see Alice too," said Charlie, getting up from the sofa.

"Who the hell's Alice, man?" Che asked, rolling up a fresh joint.

"What, the sket from Friday?" Knighty asked, clearly disappointed.

"I said I'd see her today, and I've lost her number, so one of you lot's gonna have to take me there. My motor's at Ambrose."

Che didn't take his eyes off the cigarette he was dismantling and Knighty just shook his head in disagreement at the idea, before getting up to make a fresh tea.

"I'll take ya, pal," Billy kindly offered. "You two muppets can stay here and wank each other off to Jezza Kyle," he suggested to Che and Knighty.

"Nice one, Billy. Can I have a quick shower first?"

"Course you can, son. I got a load of those snide Aquascutum tops in the bedroom still too; chuck one of those on, impress the girl," Billy proudly offered.

Charlie winced, but knew fake designer clothing was what he would have to be reduced to as the option of going back to his flat was now clearly out of the question. Che paused his marijuana rolling ritual, and quickly warned, "Don't go to get your car, dude. They'll be watching it, 'cos it's registered in your name and that. Avoid it, man, like the plague."

Charlie nodded back at his permanently stoned friend, wondering what he would do right now without his firm, his gang, his best friends.

Charlie and Billy drove slowly down Alice's road in his racing green Land Rover defender. As Charlie racked his still drunken memory for where her house was, kids played noisily amongst the concrete and rubbish; kids who looked as though they should have been at school. And slightly older kids who pushed prams, containing their own, slightly younger kids, while smoking, swearing, shouting, and sporting a vast array of cheap gold and even cheaper clothes, apparently all at the British taxpayers' expense.

"That's it, Billy, that one there, mate."

Charlie pointed excitedly towards the clean looking front garden, a shining example of pride in awkward comparison with its neighbours.

"This is about as Aleister as it gets, Charlie. You sure you wanna bird from round here?"

"You just keep your eyes on that door when she answers, Billy. You'll see why. She's a fucking goddess, mate."

Billy chuckled at his friend's soft side, and pulled the solid Land Rover up on the curb.

"You gonna be all right out here on your tod?"

Charlie asked before getting out, grabbing his new pay as you go Blackberry phone from the dash as he did.

"Do I look all right, ya soppy git?" Billy laughed. His huge, tattooed forearm rested easily on the driver's side door, a tyre wrench for the four-wheel drive not far out of reach; conveniently kept under his seat rather than in the boot where it belonged: an excusable weapon to be kept in a car in case of any prying, policing eyes.

As Charlie walked up the path towards the looming front door, he suddenly stopped dead in his tracks; a sudden wave of nerves gripping at his already tightened gut. He looked back to Billy, who watched on, confused and then, upon realising the problem, spurred him on with a laugh and a directional nod. Charlie took a deep breath, composed himself, and continued. With all the uncertainty of the past few days, he was sure of one thing: Alice, and the love she brought, would brighten his day. Sudden and reassuring visions of her visiting him in his category C prison helped him take each step up the path.

He tapped on the neatly painted red front door and waited patiently for a reply. He heard footsteps running to the door from within; gentle, light footsteps. He pushed up his bottom lip in anticipation. The door swung open and there stood a stern-looking ten year old boy, dressed in full US Army fatigues, pointing a toy rifle. His cute face looked unimpressed, as his long fair hair blew about in the cold breeze.

"Who goes there?" he demanded in a squeaky but determined young voice.

Charlie turned back to Billy, who looked on, freaked out. No answers for this one.

"Errr, I'm looking for Alice?" Charlie smiled.

The boy looked back confused, as if not recognising the name, then called for assistance.

"Mum!" he shouted up the stairs, and turned to run, bored of the situation now.

Charlie watched in amazement as the boy headed back through the small hallway, then the living room and finally through the large patio doors, back out into the small garden from where he had originally come, to continue his battle with his imagined enemy.

Alice came hurriedly down the stairs, immediately pulling Charlie's attention away from the little boy soldier. Her slim frame was wrapped in a small white towel, her hair dripping wet, fresh from the shower.

"Oh, it's you."

She looked at him in shock, reaching the door and wrapping the towel tighter around her now, as the cold air hit, much to Charlie's pleasure.

"Yeah it's me, the Spanish Stallion. Sorry for coming round like this, unannounced and that. I lost my phone," he explained nervously, no Dutch courage willing him along this time.

"Of course not, Charlie. Come in, close the door."

She quickly upped her tempo as she ushered him inside.

He quickly glanced back again, to Billy, who was moving his head about in frustration, trying to catch an eyeful of Charlie's 'goddess', but to no avail.

"Go have a seat in the lounge. I'll get dressed quickly and come straight back down," the beautiful Alice instructed as she closed the door behind him.

"I don't mind you like that," he flirted uncontrollably, gazing down obviously at her beautifully toned and exposed legs.

She looked down at him as she headed back up the stairs, more relaxed this time, welcoming his calming familiarity, and smiled.

He walked off into the lounge and sat himself down on the worn, but tidy, large beige fabric sofa. The room was decorated cheaply but tastefully, with bright colours and plenty of pictures. The pictures were mostly of the mystery boy, who continued his assault on the enemy in the back garden, completely uninterested in Charlie, who now puzzled over whether Alice was his mother. There was a small television in one corner of the room, and a half cupboard with a single slatted door in the other. Hanging from its chrome knob was a heart-shaped cushion, displaying the words World's best Mum!. The sound of a hairdryer drifted down the stairs and through the open living room door. There was a small, white flat-pack coffee table in the centre of the room, its edges chipped to reveal the MDF underneath and glossy gossip magazines strewn across its top and toys neatly stacked underneath it.

The hairdryer stopped for a moment and Alice shouted from upstairs, instructing him to go through to the kitchen, located through the lounge at the front of the house and make them both a cup of tea.

Bracing his hands against his knees to stand, Charlie did as he was told. The kitchen was almost a uniform white, clean, but showing the signs of age and use. The window over the sink was ajar, and he fumbled through the unfamiliar cupboards in search of mugs, tea and sugar, before filling the kettle at the sink.

She finally strolled into the kitchen dressed as if for a shoot in one of her magazines; make-up perfect, long dark hair perfect, clothing slightly overboard for the occasion, but perfect nonetheless. She smiled warmly as she made her way towards him; he sat his tea down on the side and stood bolt upright up in expectation. She moved straight in for the kill, as he had hoped, and without hesitation kissed him passionately on the lips. He let her melt into his arms, all his troubles drawn through the kitchen window and into the cold November air.

Suddenly they were both snapped from their loving embrace as Billy honked on the horn from outside. He'd been watching the whole thing through the kitchen window from his 4x4, and sat there laughing like a big ape and pretending to snog his hand. Charlie stuck up a middle finger, with a stern frown in shocked response.

"Is that your friend?" Alice asked, just as taken aback.

"Err, yeah. That's Billy."

"Oh. Well, why don't you ask him if he wants to come in? You can't leave him sitting out there," she offered.

"Nah, he's better off out there, trust me," Charlie explained, leading Alice quickly by the hand out of the kitchen and back to the privacy of the lounge, after giving Billy another evil and warning glance. Billy laughed back harder in response.

"So what's going on with this shooting? You weren't involved, were you?" Alice asked, biting her lip as they sat close together on the worn-out old sofa.

"I promise you, hand on heart; I had nothing to do with it. Nothing," he answered honestly and placed a reassuring hand on her knee. "But I really don't wanna go into it all now, if that's okay?" He sought mercy in her forgiving hazel eyes, pleading, "I need some time away from it, it's taking me over."

She pursed her lips, thought a second, then replied with complete sincerity, "Okay Charlie. Fair enough. Don't ask me why, but I do believe you. I mean, I don't even know you properly, but for some reason, yeah, I believe you, and that's enough for me."

"Thanks Alice. I've not stopped bloody thinking about you since Friday and that's why I came here; so we can get to know each other. I want to get to know you," he explained intensely, tilting his head to one side as if awaiting another kiss.

"Me too, Charlie. I couldn't stop talking about you at work," she replied. Then she suddenly seemed to remember herself, peering out to the garden and moving his hand gently from her knee. "Where's Hitten?"

"Who's Hitten?"

"Hitten's my boy, the soldier who greeted you."

"Oh," Charlie smiled back, the confusion surrounding Hitten still clear and unquestioned.

"I did mean to tell you about Hitten, Charlie, it's just…" she began to explain hastily, as she scanned the back garden for her son.

"Don't worry, Alice, its fine, honestly. I completely understand," he replied, joining her in scanning the garden..

"Most blokes run a mile when I mention I have a son, ya know, and I really liked you, I had a great time Friday, I only get to go out twice a month, when my mum comes round and watches him," she blurted out, trying to explain it all in one long breath, while her eyes continued to search the garden for her missing son.

Charlie stopped looking, as his hungover mind put the pieces together. "It all makes sense now," he smiled at himself, "why you had to be back on Friday night; why you pointed to the bedroom for me to be quiet when I dropped you off. I thought this was your parents' house and they were asleep up there!"

He chuckled.

"No, I haven't lived with my mum and dad since Hitten was born," she explained, glancing back at him, worry appearing on her face now.

"And the family thing you had on yesterday?" Charlie grinned like a clever detective, ignoring her concern. "You should have just told me. I don't care; he's a lovely little geezer."

"Yeah, he is, when he's not missing," she replied, getting up and heading quickly to the back door in increasing maternal panic.

He watched her stunning figure from the rear, when something caught his eye from the corner of the room; the barrel of Hitten's toy rifle sticking through one of the slats in the half cupboard door.

"Alice," he whispered.

She turned to him with impatience, and he pointed sneakily to the cupboard door in response.

"Of course," she laughed, the panic quickly draining from her.

She walked over to the door and quickly opened it to reveal Hitten's squashed little body wedged between the gas and electric meter, the door taking his gun with it as she did.

"Out you get, silly," she coaxed him. "This is my friend, Charlie. Come and say hello."

"Hello mate." Charlie waved at him, grasping his new phone in the same hand.

Hitten instantly spotted the phone.

"Wow, is that a new Blackberry?" he asked, wriggling himself out of the cupboard in excitement and then running over to Charlie.

Charlie handed him the phone in reply, which he immediately accepted with a huge grin.

"Mum's friend Shell has one of these; she lets me play the games on it," he explained, flicking through to the games without asking, then back out to the camera application. "And she lets me shoot war movies on it. I'm the main star, the hero, Sergeant Hitten!" he pronounced, standing to attention and saluting Charlie.

"You'll have to meet my mate Billy. He was a Royal Marine."

"A Marine!" Hitten replied, a huge grin spreading in excitement across his face.

"Right, give it back," Alice commanded, looking slightly embarrassed at Hitten's absence of manners, and slightly concerned about him meeting the man-mountain outside. "He's never normally this forward," she tried to explain.

"It's fine," Charlie replied, laughing. "You can have that one if you want, Hitten," he offered spontaneously, nodding at the phone.

Hitten looked to his mother for a response, a huge mixture of shock and excitement written across his bright young face.

"Don't be silly, Charlie. Hitten, give it back," she responded, firmly.

"Ooooooooow, Mum!" he pleaded, running over to her with the phone still clasped tightly between his little fingers, and then throwing both arms around her waist.

"Honestly, Alice, it's his. I've just got a few in off a mate, don't worry about it," he replied, lying. He'd just spent £300 on it with Billy.

"Please Mum… Pleeeeeeeease!" Hitten begged, almost in tears now.

"I don't know, Charlie. It's a bit much."

She shook her head with worry and pride.

"I got them free. It's no big deal, honest."

He winked at her.

"He's not gonna get arrested for it is he?" she asked, trying to work it all out.

"No, it's nothing like that, it's all legal. And it's got fifty quid worth 'a credit on it too, so he can call you when he's out in the street, or whatever. Or better still, you can call him, when he's hiding!"

She thought about it for a few undecided moments more, as Hitten clung desperately to her waist, and then nodded her head, with a huge thankful smile to Charlie. "Okay, what do you say, Hitten?"

He gawped up at her for a moment while it sunk in, then ran over to Charlie, and slung his arms around him.

"Thank you, Charlie! You're the best, ever!"

Charlie initially drew back, but then immediately warmed as Hitten squeezed tighter, realising his hug was nothing more than 100% pure affection, no strings attached. He hugged him back.

"Don't mention it, pal, it's my pleasure."

"Okay, Hitten, why don't you take it upstairs and make a video with your GI Joes while Charlie and I talk? There's a good boy," Alice persuaded him, gently.

"That is a brilliant idea Mum! Thanks again Charlie!" he replied happily, before zooming off, out of the lounge and up the stairs as though she'd just lit a tiny go-faster fuse on his back.

"He's great!" Charlie complimented her.

"Well, thanks. You've definitely won him over there," she smiled back, impressed, and then sat back down next to him on the sofa.

"So, where's his dad?" Charlie asked abruptly. He'd intended not to pry, but the question had been bursting uncontrollably to get out.

"Straight in there with the big ones then!" she laughed. "He's not around. Hasn't been since I was pregnant," she explained, all emotion disappearing as if she'd flicked an internal switch.

"Oh really? What a dick," Charlie cursed. Coming from a loving mother and father himself, he felt the boy's loss and complete contempt for an abandonment that he couldn't comprehend.

"I was fifteen, Charlie, and believe me, it wasn't what I wanted. I wouldn't change it for the world now, obviously, but yeah, I was young."

"Fifteen... Jesus, I was playing for Stambro FC, having the time of my life at that age, not a care in the world," he replied, replacing his hand lovingly upon her knee as they both leant back into the comfy old sofa.

"Yeah, it kind of put a stop to my life for a while. I found out after I missed a period one month, then my mum and dad offered to take me to Thailand on holiday to think the whole thing over when I told 'em."

"Bloody 'ell, they're cool parents, ain't they? Don't know of many other parents who would do that after finding out their fifteen-year-old was pregnant. Most would have sent you to the bathroom with a bottle of gin and a slapped ass!" he joked, highly inappropriately, then dropped his smile as soon as he realised Alice wasn't impressed.

She continued, "When we were in Thailand, I spent a lot of time in the temples getting into Buddhism and that. As I told you before, it seemed to help me so much; it just really struck a chord with me."

"So, they let you get a tattoo as well?" Charlie asked in amazement, thinking Alice's parents must be Sharon and Ozzy Osbourne by now.

"No, I got that when I went back a few years ago, with my mum, dad and Hitten," she laughed. "Anyway, I decided while I was out there I would keep him and raise him to be the best man ever - nothing like his dad." She gritted her teeth with raw emotion. "To break the cycle, you know? Something good outta something bad?"

Charlie nodded his head in reply, fully understanding of her story. Lots of girls got pregnant around Stambro; it was almost a fashion trend. He wasn't shocked by Alice's story, or the dad leaving when she was pregnant. It was, tragically, the norm.

"That's where his name comes from. Hitten means Buddhist Angel," she explained, smiling again now.

"It's beautiful" he replied.

Charlie spent the next hour telling Alice all about his life in fine detail.

He explained how he was once a promising footballer who lost his chance with West Ham when he damaged his knee in a dodgy tackle. Then how, with no decent qualifications from school, he'd had to go work in a dingy factory, where he got quickly depressed and battled that depression with drink, and watching *Tottenham Hotspur*, his childhood team at their home games whenever he could afford to. And that's where he'd met his friend, Leon Brown. Leon was a big-time face around the Tottenham hooligan scene, who could only drink in the pubs around the ground since he'd been banned from going to any of the games, and it was in one such pub that he and Charlie had got chatting one drunken Saturday afternoon. Charlie had drunk way too much, couldn't afford a ticket for the game and was being sick into a sink in the pub toilets. In walked Leon, who'd been left alone in the pub as most of his friends went to the game, and offered Charlie a line of cocaine to 'sort him out'. Charlie drunkenly accepted and instantly fell in love with the drug which would help him drink more and forget more. He later discovered that that first experience was 100 times better than anything Stambro had to offer when he tried buying some back at home. From then on, he bought his cocaine from Leon and Leon alone. Soon after, his friends back in Stambro started asking him to get them some of the stronger London product, to which he generously agreed. Charlie quickly realised he could buy more from Leon, explaining how much he could buy in bulk and then keep a bit back for himself for free. One thing led to another and he was soon buying half-ounces up front with cash, selling it on, keeping some for himself and still making a decent profit. He soon earned more money in one day than a whole week slaving away in the depressing factory and quit working there altogether.

When the demand increased, he couldn't keep up with the supply. There was no problem from Leon's end; he could get as much as Charlie needed. But Charlie couldn't be everywhere at once and decided to recruit some old, and some new friends, Che, Knighty and Billy. Each had different talents and skills to offer Charlie's growing business. Che could help shift some of the cocaine, but also marijuana, which Leon constantly offered but Charlie knew nothing about, whereas Che was an expert. Knighty again helped with the powder, but already had a decent market for ecstasy going around Stambro. Charlie got him better prices for the pills from Leon and everyone was happy. Billy was the by that time much-needed muscle; the Dunn Brothers had soon got wind of Charlie's game and weren't keen on him taking their hard-earned business away from under their greedy noses with his far superior product. And the Dunns knew Billy; he was one of the only men in Stambro they wouldn't happily start a war with, he explained to an innocently fascinated Alice.

She in turn explained how she had grown up in the shadow of the Dunns' ruthless reputation all her life, and didn't know of anyone brave enough to take them on, until now.

Charlie went on to explain how the Dunns had initially approached him to be partners, but when Charlie refused they had started threatening him, Che and Knighty with all kinds of unholy punishments he couldn't return with his existing crew. It was then that he'd brought Billy in, an old friend from school and a double-hard bastard. Billy needed the money, knew he could offer the skill set required, and happily joined the team about three years ago.

He pushed home the fact that the dealing was just a short-term thing, so he could save enough money to move to Spain, where he planned to open a restaurant with his father. He then explained how his father had owned a small pub on the outskirts of Stambro, catering more to the surrounding villages and the people with money. He had prided himself upon his fine Spanish tapas-style menu, taught to him by his own father, but had decided to sell up and move to Spain when Charlie's mother became ill with asthma and was barely breathing in polluted Stambro. His father had made the big decision that the sun, fresh Spanish air and more relaxed way of living would help her. And it had, massively, right up until he got viciously stung on a property deal for some land to develop his restaurant on. He lost a big sum of money to the bogus property developers and had no way of getting back to England, or real want to, Charlie swore to them he would earn enough money to get over there and help them out, and that's what he had done. He had enough money safely tucked away for him and his crew to retire, and was waiting to make a further £500,000 or so just for good measure, then he would leave for Spain and never look back.

"You and Hitten could come with me you know, to Spain?" he suddenly blurted out, not really thinking of the magnitude of his sudden and unexpected offer to the girl he'd met just a few days before.

She looked back at him with yearning warmth,

deep from behind her light hazel eyes. "I'd love to, Charlie," she replied, smiling softly, completely lost in the moment.

The front door suddenly thudded from outside, knocking them from their romantic dream and shattering it into tiny pieces on the living room floor. Alice sighed and reluctantly got up to answer it, picking up the pieces of the dream and weaving them back into her hungry mind as she did.

"Is Charlie there, darling?" Billy asked, in his politest of tones.

Charlie quickly made his way to the hall before Alice had chance to invite the madman in, as he was sure she would. It was definitely too soon for her to be exposed to the world of Billy Marine. These sorts of things needed easing upon a person, slowly.

"Sorry mate, I've been ages, I know. I'm coming now, just give us two secs."

He shut the door firmly in Billy's frowning face, just as he was on the cusp of a reply. He grabbed Alice with both arms and firmly pulled her into him, their lips instantly moulding together like putty, hands wildly running over each other's body with lust, whilst something else built within them both, something more honest than lust.

The innocence of her world compared to his and the amazing fact she had continued her life successfully, after being left to raise a child, and had not chosen the path of benefits and daytime television so many other young girls in Stambro had, stirred something deep within his soul, a feeling of sanctuary in her clean world, a hole being filled in his cold heart, the motherly type of woman he needed now more than ever.

She fell safely into the strength of his outward confidence, the warmth of his protection, the promise of his ability to provide. She had longed for a father figure for her son, whilst obviously worried if a drug dealing, drug using, Stambro man could really be that? But his downfalls fitted so well into the mould of all the men she'd known growing up, there was a comfort in that, and there was also a comfort she found in the compassion that came from behind his eyes, and that wasn't like all the men she had known growing up, there was something she had never seen before, back there and her heart told her she wanted more.

"When can I see you again?" he asked desperately, prying himself away.

"Whenever you want. I'm not going anywhere. I'll be right here, until you say otherwise."

She threw herself back in for one last kiss, and then quickly scribbled her number down and stuffed it in his jacket pocket with instructions not to lose it this time.

Bidding Hitten farewell up the stairs, Charlie left, painfully clutching at Alice right until the last moment, taking in as much of her life-giving persona as he could, sucking in every breath until he was back out into the cold November air and all the haunting realities it brought with it.

Billy cursed him for leaving him so long to be with a woman as they made their way back to the Land Rover. They stood either side of the 4x4, Billy boring him over the bonnet about how he recognised Alice and how he always knew everyone. It was one of his signature traits, one of which he was extremely proud. Suddenly the same white Range Rover with the private plate from Friday night screeched to a halt in the road about ten metres away.. They both froze, silent, and turned to look. Tommy, Mickey, Freddy and Frosty jumped out of the gleaming white car.

"What the fuck you cunts doing round here?" Tommy Dunn roared with aggression, like an overprotective lion defending his pride.

The four men came bowling down the middle of the road towards them, Tommy in front, the biggest and meanest, Frosty behind him, weighing in at around 16stone of muscle himself, and Mickey and Freddy bringing up the rear.

"Get in the car, Billy!" Charlie shouted as he saw Mickey pull out a long, shiny blade from inside his jacket; his already drug-battered face distorted further with venomous hate.

"Fuck that!" replied Billy defiantly through gritted teeth.

"Not here, Billy, not now. Just get in the fucking car, mate!" Charlie commanded, exerting his full authority.

Billy backed down and opened his door as Charlie did the same, the four angry gangsters almost upon them. Billy revved the engine into life, still fuming with anger. The Dunns and their new accomplice stopped just short of the car, laughing and jeering at the retreat. Billy hammered the car into first and wheel-spun off, but not before Freddy Dunn had time to pick up rather large piece of broken concrete curb and launch it at Billy's rear door, causing a huge crashing sound.

"Fucking Aleister cunts!" Billy screamed with fury, punching the dashboard, his face exploding with a red rage as they sped out of the estate. He wasn't designed for retreating.

"We should have fucking done 'em, Charlie, then and there. We let 'em beat us!"

"What the two of us, against a couple of steroid mountains, one who we know has a gun, and two nutty little cunts, one who clearly had a massive fuck-off knife on him?" Charlie shouted back, unimpressed by Billy's reckless bravado.

"Fuck their guns and their knives; I'll stick them all up their fucking shit-fuck arses!" he thundered back, still assaulting his own dashboard with all his might.

"Listen, Billy. They'll get it all right, but not before we're fucking ready, and not when we're outnumbered. But they will get it, mark my words." Charlie attempted to reassure the livid Billy, although he himself was not convinced.

Taking on the Dunns was not part of his plan, and never had been. For him it was all about the money, the turf war didn't interest him, just as it hadn't at Tottenham when Leon had got him into a few scrapes with other football firms. He didn't see the point of it all. He understood the use of violence if he needed to protect his money and his business, but he didn't see the Dunns as a threat. Their drugs were worse, they didn't steal his customers, they didn't owe him money; he just needed to keep them at bay, which was the whole reason for getting the gun from Leon in the first place. He wanted no part of unnecessary violence; it didn't sit well with his admittedly black morality.

CHAPTER 6

14th November 06:06pm.

Jack and Jenny walked into DCI Brent's oversized office and took a seat.

"Okay guys, what have you got? Why haven't we got him in custody yet?" Brent demanded, looking down his long thin nose at one detective and then the other, with a supercilious frown. "I'm getting pestered like mad from above; it doesn't look at all good for the unit."

"Well, simply, sir, he wasn't there. But it wasn't because he knew we were coming, which we know because we found a firearm, blood-stained items of clothing, fourteen grams of high quality cocaine, and a Mercedes Benz registered in his name that matches the tyre tracks at the scene," Jack replied, confidently.

"Have we matched the firearm to the bullet?" DCI

Brent asked, sitting up in his chair and rubbing his hands together in anticipation.

"Well, it's definitely same type as used in the weapon we found, but they tested it in the water tank and didn't get an exact, positive match on the rifling marks," Jack explained, clearly displaying his annoyance and disappointment. "But the bullet wasn't in the best of shape after being recovered from the victim, so we just don't go with the rifling marks as evidence, and say the bullet could have come from that gun. Which it could. I'm convinced Paccadillo is our shooter, sir." Jack paused, filling his lungs with fresh, much needed oxygen.

"Okay and the items of clothing found - have they been matched to the victim's blood?" Brent retorted impatiently, seemingly unconcerned about the match of bullet and barrel.

"Yes, positive match on that one, sir." Jack beamed back at him.

"Okay, so the evidence is overwhelming. Shouldn't be a problem in court. I think from what we have currently, this is our shooter. Is everyone agreed?"

"Yes, complete agreement, sir." Jack replied with self-assurance, as Jenny nodded with silent approval.

"Now, what about the motive?" Brent asked, leaning back, crossing his legs, and biting on a pencil he had plucked up from his desk.

"DC Pearce took an interesting phone call this morning, from someone replying to the notice we pinned to the suspect's door. He had good information and was obviously attempting to claim the reward for what he had to offer, of course."

"Well, of course," Brent sighed back, knowingly. "DC Pearce?" He turned to Jenny, sitting back up in his chair. She uncrossed her arms and sat to attention, preparing to take the floor.

"Well his name is James Vole, sir. He lives on the same floor as the suspect, and 'claims' to know him very well."

"Vole, how very apt," Brent butted in, a wry smile lighting up his taught cheeks.

"Yes, sir, indeed," she replied, with forced laughter, and then continued. "So 'apparently' our suspect is heavily involved in drug dealing. Cocaine mainly, but also marijuana and ecstasy, and 'apparently' the victim was a regular customer. So this would explain them meeting in the concealed location, and the dealing would explain the suspect's expensive tastes around the home, while claiming benefits for a bad knee."

"So, what's the motive in killing a customer?" Brent gawped back at her, clearly unimpressed with the answer.

"Well, apparently the suspect had an ongoing feud with the Dunn Brothers over cocaine sales in Stambro."

"Oh, now there's a gang of vile reprobates I've certainly heard of before."

"Some of the worst the town has to offer, sir. Well, anyway, Vole believes the victim was also using the Dunn Brothers to source his cocaine, as he brought bulk amounts and resold for profit himself."

"So we've also got the suspect on distrusting class A?" Brent butted in once more.

"Oh yes, sir. Well, if this Vole actually gets down here to make an official statement, and if that then stands up in court. He doesn't have a clean record himself, by any stretch of the imagination," she replied. "So back to the motive, 'apparently' the victim had got in a bit of debt with the suspect, and was sort of robbing Peter to pay Paul, so to speak."

"Okay, so the suspect shot him to make an example of him, to send a message to The Dunns?" Brent quizzed.

"Exactly, sir," Jack interjected on Jenny's behalf, letting her relax a bit, while giving her a wink and a nod to show he was impressed. "What we've got will hold up in court, with or without this Vole character, and we can get a guilty on the bastard, I'm sure of it. And when we bring him in, we'll match his prints to the gun and his voice to the emergency call from the phone box."

Brent looked proudly at his second-in-command.

"Excellent work. This will get them off my back for now. Do we have a photo of the suspect?"

Jenny reached into the folder lying across her lap, and pulled out the picture of Charlie and his parents in Spain. She slid it across the desk, and Brent picked it up and studied it carefully.

"She looks a bit old to be dealing cocaine and taking on the Dunn brothers," he laughed, pointing at Charlie's mother.

"The one in the middle, sir," Jack replied with a fixed smile.

"I know Jack, it was a joke!" said Brent, shaking his head, as both Jack and Jenny held their pasted smiles out of obedience. "Okay, so I'm going to get this out right away, to everyone, as the suspect we're actively seeking in relation to Friday night's murder," he explained, sitting bolt upright in his chair, lying the photo face up and his palms face down on the desk. "Well done guys. Keep up this excellent work and, for now, get yourselves off home for the night."

"Yes, sir," they both replied happily, and got up and left the office.

As they shut the chief inspector's door behind them, Jenny grabbed Jack's arm impulsively, spurred on by his previous wink and nod.

"Fancy going for a drink, to celebrate, sir?" she asked, then immediately removed her hand and began playing with her cuff in anticipation of Jack's reply.

"We've not got him yet, Jen." Jack replied, sternly.

She tilted her head downward, clearly dejected.

"But yeah, why not? I could do with a pint to unwind; it's been an intense couple of days," he quickly continued.

Jenny lifted her chin up in amazement. "Excellent guv. Only one drink, won't get sloshed or anything like that, and we can go wherever you like."

"Okay, how about that little pub on the corner of the Aleister estate, The Hen and Chickens? It's on the way for both of us then," he suggested.

"Perfect, guv," she replied, beaming.

"You gotta cut the 'guv' out though. Might sound a bit weird, Jen."

Jack clicked the fob as he slipped on his black pea coat. The car clicked shut as Jenny walked towards him. She had reapplied her makeup and hair in the car park while she waited for him to pull in, and he immediately noticed; he couldn't help but notice. She was stunning. They walked into The Hen and Chickens together, he letting her go first with a gentleman's touch. He also insisted on buying the drinks: a glass of white wine for her, a pint of Guinness for him. They sat down at a table near a flashing fruit machine inside the near empty and typically bland council estate pub. Its only other customers right then were three male regulars propping up the bar and discussing the weekend's football results.

"You come here often?" Jack joked, to ease a surprising attack of nerves.

"Oh yes, guv, I'm normally at the bar with those three," she joked back.

"No more 'guv', remember?"

"Sorry. Jack," she replied timidly. Her cheeks flushed crimson.

He took a big, long gulp of his black Guinness and pulled out his electronic cigarette.

"One law I wholeheartedly despise: the bloody smoking ban," he explained, inhaling the vapour for a quick nicotine high.

"Why don't you just give up?" she asked, abruptly.

Jack had no answer for this, and chose instead to fire a question back at her. "So why did you decide to become a policewoman, Jen?"

She took a short sip of her wine, and tilted her head to one side.

"My family, I guess. My dad was a policeman, my granddad was a fireman, my other granddad was in the air force, and my brother's in the Met. So it was the obvious choice I suppose, It's all I ever heard about growing up, although it wasn't that obvious for my parents, me being a girl and all. My dad wasn't keen at first. In fact, he was dead against it."

"Daddy's girl, eh?" Jack mocked her.

"Yeah, every girl is, aren't they?" she replied as her cheeks reddened again, not wanting to expose her softer side to him.

"Dunno. I was the only kid in our house, so I was both mummy and daddy's boy," he laughed, for the first time lifting the curtain that separated the professional from the personal.

Her pretty, tanned face responded immediately, and she leaned in to the table, ready to pry further. He leaned back, suddenly intimidated by her good looks, trying to keep up his usual defensive guard.

"So what about you, Jack, why did you join the force?" she asked softly, her moist, pink painted lips spinning into Jack's eyes and engulfing his thoughts. His defence had been shot down in seconds.

"Well, it's going to sound a bit corny, but my dad, God rest his soul, was the head teacher at my school in Cambridge. That's where we were from originally."

"Bloody hell. That must have been hard!" There was genuine compassion in her eyes, and he felt a tug at his heart strings.

"It wasn't the easiest, no, but anyway, one year, when I was about fifteen, one of the lads in my year decided to set my dad's car alight, after he'd expelled him for fighting. He blew it up, completely destroyed it. We knew who it was, but my dad couldn't do anything as he'd already expelled this lad. He was completely powerless, so he had to call in the police." Jack took another long, satisfying gulp at his now half-empty pint. "And when they came to the house, these two CID officers, it impressed the hell out of me; Their confidence, their suits and the way they finally caught the lad. I was sold from that moment to be honest, so I left school and went for it."

"Wow, that's a proper reason that is, not like mine," she replied, tipping her head down and reaching for her glass.

"But you're a bloody good detective, Jen; it's obviously in your blood." Jack's compliment was unexpected and quietly delivered. "It's more in my blood to be teaching piano or something," he added.

"Piano?"

"Yes, I'm classically trained."

"Well, get you," she responded, looking up at him with an impressed smile. "I would never have guessed that."

"Yeah, my father thought I was going to be playing concerts for a living, composing my own pieces. He wasn't too impressed with the detective idea."

"I'd love to hear you play," she announced, her pretty pink finger nails stroking at her glass.

"Ha, that is not going to happen." Jack laughed, but his defences were rising again slightly.

The change in tone didn't go unnoticed by Jenny, who decided upon a change of subject.

"So why did you move to Stambro from Cambridge? Bit of a step down, wasn't it?"

"Well, that's my dad for you. I went into sixth form before joining up, and that's when he decided to move down here, as he'd been offered a job at High Croft."

"The Crowley school?" she asked, amazed.

"Yeah, he wanted to work with less privileged kids. He wasn't even the headmaster, only deputy head, but he loved it, you know. He was a very giving man." He replied proudly and knocked back another quarter of his pint. "Anyway, I left school then. I didn't want a whole new load of abuse from a whole new load of spotty teenagers, so I got a job. Then, when I turned eighteen I joined up. And the rest is history, as they say."

"Yeah, good job an' all. That's a right rough school, that one."

"Don't I know it, Jen. He had some shocking stories, which contributed to me wanting to be stationed around here."

Just as he was about to finish his pint, a buzzing came from his trouser pocket: Mum Calling. He excused himself and stepped outside.

"Hello darling, it's mother."

She sounded unusually upbeat.

"Hi, sorry Mum, I should have rung. Just stopped off for a drink after work, I will be home shortly though," he explained, a guilty look drowning his face.

"Don't worry, Jacobe, you enjoy yourself. Let your hair down, you deserve it. I just wanted you to tell you that I love you."

He looked shocked, expecting an interrogation on his whereabouts and a lecture about his cold dinner.

"I love you too, Mum. What's brought all this on?"

"Oh, nothing really. I just wanted you to know, and your father loved you too, you know. He was so proud of you becoming a detective."

"Really, Mum? Wouldn't he have preferred Jacobe the composer?"

"No, don't be so silly. You followed your own dreams and he loved you for that; we both did. You're the best son any parents could ever have dreamt of," she replied, the emotion clear in her voice, as if tears were only a moment away.

Jack was concerned. "Have you been drinking

again, Mum?" he asked nervously.

She laughed back, warmly. "No, well, maybe a little. I just want you to know, as long as you're on this earth, how much we both loved you."

"I do Mum, of course I do, and I love you both too. Even though Dad's gone, I'll always love him. He was a great man. Now stop being so silly, I'll be home in about half an hour."

He looked to the wristwatch on his free hand; it was already eleven minutes past nine.

"Don't rush, Jacobe, enjoy your life. You only get one."

Just as he was about to reply, Tommy Dunn's white Range Rover pulled into the car park and screeched to a halt, taking up two spaces, music blaring.

"Okay Mum, gotta go. See you when I'm back."

He hung up the phone and rushed back inside to Jenny.

"Guess who just pulled up?" he asked, excitedly.

But before she had time to reply two of the Dunn brothers, Freddy missing but Frosty by their side, crashed through the door. They stomped their way to the bar and ordered a round of drinks before rudely demanding the barman bring them to their 'usual' table.

"Put some fucking music on too, you sour old melt, it's like a fucking morgue in here" Tommy demanded with a harsh snarl.

"Charming," Jenny whispered across to Jack, who was watching the group with a disdainful glare.

"Think that's our cue to leave, Jen, don't you?"

"Definitely, guv."

He looked at her, grinning, squinting one eye.

"Sorry, Jack." She giggled, like a schoolgirl with a crush.

They both sipped their remaining liquids, and Jack took the empty glasses to the bar, thanking the landlord as he did. He then made the spontaneous decision to approach the group of laughing Neanderthals. Jenny immediately noticed and followed close behind without questioning his motives. He pulled out his badge from an inside pocket and held it in front of him as he approached the table. The three stopped talking and turned hostile glares upon him.

"Hello, fellers. Detective Inspector Jack Cloud." He introduced himself confidently, with no fear whatsoever of the group of men whose wild and aggressive manner would make most other men look away and duck for cover.

"Just wondered if you had any information on Friday night's shooting? Or the suspect we're after? Charlie Paccadillo?"

All three men kept straight-faced, unmoved by the badge or the man, and then Tommy spoke up for the group.

"Listen, we're all Muslims, pal," he explained, to Jack and Jenny's bemusement. "We don't do pork, so fuck off!"

The table erupted with laughter, as Frosty followed his leader up. "Yeah, fuck off back to the sty, before you stink the boozer out."

His nasty tone and nasty persona proved there was not one ounce of good in this man. His gnarled face, short stubbly hair, wide shoulders and fascist tattoos screamed hate from every angle. Jack instantly knew he was wasting his time.

"Well, if you do change your minds, gentlemen, you know where to find me," was his calm reply. He gave them a guileless smile, and then turned and walked away, with Jenny following close behind.

"She can stay though!" Mickey shouted, his face a grotesque picture of lust. "I'll show her a real man."

Jenny turned back to face the group, red faced, and snarled, "A real man, you say? Bet you can't even get your little chipolata up with the amount of shit in your system, mate." Her words were guaranteed the venomous sting of a king cobra to a weak man like Mickey Dunn.

Tommy and Frosty instantly cracked up with laughter, stopping Mickey dead in his tracks and leaving him visibly wounded. Jack gently coaxed Jenny away and led her out to the car park as the group of gangsters made farmyard 'oink oink' noises in the background.

"Bloody hell, Jen, you soon shut him up," said Jack admiringly as they headed for their cars.

"I've had to deal with little runts like him all my life, Jack, growing up around here, and then working the streets as a uniform. He's a joke, just hiding behind his big meathead of a brother," she barked.

Jack laughed and reiterated his approval. He hadn't yet seen this side of Jenny, and he liked it. A lot. They bade each other a rather fonder farewell than usual, and looked forward to the morning, when the hunt for Paccadillo would commence.

Jack walked up the drive, shouldering his work bag

and wearing an unusual smile on his strong face. He wondered if he would reveal tonight's 'date' with Jenny to his mother or keep it private. As he pondered the difficult choice he closed the front door behind him. He knew his mother would want the full lowdown on Jenny and he didn't know if he wanted, or could be bothered to do that. He really just wanted to go to his room and think about every second of the 'date' in minute detail. He shook his head at his excitable feelings and laughed out loud.

"It's only me, Mum," he announced.

The antique record player sang out from the living room with the start of *Tchaikovsky's Swan Lake, No.10 Scène (moderato)*. He shook his head with a frown now, knowing the all too familiar scene: a drunken mother listening to loud classical music and wallowing in her own self-pity. The symphony eased its way effortlessly into the uplifting string section of the song as he made his way to the kitchen, poured himself a glass of water and looked to the living room.

"Mum, I'm home!"

He yelled, but to no reply. The strings rose in pitch now, drowning out his words.

All he could see through the service hatch was his mother's arm hanging from one side of her chair which faced the record player, its back to him. He sighed as he realised she had fallen to sleep drunk again, with the song playing on the record player's repeat mode. He walked out of the kitchen and around into the lounge, and as he did the music appeared to follow his steps. He turned into the lounge as the booming, gloom-ridden horn section took its turn, the powerful, commanding tones opening his eyes, his ears, all his senses at once. And then he saw the empty pill bottle on the floor and his heart sank along with the pace of the music, which returned to the strings, the now sombre, haunting strings.

"Mum!"

He raced around to her side, but it was too late. Her motionless body lay slumped in the old dusty chair, the picture of his father from atop the piano clasped between her lifeless fingers.

"Mum! What have you done? What have you done?"

He reached down for the empty pill bottle, Mrs Cloud, Codeine Phosphate, 1 to be taken when necessary, with food. He had only just picked the prescription of 50 tablets up the previous week. He fell to his knees, his eyes glancing towards the bottle of gin on the table next to her as he did. His head fell into her lap, his eyes streamed with tears, he jerked at her thighs,

"Mum, please, wake up, please wake up."

Her cold body gave no response, not even a speckle of hope; her blue lips and icy hands told Jack what he already knew deep down. This wasn't the first overdose he'd seen, and wouldn't be the last. But it was the first time he'd seen his beloved mother in such a cruel, undignified, un-motherly fashion. He cried aloud, his stomach flapping like a sail in a 100mph perfect storm. He turned away, and then sank down further to a seating position, leaning his back against the old chair. He reached inside his blazer and pulled out his mobile phone and shakily typed 999.

"Hello, this is DI Cloud of BHMCU. I need an ambulance right away to thirty three Masons Way. It's my mother, she's taken an overdose. Codeine and alcohol. Please hurry."

He dropped the phone to the floor as the record, reaching its end, automatically jumped its way back to the beginning. Pulling up his knees and sinking his head into them, he wept as Tchaikovsky's strings filled the room. He snorted and coughed as salty tears rolled into his mouth and down the back of his throat, and he squeezed his body in tighter. Finally falling sideways to the floor he curled into the foetal position. His mother's womb now too small and too dead to re-house him. His body trembled, alone, broken, betrayed, let down,

"Why?"

The words repeated over and over from the murky depths of his lacerated, blackened soul, as Swan Lake reached its climactic crescendo again, and again he sobbed, sniffled, and bawled.

"Why?"

CHAPTER 7

15th November 09:11am.

Charlie slammed his foot into the door of the Ambrose Court roof space, smashing it flying open, destroying the padlock with ease. He ran up the stairs two at a time, almost flying as he did. He broke through the next door, out into the open. The air was a crisp light blue; he could see the whole town, roofs, trees, roads, cars, life, and he felt the worry tear through his insides. He ran to the edge, wanting to stop, but unable to. He left the edge, his stomach taut with angst and fear, and then he flew, down, down, down he went, soaring through the freezing cold air, the ground below zooming itself closer, control lost, fate sealed, death and sanctuary mere moments away,
"Charlie."
Billy, tapped on his shoulder, "You 'aving a bad

dream, pal?"

He opened his eyes to see Billy standing there, hulking over him, his grey tracksuit on, hood up, his forehead pouring with sweat at an alarming rate.

"Yeah. Yeah, bad dream, Billy," Charlie panted. "The fuck's going on? Why you sweating like that? You're leaking, mate." His brain still in dreamland, perplexed.

"Been for a run, ain't I?" Billy answered, heading for the kitchen. "You want some grub?" he offered.

"Nah, I'm fine for the minute, mate. Cuppa tea would be nice though."

"That ponce Knighty finished the last teabag, didn't he? Got coffee though. You look like you could do with it black, to be fair."

"Yeah, whatever Billy." Charlie tried desperately to pull his brain back into the real world.

He scanned the cold room; it was tidier than the last time he woke up there. No Che, no Knighty, no pile of cocaine, just a few empty beer cans, and a fried chicken bucket. He mused on the dream and what it meant, and then the fear came rushing back to the pit of his stomach as he was once again reminded of the brutal actuality of his predicament. He sighed and reached for his cigarettes, lit one up, and a long, heavy, malevolent drag filled his lungs to capacity, relieving his anxiety for a millisecond. Then it came flooding back, with lightning aggression, as sure as night follows day. Billy came back into the room with a steaming black coffee and placed it on the table in front of him.

"Filthy 'abit that."

He pointed to the cigarette while waving away the smoke with his hand.

"What and bag, booze and brasses ain't?" Charlie replied, bitterly.

"Well, that's why I go for a run, don't I? Sweat it all out, mate, none of that shit in my system now, clean as a whistle, son," he informed him, proudly.

"You can't sweat out all those dirty brasses mate."

"Yeah, but they come, I love 'em, they go. I don't get any of that emotional attachment, like what you got at the minute with that Aleister bird."

"What's wrong with emotional attachment?"

"Love makes you fat, everyone knows that."

"Yeah, but she's worth getting fat for, ain't she?"

Billy giggled in reply and perched on the edge of the sofa. "Yeah, I 'spose. I wish I could remember where I knew 'er from, it's doing my 'ead in." He rubbed his hand on his chin, deep in thought.

Charlie sipped the warm coffee, and smoked the tarry cigarette.

"I was having one mental dream then, Billy; I was just about to die when you woke me up. What's that all about?"

He looked to his huge friend for answers, but Billy was still rubbing his square jawline and thinking about Alice.

So Charlie continued, "It really felt like I was going to die, do you know what I mean? Like real fear, but then also relief. That's the part that's freaking me out, the relief."

"I got it. Fuck, I got it!" Billy jumped to his feet with excitement. "I saw her visiting that wanker Frosty in the nick."

"What? What you on about?" Charlie replied, too tired, too confused and too anxiety-ridden to take in what his excited friend was revealing.

"I'm telling you, mate. I never forget a face; we learnt that in the marines, reconnaissance photos and that, how to remember a face."

"Get on with it Billy!" Charlie bellowed. What Billy had just told him was sinking in now and he was in no mood for hearing the ex-marine reminiscing.

"I remember her and she visited him in there when I was there. One hundred fucking per cent, mate."

"Why the hell would she be visiting that prick?" Charlie demanded.

"Probably his bird, I dunno. But I remember all the lads going on about her now; we always talked about the tasty bits of crumpet mate. Blokes in prison, you know, obviously," he explained, calming himself and sitting back down as he noticed the distraught look etched awkwardly across Charlie's face.

"Are you sure Billy? You might have just mixed her up."

"When have I ever been wrong? Faces, names, numbers... tell me once you've known me to be wrong."

Charlie knew he was right. Billy had the incredible gift of a photographic memory. Whether he'd learnt it in the marines or not, he knew he could rely upon his flawless powers of recollection.

"Might not have been his bird mate, might just be pals. I dunno. They're both Aleister, ain't they?" Billy tried to pacify the situation as Charlie's mind visibly raced.

"You, you don't think she told him where I was going the other night, do you?" Charlie asked, his face creasing up and begging Billy to go easy with his answer.

"You said you didn't tell her where you were

going?" answered Billy, puzzled.

"Yeah, well I did. She heard my call to Harry."

"Well it's fucking her then, Charlie, of course it is, it all makes sense, mate."

"No, it can't be, she ain't like that, Billy. I'm telling you, she's not that type of girl," he pleaded.

"Oh yeah, none of them are mate, none of them are. This is what I was just talking about, pal, the brasses thing, emotional attachment." He backed off again, seeing Charlie clearly upset, the frown of a fool weighing his brow down like it had been pumped full of lead.

"I can't believe it was her. I don't believe it was her. Why would she do it?"

"She's a young girl with a kid mate, probably works for them bunch a cunts, doing bits and bobs. She was there with that Freddy's 'orrible bird for fuck's sake; they'd been sent there."

Charlie could not believe it. He could not have been sucked in so easily by someone like that, and he still didn't believe Alice was the type, whatever Billy said. He was a good judge of character, he'd thought. The doubt eating his brain, he blurted, "Fuck it, I can't deal with this now. I'm gonna call her later and just ask her outright."

"Best bet, mate. 'Ave it out with 'er," Billy agreed.

There was a familiar knock at the door, in the fashion of Kumbaya My Lord. They both looked at each other.

"Che."

Billy got up and answered the door. "My word!" He roared with laughter.

"Look at the state of you, this has gotta be the earliest you've ever been up, ain't it?"

Che pushed past the laughing mad ex-marine and walked in, his long black hair a big frizzy mess, his clothes thrown on; he looked like he'd just stepped out his cardboard box after a long cold night on the street.

"I had to get round, dude, have you seen this?"

He threw the national paper down on the table, folded open about five pages in. It was a big, clear picture of Charlie's face captioned with the words, Police pursue suspect in suburban shooting.

"Fuck's sake!" Billy announced.

Charlie sunk his head in his hands.

"I'm going back to sleep." He declared, as his brain shut down and gave up. He closed his eyes and let the warm couch swallow him back up, hoping to get back to his dream, flying from the roof of Ambrose court to the relief awaiting him below.

Charlie opened his eyes with careful adjustment as Billy's cold flat came back into view; the dark had worked its way into the air. He'd been dreaming of Spain, sitting at the bar with a cold beer in one hand and Alice's hand in the other, his mother and father smiling from behind the bar as happy customers tucked into delicious meals. He then realised what had woken him, Billy and Knighty coming back into the flat, and the cold air and loud bang that came with them.

"Fuck me, taters out there." Billy bellowed in his deep gruff voice, stopping then to look at Charlie, who remained in the same position he'd left him.

"You only just woken up, you lazy cunt?" he mocked and then pointed to Che, still asleep on the other couch. "You're as bad as that fucking 'ippy."

Che had got stoned, as usual, when Charlie had gone back to sleep, whereas Billy and Knighty had gone to 'work'.

"Got nuff cheese in today, captain, lovely lickle surprise to wake up to."

Billy gave Knighty a deathly glance as the lankier man declared today had been a good debt-collecting day. It was the kind of glance only a man who had been sat in a car with another man he didn't really care for for six hours could give.

"Really? Well, at least something's going to plan. Let's get the iron out and get it tidy," Charlie replied optimistically, as he slowly pulled himself up from the sofa, rubbing the sleep from his eyes, and then massaging the pleasant dream away from his mind with his palms on his side temples. Reality was the truth now, and reality was the only thing that could get him to that dream. Reality also reminded him quickly of the Alice situation, but he put it to the back of his mind, to deal with later.

"So they all paid up?" he asked, as Billy stomped into the kitchen, making his need for a beer known with the vulgar use of various profanities.

"Yep, well nearly all, but check this, bruv," Knighty exclaimed happily, emptying a huge heap of money down on the table in screwed up rolls and separate, rather cleaner looking elastic-banded packages. "'Bout eighty-four K there, bruv."

"So, we're missing ten off what we should have?" Charlie immediately pointed out, his calculator brain working as hastily as ever.

"Yeah, well that's the nearly bit, init?" Knighty began to explain, sitting himself down next to the still sleeping Che. "You know dat wannabe fool from Duncan Street?" He asked, as he reached for Che's last half-smoked reefer, which was sitting patiently in the ashtray, before lighting it up and tugging it hard back to life.

"Duncan Street? No, who is he?"

Charlie racked his brains for 'wannabe fools' from Duncan Street, a particularly untidy little cul-de-sac even by the Crowley estates standards. The Stambro council seemed to house a lot of young, single mums from troubled families in this little area, and the smashed-up kitchen appliances and broken children's toys that littered the gardens in front of the unkempt houses did nothing to disprove this well-known fact.

"C'mon, bruv, the one we brought into Turner's place. He lives up there with that 'orrible little sket he got up the duff, young guy, bout twenty, ginger ninja, just discovered the 'roids."

"Blaze?" Charlie laughed back, remembering the humour of the one and only meeting he had had with this character, as his bright orange hair had matched his name so perfectly but unintentionally.

Blaze had apparently got his name because he had liked to 'blaze up' spliffs throughout his brief secondary school career; in classrooms, in the headmaster's office, wherever he had deemed the most outrageous. This act of blatant defiance for authority was one of the most memorable tools in his ruthless young armoury of not giving a shit, for making waves in the Stambro Who's Who of naughty young men. He quickly got noticed by some higher up lads in the estate's naughty book when he got expelled for 'blazing' at his own mother's final meeting with the headmaster to decide whether to expel him. Then he went on to selling small bags of weed for them to school friends on their lunch breaks and began learning the kind of education only the street could teach him. He had come to Knighty's attention after ruthlessly attacking one of his young dealers over some fake pills that Knighty had apparently had nothing to do with.

In the four years since his expulsion, Blaze, along with a small firm of young men from his year at school, had set up their own thing selling E's at all the local raves. And they had started to make some pretty decent money. Along with the money and notoriety at the raves came the head of this little firm's need to show he wasn't to be messed about with. Although it was thought among the drug dealing world that raves were the easiest place to make a penny, as everybody had money on their hip and was off their face and not keeping check on what they spent. There was also no need for 'ticking' or large payments, as pills went for as cheap as seven for five pounds; enough to keep even the most hardened rave rat happy for a few hours of hardcore trance dancing, and more than affordable to the mostly young dole-hungry crowd. Sometimes the easygoing ravers would be joined by not so easygoing traveller kids though, also trying to make a quick buck selling anything from stolen alcohol to tax-free cigarettes. The travellers, or 'pikeys' as they were more affectionately known, didn't generally get involved in the selling of drugs, but would buy pills from Blaze and his mates all the same on odd occasions. Blaze had started weight training and steroid taking when he was about 19, and quickly bulked out into a short, red haired lump of muscle, with poorly inked tattoos on his forearms and neck to match. He looked the part, but no one really knew if he could act the part, not until Knighty's dealer had sold him a bag of 5000 pills. Those pills had apparently pleased everyone at a certain rave held in a certain abandoned factory, apart from the pikeys. They came at him and his little gang of rogues with pick axe handles and broken bottles, screaming that the pills were fake, and demanding their money back or else. Blaze, being heavily outnumbered, and out-armed, had had to refund the crazed travellers, plus interest, which gave his hitherto flawless reputation at the raves an undeserved bashing. He left the rave early that night, in a car with one of his accomplices, and went straight to Knighty's dealer. Whether the pills had been good or bad was irrelevant at this point, as Blaze had lost face and now had to regain it.

Blaze and his friend broke into the dealer's mother's house just after midnight that same night, dragged him from his bed despite his screaming mother's pleas not to, for which she received a shove to the floor and a broken wrist. The mid-level dealer was dragged outside and beaten, by Blaze alone, to a quivering bloody mess and left for dead. Obviously this news travelled up the ladder to Knighty the next day, and then Charlie and the rest of the firm. Blaze was quickly paid a visit by Knighty and an angry Billy and Charlie. They'd tied him up in his trampy Duncan Street living room, Charlie had given his girlfriend some shopping money and told her to take their small baby and leave for a few hours. She'd happily obliged, leaving the terrified Blaze, quite unhappily, to face his fate alone.

After a few slaps from an angry Billy the full story had come out, and after Charlie had quizzed Knighty on the pills authenticity alone in the kitchen, they came to the conclusion Knighty's dealer may have mixed and matched some of the pills he'd been given to sell with decent looking fakes. The fact the young lad had shown balls to do what he'd done had earned a tiny bit of their respect. In his earning of their respect, Knighty's dealer had lost it and Blaze was offered his rung on the ladder, along with his little posse, which he'd quickly accepted. He was to deal with Knighty, and do exactly as he was told when he was told, and everyone would get along just fine. Handshakes and an eventual untying by a put-out Billy (not enough punishment had been dealt in his books) put the matter to rest and that was the last Charlie had heard of young Blaze, until now.

"So what? That little shit's come up short or something?" Charlie asked, still laughing at the memory, and the name.

Billy walked back in from the kitchen at this point, glugging down a cold beer. "He hasn't come up short; he's just blatantly refusing to pay, saying he ain't paying a 'dead manz'," he growled, putting on a fake street accent..

Blaze was also one of the younger generation who drank in the new Jamaican Yardie/American rap culture; white but black wannabes with all the lingo to go along with it. Blaze and his little crew of wannabes had also got into making rap records and posted a few on YouTube; a constant source of amusement for any older chaps on the estate. Even Knighty, who was clearly part of the same culture albeit for more legitimate reasons (his own father being an original Yardie from Jamaica), would cringe at people like Blaze.

"What the fuck does he mean, 'dead manz'?" Charlie replied, still laughing.

"He's on about you. Word on the 'streetz'," Billy broke into mimicking the street slang again, "iz you either gonna get busted by the fedz or murced by the Dunns."

Charlie's smile quickly dropped and the all too common of late frown line appeared between his angry eyes. He knew what verbal attacks like this meant to his reputation on the street, which was now more desperately important than ever. The street was always watching, waiting for the big boys at the top to slip up so any up and coming thug could take their place. It was a constant worry and danger for men like Charlie and he knew he had to nip it in the bud, Wanted Man or not. His plan to flee to Spain involved collecting all debts in that were still owed, including ones like the ten grand from Blaze; not a small hole in any man's pocket.

"Right, where is he? Charlie asked sternly, without wasting another thought.

Knighty quickly interjected, before Billy had chance to reply. "We've heard da little prick is in dat boozer down the end of his street, The Emperors Head. Apparently 'im and 'is little crew up there every night, giving it large. I always meet him in the car park there too, so it makes sense."

Charlie sat for a moment, head in hands, hatching a plan. "Right, what tools we got about us, Billy?"

Billy smiled menacingly and headed off towards his bedroom, then, as quickly as he'd gone in, came back out with a black duffel bag which he dumped on the floor in front of Charlie. Charlie quickly unzipped it and checked the contents; there were Taser guns, knuckle dusters, extendable coshes, CS gas canisters and sprays. It was a gangster's paradise of weaponry. He fingered through each deadly weapon thoughtfully, as a painter might debate the right colour for a landscape. He settled upon the extendable cosh, pulling it out and setting it down next to him, then zipped the bag back up and slipped on his black leather jacket. He slipped the cosh into a large internal pocket in the jacket. "What ya zipping it back up for?" Billy growled in concern. "I ain't picked my baby yet."

"I'm going alone, Billy." Charlie explained, with authority.

"Are you fuck, Charl,"he growled back once more, grabbing for the bag.

"Billy! Charlie shouted, stopping the other man in his tracks and reminding him who was head of the firm. "I'm going alone. That's the way this needs to be done, end of."

He headed off towards the door, grabbing Knighty's car keys as he did.

"I don't like this Charlie!" Billy roared with persistence.

Charlie paid no attention and walked straight out the door, slamming it shut behind him. Knighty, knowing Charlie's stubborn glare when he saw it, left him to it. Che had awoken, dazed and confused by the shouting and banging door, and piped up in dry, rasping tones, "What, what's going on man? What's all the bad vibes in here? It's like fucking, fucking, hell or something, man. Where's Satan hiding, dude? This room is burning up with evil, man."

"Satan's just left the building, blad," Knighty informed him.

Charlie sailed the new black Lexus IS200, kitted out with blacked out windows and black alloy wheels, ominously through the worn-out Crowley estate. He checked every road he passed for idle police vehicles whose occupants might fancy pulling over such a highly conspicuous luxury car. He turned on the fancy, custom-made in-car stereo system, which, without warning, lit up like the Manhattan skyline. James Brown's *The Boss* kicked in, loudly. Knighty's love of soul was no disappointment to Charlie, who smiled and tapped his left foot on the clutch as he cruised along. The words resonated in Charlie's impressionable mind, as he thought of himself as the boss of his little crew of criminals, and then, even more egotistically the boss of Crowley. It was a small estate in a London overspill that no one else in the world cared about. But he did. He'd grown up there, he knew everyone worth knowing, and most knew him, most even feared him, and that made him feel strong, powerful and untouchable. The depression he'd known after his failed football career was quickly blasted away by the fame being Crowley's top drug dealer had brought him.

He nodded along to the laidback drum beat now, leaning back in the chair, holding the steering wheel with one hand, looking around menacingly at the rundown streets he passed. In his own distorted mind he owned those streets, and he loved that imaginary ownership; it was addictive and empowering. But then, like a bolt of lightning striking the roof of the forty-thousand pound car, ripping through its shiny black roof, and hitting him directly on the crown of his inflated head, Alice popped up. Not the paranoia about who or what she really was, but the words she had said to him, do good get good, and the whole karma-based philosophy she had told him about. He wasn't doing good; he was doing bad. He was en route to do bad; would that bring more bad? He didn't know, but as The Emperor's Head public house came into view at the end of the street, he also didn't care; he could take on whatever bad came his way and deal with it the way he was about to deal with Blaze. He was a Boss, a gangster, and doing bad was what he was all about.

He pulled to a halt outside the pub. He pulled a small bag of cocaine from his jeans pockets, and scooped a bit out onto the end of the ignition key, then quickly snorted it up his left nostril, before doing the same with his right. He then jumped out of the car with a cocaine rush, locking the doors behind him via electric key fob. He then slipped the keys into his outside pocket, before slipping the cosh from his inside one up the jacket's sleeve, where it remained gripped firmly in his clenched fist so that its telescopic motion could be flicked out and into action as quick as he needed.

He bowled straight on into the empty pub, where he was greeted with the sight of two or three old locals sitting around enjoying an early evening's drink. Fearlessly striding forward, he knew what had to be done. This was business, and one thing Charlie knew how to do was conduct his specialised line of business. He spotted the lump of unearned muscle standing at the bar with two cronies, and before he himself could be spotted, flicked the extendable cosh out into play with a quick snap of his wrist. Its three tiers of black metal pain locking into place grabbed the three previously cool, bar-leaning young men's immediate attention. Their pints of beer lowered, along with their happy expressions. The only bar hand, a pretty young 18-year-old local girl, backed away from her place behind them at the bar on recognising Charlie and the weapon in his hand.

"Ch... Cha... Charlie..." Blaze stuttered in shock, his face a ghostly white now as the blood drained from it.

But before he could utter another stunned word, Charlie was on him, the cosh brought up now and resting against his shoulder, the arm holding it bent at the elbow ready to strike, his opposite shoulder and foot toward his target. Blaze immediately raised his arms up over his face and head in defence. His first mistake. Charlie whipped the baton down and across with extreme force onto the side of Blaze's exposed rib cage. A sharp crack echoed around the now completely silent pub, and Blaze let out a yelp and rolled over onto the bar to protect his broken ribs, his forearms still up protecting his head. Charlie pulled the cosh back up and straight back down at speed, this time aiming for the side of the knee. The very end of the metal stick hit its target spot on, causing a dull slap this time, and a louder cry from Blaze, who bent over, clutching at his damaged knee. Charlie smashed the base of the cosh into the side of Blaze's exposed face, and with that the lump of chemical muscle fell heavily to the floor, moaning in pain, blood pouring down his face. His friends, wanting none of this unexpected display of violence, stood back from him, their hands raised up in surrender.

"The only dead man round 'ere is gonna be you! You open that muggy trap again, right?"

Blaze didn't reply, just whimpered and caressed his wounds from the sticky, dirt of the pub floor.

"Ten grand this time tomorrow, to Knighty, no excuses!"

Charlie gazed fiercely into the eyes of the two friends, who both quickly looked away, not wanting to bring any of the madness they'd just witnessed upon themselves. Charlie paused a beat, let the message sink in really deep, and then turned and began to walk away.

"Fuck you blad, I'm with the Dunns now, and they gonna slice you up when they get you!" Blaze shouted at Charlie through the blood and whimpers. His second mistake.

Charlie ran back over and kicked the meathead's stomach, then again, then again, then a bit harder, then rested his hands on the bar and kicked some more. Bang, bang, bang, until Blaze was silent, not whimpering, not moaning, out cold. His leg fidgeted slightly, as warm urine begun to seep through his jeans and start a big wet patch around his crotch.

"Big fucking man, big steroid junkie man! What you gotta say now?" Charlie pushed himself up from the bar, slightly out of breath now, looking down with pure disgust at what he saw beneath him. He slammed the end of the cosh into the bar so it slid back down into a compact tube, and then shoved it back in his inside pocket. He turned his attention to everyone else in the pub, with slightly less disgust.

"Anyone says anything to the old bill, they get the same treatment."

Puffing and panting, he headed back out the same way he'd came in, reaching for the Lexus keys as he did, his eyes wild with rage, his mind rushing with the hit of cocaine-fuelled violence.

The black saloon crept down the dark farm track, gently bumping through the muddy puddles, its headlights set to park.

Rain washed down the front window as the wipers cleared Charlie's straining view; he quietly drove his way to a set of barns at the end of the track, trying his best not to alert any suspicions from the nearby farmhouse. He knew the son of the farm owner and had his permission for a small fee to use one of the barns as a safe house, but the father would have quickly let off his shotgun in Charlie's direction had he known he was there, let alone what he kept there. The Lexus rolled to a standstill in front of the end barn in a cul-de-sac of five.

He slunk out of the car, quietly shutting the door behind him, and then tiptoed over to the barn, carefully avoiding the puddles. He pulled out his keys and opened the large padlock sealing the huge double doors shut. He then slid them back and crept inside, tapping in the beeping alarm code before it went into a merciless wail, alerting everyone he did not want to meet.

He turned on a small LED key-ring torch and then

made his way to the back of the barn, weaving past various parts for various farmyard machines. He removed some old boards which were loosely nailed to the rear wall. From inside the cavity, he pulled out a large black duffel bag, along with several sticky spider webs and a generous helping of dust. He shook the bag until almost of the web and dust had fallen clear, and then sat it on a work bench to his left, trying his best to avoid the greasy tools and parts. He gently drew the thick metal zip along the length of the bag, his teeth revealing themselves through smiling lips as he did so, the comfort of his well-hidden monetary get out clause warming him from the feet up. The £500,000 in used notes was his means of escape; split four ways between the gang it was £125,000 each. Not as much as he had hoped for, for his new life in Spain, but with what Billy and Knighty had rounded up earlier that day, it would definitely be a good start. He knew his luck was up in Stambro now. No way out, but get out. He quickly zipped the bag back up, before pulling the used cosh out from his inside pocket, and placing it carefully behind the boards, and then quietly replacing them, as if he'd never been there. He slung the bag across one shoulder, and headed back through the dimly lit barn, his wide smile lighting the way.

Charlie pulled the blacked-out car into a quiet lay-by just past the exit for the farm track, and then reached for his phone from the glove box.

"Yeah, who's this?" the thick cockney accent asked.

"Leon, it's me, Charlie."

"Yes, Charl, 'ow are ya me ol' china? I've been worried about ya, cock, ya face is all over the news. Woss the crack, san?"

"A big fuck-up, mate. It weren't me, that's all I'll say right now until I see ya, but I need a favour."

"Name it, san," his London contact chirpily replied.

"I need a passport, mate. I'm off."

"What, a snide?"

"Yeah, British and that obviously, but whatever name, I ain't bothered. I just gotta get out the country, mate, ASAP."

"Okay, Charl, okay. I gotta geezer that can sort it. Need a photo though. You get that sorted, and I'll get ya a price on it, short notice ya probably looking at a bag a' sand though, at least." Leon explained, using rhyming slang to refer to a grand.

"Whatever the price is mate, I'll pay, not a problem. I'll send someone up with a photo and the money."

"Sound as a pound, cock. Listen keep ya facking nut down, yeah, and be luckee!"

Charlie ended the call, with a promise to do just that, and dialled again.

"Mum, it's me, Charlie. I'm coming over in the next few days."

"Charlie!" the fragile voice replied, excitedly. "I thought you weren't coming 'till Christmas, my boy?"

"Yeah, well, something's happened at work Mum, and I'm coming now. I got the money too, so tell Dad not to worry, everything's gonna be all right."

His mother went silent, as the unexpected information set in. "Where did it come from?" she asked worriedly.

"I'll tell you all about it when I'm there, Mum."

"But Charlie!" she pleaded.

The phone buzzed in his ear; he pulled it away to look: call waiting - Billy.

"Mum, I gotta go. Please don't worry, everything's gonna be just how we planned. Just get ready for me."

He ended the call without another word and answered Billy's call.

"Charl, where the fuck are ya, pal, what happened?" the gruff low tone demanded, the worry in his voice unusually clear.

"On my way now, Billy. I took care of our ginger mate, don't worry."

"Nice one son, but I got more bad news I'm afraid. Now, when I was back in the army, we had a saying…"

"Just tell me, Billy." Charlie demanded, impatiently.

"Right, okay, I'll get back to the saying later, you'll love it," Billy assured him, before continuing, "Firstly, those Dunn cunts have been round the whole firm, everyone, trying to get 'em on board. Most of 'em stood their ground and a few have even took a good hiding, so we gotta do something about 'em, mate. We gotta strike back hard and fast."

"Okay, so what's the other bad news?"

"Right, that bird, Alice. Her name ain't Alice. It's Hayley, Haley Frost."

"Frost?" Charlie spluttered, his mind beginning to reel.

"Yep, one and the same. That two-bob Frosty's sister, that's why she was visiting him in nick. I hate to say it Charl, but she's fucking stitched you up, pal."

He immediately ended the call without a reply and threw the phone onto the passenger seat, where it instantly started buzzing with Billy's name again. He smashed his forehead down on the steering wheel, ignoring the call.

"Bastards! They've done me over, the conniving bastards!" he screamed through gritted teeth, clenching his fists until they went white, butting his forehead onto the hard leather of the wheel, in quick, short successions.

After several minutes of uncontainable rage, he lifted his head up from the steering wheel and took a long, deep, calming breath. He pulled the sanitizer from a coat pocket and gave his hands a deep cleansing rub. He focused on Spain, visualising sunshine and cold beer as he forced himself to think forward to a new life, then looked to the black duffel bag on the passenger seat and restarted the car. He wheel-spun it in a flurry of flying gravel back onto the main road and sped back to Stambro. With his fists wrapped tightly around the wheel and his nostrils flared, he found a new determination for self-preservation. He'd show whoever was trying to stop him that he was unstoppable.

CHAPTER 8

15th November 07:07pm.

The amber liquid swilled around the cracking ice cubes as Jack placed the crystal tumbler down on the coffee table to reach for a fresh cigarette. He lit one up, leaned back in the antique armchair and sat staring at the spot where his mother's chair had previously been. It was now soaked by rain in the back garden; he'd chosen to move it outside earlier in the day, the pain of its presence too much to bear. The necessary phone calls had all been made, like the organised detective he was; some to old friends in Cambridge, some to new ones in Stambro and even some to distant relatives in Canada. The station had been informed of his bereavement and he'd been instructed by DCI Brent, quite firmly, to stay at home and get some rest. So now he sat and he drank and he smoked, alone. Alone with his memories, memories made all the more tangible by the photos, the furniture, the objects, the things surrounding him in the old damp room. He reached for the whisky glass as he blew out a thick plume of grey smoke through his trembling lips, then immediately busied them with the cold edge of the glass, the ice cubes sliding down it and clashing with his teeth. He let the cold liquid drizzle past them and down his dry throat. The 21-year-old Scotch swaddled his shivering soul as he immediately pulled on the cigarette, the end of which glowed red hot and dropped its messy ash into his lap. This he utterly ignored, his gaze still too fixed upon his mother's final living spot to care.

He was knocked clean out of his morbid stupor by a sudden and intimidating rap of knuckles at the front door. He quickly sat the whisky back down, pulled himself up straight, took a quick puff of the cigarette and then pulled his black jumper up to his eyes, wiping away any stale, salty residue. He hurriedly stubbed out the cigarette and headed to greet the unwanted guest, and the knuckles rapped again. He paused at the door, wiping his eyes again, but just succeeding in making them redder and more obvious a declaration of his pain. He took a deep, calming breath, before slowly opening the door. To his pleasant surprise, Jenny's saddened, yet utterly delightful face was revealed; her make-up toned down for the occasion and her shiny blonde hair tied back in a knot.

"Hello, Jack."

She smiled lightly.

He stared back achingly, a lack of confidence quashing the impulse to reach out and grab her, to pull her warmth in close, to wrap his tired arms around her radiant and elegant body, to ease his pain.

"I'm so sorry, Jack."

She reached out to give him the enveloped cards of condolence tightly gripped in her petite, tanned and perfectly manicured hand. He accepted them dully, managing to raise a half-hearted smile and then placed them gingerly on the shoe rack beside the front door. The pair both dodged eye contact for an uncomfortable minute, until he broke the silence and mumbled, "Thank you, Jenny, would you like to come in?"

He looked up into her eyes, the sorrow bursting out, crying for her feminine touch.

"Of course, if you don't mind?" she replied with a smile he hadn't expected.

"No, not at all, come in, please."

He stepped aside and took her coat, while she took in her surroundings.

He showed her through to the lounge and offered her a drink. She requested water, and he persuaded her to go for wine. She sat down in the only spare armchair, placed over the other side of the room to his, near the piano, noticing his half-empty whisky glass and still-smouldering cigarette along the way. She quickly studied the happy family photos sitting on the old piano, as Jack returned from the kitchen and handed her a large glass of red wine. She responded with an upturned smile. He sat down and reached for his cigarettes.

"Smoking in the house?" she gently mocked.

He replied with a wry smile as he lit one up, and then reached for his own glass. He sank back a huge warming sip, then looked directly at her, sighing out a massive and heavy explosion of mourning from his chest as her mere presence easing his desperate agony within minutes. She smiled back, softly, her natural tenderness firing on all cylinders.

"So, are you okay?"

He paused before answering the question; a simple, yet daunting one. He knew he wasn't okay, but didn't want to burden her with it and at the same time risk losing any respect he thought she had for him due to his apparently superhuman emotional strength.

"As good as can be expected. Just still a bit shocked by the whole thing, you know?"

She nodded in reply, her eyes sympathetic, and sipped at her wine.

"So you had no idea your mum was feeling this way?" she bravely ventured.

"Yeah, I knew she'd been like this since my father passed last year. I just never expected she'd go this far; I thought it was grief, a natural process." He paused to drink some more. "I guess I've been pretty wrapped up in my own grief, and work. Maybe too much to notice the warning signs," He added regretfully, after a long swig.

"You mustn't blame yourself, Jack. We never know what's going on inside other people's heads, even if you see them every day. It's impossible. How could you have known?"

He nodded back in agreement, albeit clearly unconvinced, while inhaling deeply on his cigarette. This time he quickly moved it to the ashtray before it had chance to drop its ash on his lap.

"I just wish I could have been here. If we hadn't gone for that drink, I would have been here, I could have…"

"Stop it, Jack!" she interrupted.

She gulped at her wine, got up from the creaking chair, and then went and knelt down next to him.

"You know as well as I do, when people wanna let go, they let go. If you had been here, your mum wouldn't have told you anything different. You would have just delayed the whole thing for some other time."

He looked to her with squinted eyes, tears forming behind them; the sudden closeness breaking down his ice-cold barrier.

"But she was my mother, Jen. She was supposed to be strong."

He finally broke as the tears rolled down his cheeks without mercy. He quickly sat his glass down and put his head into his hands, trying his best to shield what he perceived as weakness. She moved in response, edging herself closer still to the thin arm of the chair, and then wrapped her arm around him, squeezing out the pain.

"Our parents are human beings just like us, Jack. They have feelings and emotions. We want them to be superhuman, but they're not, they're just not."

He wept quietly, as his head hung low. "I'm sorry," he announced, in as robust a voice as he could muster.

"For what?" she asked, raising her tone to a low level of anger.

"All this self-pity crap."

"Don't be so bloody silly, Jack. You are human too; you have feelings and emotions and it wouldn't be natural if you didn't."

He slowly brought his head to face hers with widened eyes, completely belonging to her and her alone in that one honest moment. Her chiselled cheeks rose with a warming smile, melting the final pieces of frozen air between them.

"It's okay to cry," she assured him, rubbing his shoulder.

But the tears had stopped now, as another emotion surged through his wounded soul. Love. He narrowed his red eyes, as she did hers, their focus fully locked into each other's existence and nothing more.

She moved down towards him, as he let her in, one arm reaching around her waist, the other her shoulder. She slid her free arm around his back, dropping the wine to the floor, where it spilled across the paisley carpet. Neither battered an eyelid in its direction. She moved her lips down onto his as he moved his up to her, and there they met, dry and afraid at first, but soon overcome with passion. Their tongues took turns dipping into the other's mouth with the energy of all the built-up tension and pain and frustration, speaking a thousand words their hearts hadn't dared to. She climbed onto his lap and straddled him, as he pushed up her white buttoned shirt to reveal her petite waist, her stomach clenching inwards as his hands gently worked their way up her body.

She forced her lips away from his, sat up and ripped her shirt free, the buttons popping all around, and threw it to the floor, revealing ample, soft breasts behind a white laced bra. His jaw dropped in awe. It had been a while since he'd witnessed such a serene vision of the female form.

Her lips plunged back to meet his, while he fumbled around with her bra-strap, trying with one thought to enjoy the overwhelming passion of her sweet kiss, while another desperately concentrated on trying to release the loveliness that lay behind the bra.

She, meanwhile, lifted his jumper and hooked it over his head, barely moving her lips from his as she did. She exposed his perfectly toned chest muscles at exactly the same moment he set her luscious breasts free; and their naked torsos melted into one perfect being. She groaned with pleasure, biting his bottom lip as he fondled her welcoming breasts. As she fumbled down further for his belt, he responded with the same action, and begun unbuttoning her skirt. After a few moments of unsuccessful fumbling, and still fervently locked at the mouth, she jumped off him and slid down her own dress, while he ripped at his trousers with a speed of lustful possession. She paused as she stood bolt upright in front of him, nothing but her white laced knickers left on. She slowly slid her fingers into the underwear elastic, and then began to ease them down from around her toned thighs with the sultry elegance of a medieval temptress. Then she reached down and slipped his boxer shorts off in the same erotic manner. He wasted no time in pulling her back onto him, entering her with throbbing lust. She threw her head back and yelled in ecstasy, the pressure of the previous month's sexual tension between the two exploding like a fireball into the cold winter night.

Jack held Jenny tight in his strong arms, as she curled her warm naked body up on his lap, her head tucked deep into his chest, the old armchair supporting them both with ease.

"That was amazing, Jack."

He smiled as if for a thousand men. "You're not

wrong, I've never," he paused, suddenly holding back and not wanting to come on too strong.

"Me neither," she reassured him, lifting her head up to his and sealing the promise further with an adoring kiss.

He stroked her soft, blonde hair as she melted back down into his chest.

"I'm going to find this bastard," he suddenly and sternly announced.

"Who?"

"Charlie Paccadillo."

She brought her head back up and looked firmly into his eyes.

"Me and the chief inspector are on it now, Jack, you need time."

"I need no such thing. He's mine and it's my job and my duty. Moreover, it's what my mother would want."

She looked unsure, her eyes darting inquisitively across his, looking for a chink in his reformed armour, but there was none.

"Well, in that case, 'we're' going to get him, Jack, you and I."

CHAPTER 9

15th November 9.00pm.

Charlie's phone buzzed away from its silent setting; how he'd purposely left it. Alice flashed up on the screen.
"That 'er again?" Billy asked, shaking his head.
"What do you reckon?" Charlie retorted, rubbing his forehead and then sipping at his can of warm lager.
"Fuck, dude, you should just answer it and have it out with her, man," Che suggested, slouched on Billy's comfy sofa.
"Personally, if you arks me," Knighty joined in, from his seat beside the stoned hippy.
"I didn't though, Knighty," Charlie cut in, glaring menacingly at him. "Did I?"
"All right, chill out bruv. Fuck's sake." Knighty replied sulkily while prodding Che for the joint he was currently smoking.
"I need some fucking gear. Get on the phone, Che, sort something out will ya?" Charlie ordered, desperately wanting to relieve the stress.

"From who, man? Everyone's waiting on us."
"Bollocks," he growled in reply, squeezing his can.
"Maybe you should drive up and see Leon tonight?" he suggested, the hint of addict in his tone.
Billy quickly interjected,"For one, you ain't got the picture done yet, and for two, you said no more gear until it's all sorted and you're safely tucked up in Spain, you nutter."
"I know what I fucking said, Billy. Ain't I allowed to change me mind or something?" He bolted out of his chair and headed over to the window. "Jesus, I just wanna get out of my nut. Is that too much to ask? I can't take all this shit sober."
He lashed out on Billy's punch bag hanging from the ceiling with his clenched fists.
"Chill out, Charl, will ya?" Billy demanded, in his deepest growl. "Don't forget, we're all in this with ya."
"You lot ain't being hunted for a murder you didn't do though, or, being fucked over by some bird, are ya?"
Billy stood up from his chair and threw his can of beer at the table. "Listen, we ain't the enemy, Frosty or fucking Blaze. Every one of us here in this room is brothers; one of us is in the shit, we're all in the shit. Now fucking grow a pair will ya? You think you're the first geezer to get fucked over by a bird?"
Charlie glared back at him, dead in the eyes and then wisely backed down, realising there was not one ounce of untruth in his friend's honest words.
"All right, you're right. I'm sorry, I gotta man up. Sorry, all of ya."
He looked at each in turn and then sat back down in his chair and reached into his pocket for hand sanitizer.

"Billy's right, dude, we all love you man. One for all and all that Dog Tanya stuff, yeah." Che added, in a long stoned slur.

The tense atmosphere in the room immediately dispersed.

"Dog Tanya, who the fuck is that, bruv?" Knighty asked with a smirk. The others waited expectantly.

"You know, the Three Musketeers or whatever? The cartoon with the dogs who fight with swords and that?" Che questioned, doubt entering his drugged mind.

"That's Dogtanian, you complete muppet!" Billy bellowed, as the room erupted with laughter.

"Dog Tanya sounds like some bird you'd take home on a Friday, Che," Knighty added, bending over with laughter now.

Che shook his head, unamused. "Well, I'm glad I could lighten the mood eh? You need to clear that beer up Billy, you muppet."

"Oh shit!" Billy roared as the beer seeped dangerously close to the huge pile of money lying helplessly on the living room table. The laughter died down slightly, as he darted off to the kitchen for beer-soaking apparatus.

Charlie's phone buzzed again from the sofa: Alice.

"Fuck it, I'm answering," he announced, refreshed by the laughter at Che's expense.

He grabbed the phone and headed out the front door, slamming it shut behind him before anyone could say a word.

"Charlie, it's me, Alice?" she explained hurriedly down the phone.

"I know who it is, you've rung ten times," he replied, harshly.

"I thought you'd been arrested?" she explained further, dejection clear in her voice.

"No, Alice, your plan hasn't worked yet."

There was a sudden silence as she took his spiteful words in.

"My plan, what the hell are you on about Charlie?"

"You know exactly what I'm on about, Alice! Or should I call you Hayley?" he hissed back.

She paused again, his words hitting home hard and fast. "Oh. Who told you?" she asked in a guilt-ridden tone.

"Does it matter? I'm no mug, I'd have found out one way or another."

"I know you're not, Charlie, I was going to tell you," she tried to explain.

"Tell me what? You and your cunt for a brother and his cunt for mates were setting me up? Sure you were, 'Hayley', sure you were."

"My brother? Set you up?" she blurted out, the confusion clear in her voice.

"Don't play dumb. The game's up, it's over. You ain't gotta pretend anymore."

"Charlie, I swear on Hitten's life, I have no idea what you're on about."

"You're fucking sick, Alice, Hayley, whatever it is, bringing ya' young lad into it - sick!"

He hung up the phone and stormed back into the flat past Billy, who'd been holding the door open and trying to eavesdrop..

"What she say, the lying bitch?" Billy growled.

"Still trying to deny it, swearing on her boy's life and that. She's off her rocker, mate."

He sat back down on the couch and opened the fresh can of beer Billy had sat down for him.

"Why though?" Che asked from his stoned stupor. "Why still deny it? Doesn't make sense. Maybe she is nothing to do with it," he reasoned, feeling for his old friend as he watched the heartbreak Charlie was trying so hard to hide behind his fury.

"Of course she fucking is. She's a sket. None of dose Aleister gals can be trusted, I told him this!" Knighty butted in.

Charlie didn't reply, doubt creeping back into his mind after the call. Her voice had melted his heart once more, and he too wondered why she would still keep up the lie, if it was one at all? He looked down to his phone as it buzzed in his hand, a text message. Charlie, please come round so I can explain, Hitten is in bed and I'm alone, please, I'll tell you everything.

"What's she saying?" Billy nosed over his shoulder, trying to read the text.

"She wants me to go round there," Charlie explained, deep in thought.

"It's a fucking set-up, Charl!" Billy roared at him. "Either those Dunn slags or the filth will be waiting, don't trust her!"

"He's right ya know, bruv," Knighty concurred.

Charlie ignored them both and ran the situation through his mind, as he sipped at his beer. His head told him Billy and Knighty were correct, but his heart argued the opposite. It screamed at him that she was the one for him and that he had to go to her now, without delay.

"I'm going to see her." He announced as he stood up and quickly grabbed Knighty's keys off of the table.

"Are you mental, man?" Knighty screamed.

Billy tried to hold Charlie back, but he pushed his way past.

"What the fuck are you doing, Charl, use your brain! This ain't like you!" he shouted.

But Charlie had already flung open the door and left, so Billy ran after him.

"Fucking let me come with you then, ya crazy bastard," he demanded as he ran to the passenger side of the car.

Charlie looked up at him as he opened the car door. Seeing that that bigger man wasn't going to leave, he agreed, on the one condition that Billy remained in the car while he spoke with Alice.

Charlie stood shivering in the unlit bus stop with a hooded jacket from Knighty's car pulled up over his head; a simple Stambro lad waiting for the bus, as far as any passing patrol cars would be concerned. Billy, who'd dropped him there five minutes earlier, pulled back up at the kerb. Charlie quickly made his way around to the passenger side and jumped in, rubbing his hands and blowing into them, looking to Billy for an answer.

"Can't see any of the Dunns/ motors, or old bill mate. No one sitting in any cars, nothing. Looks clear to me, but then who fucking knows? They could be waiting in an upstairs bedroom over the road for all we know."

Charlie thought on this for a moment, but his mind was already made up. He trusted Hayley although he didn't know why..

"Okay, let's go."

"What, back to the flat?" Billy asked, hopefully.

"No to Alice's."

"You mean, Hayley's," Billy corrected him.

Charlie didn't bother to reply; just kept his focus and looked straight ahead.

Billy reluctantly pulled away from the kerb.

The blacked-out Lexus slowly pulled up outside her house, the pair carefully surveying the area like a trained army unit. It appeared to be a normal street, in a normal council estate, on a normal week night. Knock, knock. Two taps on the window made them both jump with a sudden fright. A spotty teenager stood bent over at Charlie's window, his face almost pressed to the glass, smiling, his skinny baseball cap peak turned up with a greasy tuft of hair poking out. Billy lowered the electric window from his side.

"Yes, boss, got a light init?" he asked innocently, still grinning like a Cheshire cat.

Billy immediately answered, his eyes aglow with rage, his tone low and terrifying, "I'll give you exactly ten seconds to get outta my sight, and never, and I mean never, speak to, come near, or even look at either of us two again, do you understand?"

The kid's cheeky smile instantly dropped as he realised the scale of his silly mistake and spotted the size of Billy's arms.

"Sorry, big man, I was just..."

Billy stopped him before he could continue by beginning to open his door.

"One. Two..."

The spotty teenager immediately turned on his heels and ran, and he was clear out of sight before Billy could count to five.

"Little cunt," he snarled, relieved it wasn't the police,

but annoyed it wasn't the Dunns.

Charlie just shook his head and blew out his cheeks. "Right, I'm going in."

He opened his door and pulled himself out. Billy reached across and grabbed his arm.

"You come back to that door as soon as you're in and give me the thumbs up, or I'm kicking the bastard down, and ripping off any head that ain't attached to your body, then eating it."

"I got it, Billy, now chill out and wait for the signal. You're making me nervous."

Charlie slowly worked his way to the front door, looking all around him as he did, up at the surrounding windows and across the street to the ones behind. Billy's warning of policemen waiting in neighbouring houses raced around his fragile head. But there was nothing, not a sound, not a movement. He paused as he reached the door. The police threat seemed non-existent. Now to see who, if anyone, was waiting inside. He took a long, deep breath, and gently knocked twice on the door. Almost as soon as he'd put his cold hands back in the hoodie's pockets, the hallway light came on and a shadow moved towards the glass panelled door. He quickly glanced back to the car, where Billy looked on with quiet trepidation; no smiles like the day before, just pure angst as the whole situation rose to a head. He brought his focus back to the front door, as it suddenly opened.

Hayley stood there in a fluffy pink dressing gown wrapped cosily around her small frame, pyjama bottoms covering her lower half and fluffy pink slippers to match on her feet. She smiled nervously, as Charlie was yet again stunned into silence by the sheer beauty which stood before him. He quickly snapped out of it and looked past her, through the hall and into the living room, then poked his head round and into the kitchen. No one.

"Who are you looking for, Charlie?"

He didn't answer, just kept a stern, unforgiving look on his face.

She moved aside and ushered him in. He walked past her and quickly made his way into the lounge. It was empty apart from the characters of a dreary soap chatting away on her small television in the corner of the room. He noticed a half-finished cup of tea and a packet of biscuits on the table. She appeared to be alone.

"Who's upstairs?" he questioned her firmly.

"Hitten. In bed, like I told you," she replied, her tone becoming a little aggressive now. "You wanna go up there and check? Wake him up while you do?"

Charlie thought about it, then declined. If the Dunns were there waiting, they'd surely have grabbed him straight away, not hidden upstairs. He went back to the front door and gave Billy the thumbs up, who nodded back half-heartedly, still on full alert.

Hayley closed the door and led him back into to lounge, wrapping her dressing gown tighter around herself as she walked. He quickly went over and checked the patio doors leading to the garden. They were locked.

"Right, happy now?" she asked.

He nodded solemnly in reply.

"Good, do you want a cuppa?" she asked, half smiling.

"No, Alice. I mean, Hayley. I want some answers."

He wasn't softening that easy and still had no idea what was going on; all manner of paranoid thoughts gnawing at his weakened mind.

"Okay, well, sit down and I'll tell you what you wanna know."

He did as she instructed. She walked over to the television and switched it off, and then came and sat down next to him. They were in the same positions as the day before, yet the atmosphere was the polar opposite. He still couldn't help but marvel at her natural beauty though, its glowing aura assuring his heart that she was okay, but his mind still held reservations.

"So, you wanna know why I lied about my name?" she asked, looking openly into his questioning eyes.

He slowly nodded and she broke his gaze and looked to the floor.

"Well, ain't it obvious? My brother's Lee Frost. It's not the sort of thing you go telling a guy you just met. I didn't know anything about you and you didn't know anything about me, I liked it like that, Charlie."

She looked back up to him, her eyes as honest and pure as the first drop of snow on a Christmas morning.

"Plus, I've got Hitten to think of. I have to protect him. I was drunk, I slept with you on the first night. I don't normally do that, you know, but I liked you."

"Okay, so when I was round here yesterday and I thought we were getting to know each other, I'd met Hitten, I knew all about him, you having him at 15 and all that, why didn't you tell me then?"

"You'd already told me all about the Dunns and your stupid war with them. I thought you'd get up and leave if I told you my real name. I knew Lee had been friendly with Tommy Dunn in prison and how they were doing things together now, and I didn't want you to think I had anything to do with him, or them."

"So you don't have anything to do with your own brother?" Charlie asked, confused, but more relaxed now, allowing himself to believe her every word..

"No. And he's only my half-brother. My mum was with a disgusting old drunk before she met my dad. She had a son with him, Lee, and then he drunk himself to death, leaving my mum to bring up Lee on her own. Then she met my dad, they got married, and he took Lee on as his own, got his name changed to Frost and everything."

Charlie let the information sink in. It all seemed to make sense.

"Okay, Alice," he paused to correct himself. "Why Alice, by the way?"

"Alice Liddell. I thought you'd get it when I told you in the car. I was too drunk to think of anything better."

"Who's Alice Liddell?" Charlie shook his head in ignorance.

"She's the little girl who inspired the book Alice in Wonderland; it was my favourite as a kid."

Her cheeks turned a light and flattering shade of red, and she looked away.

"Stupid, I know, but as I say, I was drunk and, yeah."

Charlie broke his barrier down with a genuine smile as she looked back to him.

"Don't worry, it's not stupid. I mean, I had no idea, I'd have offered you the red or blue pill if I did, or asked to come to a dinner party with that mental bastard the mad hatter!"

They both chuckled as the fire between them relit with a sudden spark.

"So how come you used to go and see him inside, if

you have nothing to do with him?" Charlie asked, wanting all his questions out the way before he could completely relax with her again.

She looked back down at the floor, her smile evaporating instantly as her brother was brought back up.

"I went once, that's all, just to get him off my back."

"Get him off your back for what? I mean, he's your brother, why wouldn't you visit him?"

"He kept writing me, he wanted to see Hitten."

"His nephew, yeah, so what?" Charlie asked, honestly confused.

She once again brought her gaze back up to meet his. This time though it was different, a great horror had engulfed her, a horror Charlie could never have expected to see expressed so starkly through those sweet hazel eyes.

"Not just his nephew, Charlie, his son."

She suddenly burst into tears and threw her head into her hands.

Charlie reeled back in shock, the weight of what she had just divulged hitting him like a ten-tonne wrecking ball. All sorts of questions flew around like awoken bats in the dark cave of his mind.

"How, I mean, how can he be his father?" Charlie mumbled.

"He raped me, Charlie. Don't you get it?" She wept quietly into her folded arms.

He didn't 'get it', but quickly put aside his own cracking mind to put both arms around her. She crumpled into him as they both fell back into the old worn sofa. Her head buried into his strong chest, he squeezed her with all the love, kindness and protection he could muster. She cried like she was 15 again, the past rising back to the surface and tormenting her once more. He continued to squeeze and stay silent, as he gently kissed her soft dark hair. The guilt of forcing her to relive such a horrible memory ripped at his gut, but he ignored it and continued to embrace her.

After several long minutes of torturous tears and strong cuddles from Charlie, she had begun to recompose herself. He wiped away the last of her tears with the sleeve of his hoodie.
"I'm so sorry, Hayley," was all he could think to say.
"Why are you sorry? You're not him."
"No, I mean for making you tell me all this."
"You needed to know, didn't you? How could I not tell you, if we're gonna see each other? How could I not?"
"Well, I'm glad you trusted me enough to tell me."
"You're the first person, other than my parents and Shell, I have ever told. Oh, and all the solicitors, and the jury, and yeah everyone in the courtroom."
"So that's what he was in prison for?"
"Yeah. I heard he said he was in there for murder or some rubbish, but no, it was for raping his then fourteen-year-old sister. Nice eh? I bet everyone wouldn't think he was such a lad if they knew."
"They should know. He shouldn't be allowed to live around here, it's wrong."
She suddenly shot up from his grip.
"No, Charlie! No one can know. I'm trusting you with this, it's the past and that's the way I want it. When I went to see him that time in prison I made it clear that if he didn't stay away from me and Hitten, I'd make sure everyone knew exactly what he had done and he

agreed, and he has done ever since."
"Okay, okay, fair enough," Charlie assured her earnestly.
She slid back into his arms and locked into place like she was made to fit there.
"Does Hitten know?"
"No, I don't think I'll ever tell him either. What good would it do him? As far as he will know, his dad left me when I was pregnant, and that's that."
She squeezed her arms around his waist and he squeezed back, kissing her forehead as he did.
"It must have been so hard for you, I can't begin to imagine."
She didn't reply, just squeezed harder.
"So, is that why you got into the Buddhism in Thailand, and why your parents took you there and stuff?"
"Yeah, when we found out I was pregnant; he was on remand by then. They took me there to relax. We'd planned to, you know, have an abortion, but the Buddhist monks taught me life is sacred and I believed them. I still do, and now I've got Hitten. I'd never change that for the world, as I said to you yesterday, it was something good from something really bad."
"Yeah, it all makes sense now," he answered. Curiosity got the better of him and he tried to delve a little deeper, tactlessly rather than callously.
"So, how did it happen? Did he, you know, do it all the time or..." His words tailed off as Hayley lifted her head from his chest and looked at him with a determined expression.
"I promised to tell you everything, so I will and then I never, ever want to speak about it again, okay?" she

said, firmly.

"Yeah, of course."

"I mean it, Charlie. Buddha said holding on to anger is like holding on to a hot coal with the intention of throwing it: you're the only one who gets burnt."

"Yeah, I'd like to shove a hot coal up Frosty's…"

"No, Charlie, I'm serious, that's it, end of."

"Okay, I'm sorry," he quickly replied.

She put her head back down on his chest.

"I was fourteen; he was supposed to be looking after me while my parents went out for the night, as he was eighteen. But instead I was sent to bed at eight and he invited his friends round. They were drinking and doing coke, but they all went home before my parents got back. Then he came up to my room, chewing his face off, high as a kite. Maybe it was the first time he'd done it or something, I don't know,"

Charlie's stomach knotted with disgust as he remembered doing cocaine in front of her after they had made love, even teasing her for not doing any herself.

"Anyway, he forced himself onto me. I tried to resist, but he was already heavily into the steroids and the weight training by then. I didn't stand a chance, and yeah, it hurt a lot. It probably didn't last long in real time, but it felt like hours to me. I bled, everywhere, and he went to bed like nothing had happened. My mum came in to check on me when they got in, saw me in a quivering state, saw the blood. I told her what he'd done and that was it, my dad nearly killed him. Luckily for him, the police arrived into time to stop him and the rest is history."

Charlie kept quiet once more. He had no words of condolence for that kind of tragedy; all he could do was hold her and be there by her side.

"So that's it now, yeah? she asked, squeezing him tight once more and nuzzling her head deeper into his chest.

"Of course," he answered.

"Good, I never ever want to speak about it again. I've moved on from it, it took a long time, but with Buddha's teachings and my own meditations, I've managed, slowly. My life's good now." She looked up at him, with a sudden loving shine in her eyes. "Even better now I've met you."

He leant down and kissed her softly on the lips.

"As is mine is for meeting you. Trust me, you're the best thing that's happened to me in a long time," he explained, genuinely. "I just gotta get a passport sorted and we're all off to sunny Spain, as they say. If you still wanna, that is?"

"You really mean it, Charlie? You're gonna take us with you?" she asked, innocently.

"More than I've ever meant anything in my life. It'll be great, a fresh start."

She put her head back down and they embraced once more, the invisible force field of love pulling them closer with each passing second.

Charlie's phone buzzed away in his pocket, waking him up. He looked down at Hayley, who was fast asleep and still gripping tightly around his waist. He tried to reach for his phone without waking her, but to no avail. She woke and rubbed her eyes, then smiled at him, happy he was still there and it wasn't a dream. He pulled his phone out: Billy.

"Charl, how long you gonna be pal? I've been sitting out here for a fucking hour."

"Shit, sorry mate, I'll come out and see you. I fell asleep."

He hung the phone up.

"I forgot Billy's sitting out there in the car."

They both laughed.

"Bloody hell Charlie, that's twice now, the poor sod."

"I know. Shall I tell him to go and I'll stay here tonight?"

She pondered on the question, wanting to say yes, but, "No, you'd better not. I don't want to confuse Hitten in the morning; this is a normal school night for him. I gotta sit him down on my own, and explain all this Spain stuff, and you, and just everything, you know?"

"Sure, I understand," Charlie lied, a selfish and childish feeling of rejection washing over him.

"I'll see you tomorrow though, yeah? Come back round at night?"

"I wouldn't miss it for all the," he was about to use his line of all the coke in Columbia, but thought back to what Hayley had revealed to him. "I'm sorry for doing bag in front of you and that, Hayley."

"What do you mean?" she laughed sleepily.

"Well, you must have been, you know, after Frosty doing it that…"

She cut in, firmly, before he could continue. "Charlie, when I said I never wanna talk about it again, I meant it! I knew this would happen if I told you,"

She looked to the floor in despair, fully awake now.

"No, no, calm down! Honest, I will never bring it up again, I just wanted to apologise for doing it in front of you and for taking the piss when you didn't do it, that's all."

"Charlie, this is Stambro, everyone does it. I told you I don't care, and I don't. The drug didn't make what happened happen, I just don't like it, personally."

She smiled back to him warmly.

"Okay, end of discussion, I promise," he answered, not fully convinced the drug didn't have a hand in Frosty's disgusting behaviour. And that gave rise to doubts over the times he'd defended the drug over the last four or five years.

Charlie got back in the car with Billy, who wanted answers, just as he had an hour ago. Charlie explained the half-brother truth, but left out the rest, explaining she hated him and had nothing more to do with him, and visited him in prison for family reasons. Billy took his friend's word and said no more about it.

"So what's next? He asked.

"Next, we go get my passport picture done at Tesco, then Che goes to London first thing, then as soon as he's back, we sort this shit out with the Dunns, and then I'm off, mate. You lot tie up all the loose ends here, then meet me in Spain when you're done and I'll have everything ready and waiting for you."

"Sort it out with the Dunns how?" This seemed to be the only part of the plan in which Billy had any real interest.

"You got your wish mate: we sort it once and for all. And we're gonna proper have it with 'em too, on the cobbles old school style, four of them, four of us."

"Fucking outstanding my son, but good luck with

getting Che in on it!" Billy roared with excited laughter.

"I'll handle Che; he can have that junkie Micky cunt. We'll make sure we tell 'em: no tools, proper old school, fists only. Che will surprise ya, trust me."

"So who do I get?" Billy asked, his eyes alight..

"You get Tommy, Knighty gets Freddy; two pretty boys, makes sense, and I want that cunt Frosty."

Charlie's face suddenly turned to a picture of pure hate, as the thought of avenging his violated angel entered his already tormented mind.

"He can 'ave a row, Charl. He's a big lump, you see 'im the other day," Billy informed him. "But you'll do him pal. Like I always say, can't build muscles on ya chin."

Charlie smiled back at him; no fear in his heart, just pure and burning vengeance.

16th November 12:12pm

Che stumbled through the door to find Charlie, Billy, and Knighty sitting impatiently awaiting his return, each of them pumped full of adrenalin and ready for what was to come.

"Okay, man, all squared up with Leon. He's got the photo, he took the piss, and said you look like a convict, and that I was to tell you that, then said it'd be ready for you tomorrow morning at his."

"Nice one, Che. I'll grab it on the way to Heathrow. Now sit down, I got something to tell you."

Charlie revealed the violent and courageous plan to an

unimpressed Che.

"Fuck's sake, Charlie dude, I'm a lover, man, not a fighter, and you know that!" Che tried pleading his case after being informed of the day's already arranged meet.

Billy had made a call to Tommy Dunn, who had agreed with the same insane excitement as Billy. In response to Billy's accusations of setting Charlie up, Tommy had claimed to have had nothing to do with the murder. Wild, disturbing threats were then hurled down the phone, before the meet was arranged, through coded speech, for a shut-down builder's yard just outside the town centre.

"Che, I know you can row mate. You looked after yourself fine all those years at school, before the fucking pot got hold of you."

"That was a long time ago, man! Shit changes, I'm not with it now, man; I don't dig fucking fighting dude, and besides, if they've set you up once, why not again? How do you know the frigging cops won't be waiting?"

"That's not their style, Che, they honestly believe they're the top boys in Stambro. They may have just took Harry out for other reasons, might not have tried to frame me, but whatever it is, I'm getting stitched up for something I didn't do 'cos of these cunts. And they've stole all our fucking punters, it's gotta be settled."

"Why can't we just fuck off to Spain and be done with them, man?" Che demanded.

Charlie wished he could reveal his ulterior motive regarding Hayley, the rape, but he'd promised and didn't break promises like that lightly.

"I dunno if I can do it, dude."

"Well, you're just gonna have to, and you're getting that Mickey cunt. You'll flatten him in a heartbeat. Now get practicing on that bag."

Charlie pointed to the bag hanging from Billy's ceiling, wrapped in grey duct tape.

"Oh great, I get the knife-happy crack head," Che replied, not even looking at the bag.

"No that's been arranged, no tools."

"Oh and you believe that?"

"Listen, as much as I hate those cunts, I know they're not gonna wanna look like mugs by turning up to a proper straightener with tools, when tools have been banned. They'll look like clowns to the whole town, like they can't have a proper row."

Che just shook his head and reached for his cannabis tin.

"No, none of that either," Charlie instructed.

"What?" Che replied in utter disgust, as if Charlie had just told him he would not be allowed to breathe for the day.

"Just until after the straightener, that's all," Charlie reassured him.

"Fine," Che sulked, throwing the tin down on the table. "When's it happening?" He looked up, not an ounce of fear in his eyes.

Billy looked impressed and nodded approvingly to Charlie.

"Half twelve, so get ready," Charlie replied.

"What, half a fucking hour? Jesus, man, you take the piss, Charl, you really do." Che bitched, shaking his head and looking longingly at his tin.

Billy didn't look so impressed this time and frowned at Charlie, who winked knowingly back.

The blacked-out Lexus pulled up to the building site dead on time, and the Dunns' white Range Rover was already there and waiting. The three Dunns and Frosty stood outside it, glaring with all the hate and vileness they could muster at the approaching car. No one else was in sight or earshot, and the old disused yard was walled off all around, with just the one way in and out. Charlie cast his eyes over the awaiting participants, looking for weapons. There were none, just fists. Tommy and Frosty wore only vests on their torsos, Frosty's racist tattoos on display for anyone to see.

"Look at those couple 'a wankers in vests! It's fucking winter!" Billy laughed, completely unfazed by the current situation. Sporting his usual rather tight Lacoste polo shirt himself, he was scarcely more appropriately dressed.

Che and Knighty, on the other hand, sitting in the rear seats, were understandably and visibly nervous, adrenalin and fear already coursing through their veins. Charlie, who would on previous occasions have been in a similar state, having to face a man mountain like Frosty, was silently focusing on his main objective. Revenge, partly for being stitched up for a crime he hadn't committed, but mainly for Hayley.

Billy pulled up next to the white Range Rover and turned off the engine, then turned to the back seat.

"Everyone stands and fights. No running. We end this today, man to man. Now come on!"

He tried his best to rally the troops and it seemed to work, as Knighty and Che shook their heads front to

back and clenched their fists. The atmosphere in the car was one of pure electric thrill, contagious, and very useful.
Billy jumped out first, ripping forward his seat to let the rear passengers out, nearly tearing it from the chassis as he did. Charlie jumped out the other side, pumped, and ready to go, his gaze fixed firmly on Frosty, who noticed it instantly and glared straight back. That match was set. The three Dunns, Tommy leading the charge, stomped forward. Frosty was off to the left slightly, heading for Charlie, who was also heading directly for him.
"Let's fucking 'ave it, you Aleister slags!"
Billy screamed at the top of his voice as he ran straight for Tommy. He went in low and hard, like a crunching rugby tackle, bracing his shoulders and lifting the other man clean off his feet from the waist as effortlessly as a prop forward takes out a scrum half. They both crashed to the ground in a dusty heap, but Billy was quickly on his knees and on top of Tommy. He proceeded to slam hard fists, one at a time into the side of Tommy's large, square head, as he tried desperately to try and block the sickening blows.
Charlie and Frosty met next, their stares doing the only talking. Charlie walked straight towards Frosty with no hesitation in his stride. Frosty, this huge hulk of a man, wasn't used to this kind of confidence coming at him. His size usually instilling enough doubt in other men that they would be on the back foot, allowing him to go on the attack and usually win. But Charlie had no intentions of backing down. This was war and war with a moral purpose, for him anyway.

Che and Mickey sized each other up, hesitating to make the first move, while the pretty boys, Knighty and Freddy, had a war of words, shouting every expletive under the sun at each other.

Charlie finally reached Frosty, who stopped abruptly, Charlie's confident, aggressive approach momentarily stunning him. And that was all Charlie needed. He swung a fast and powerful right hook for Frosty's large, Desperate Dan-like chin. The boxing lessons Billy had given Charlie over the past few years, showing him where to hit, and how to hit, were replaying at the back of his mind. He'd never had to use them before and often wondered if and when it came to the crunch he'd be able to put them into action. He'd never imagined, though, that the first test would be against a man nearly twice his size, with arms like tree trunks. But it worked. The punch connected perfectly on the side of his jaw and the crack of it breaking snapped around the yard's bare brick walls, as Frosty's huge frame fell to the ground like a ton of concrete blocks kicking up small clouds of dust.

Billy was still on top of Tommy, who hadn't managed to return a single blow yet, but was taking the repeated punches to each side of his head without passing out and even managing to scream back some muddled abuse.

Che and Micky were now locked into a full blown exchange of flying windmill punches and kicks, catching each other and causing various cuts and bumps as they did. Freddy, meanwhile, had somehow got the better of Knighty and was on top of him, pushing his head down into the dirt, as Knighty reached up and clawed away at his face in a frantic grapple to regain control..

Charlie was now stood above the cowering Frosty, who was trying his best to cover his head and broken jaw with his arms as Charlie launched a vicious assault of kicks to every exposed part of his curled-up body.

"Dirty fucking rapist!" Charlie screamed at the top of his voice. All control was gone; this was pure, unrestrained rage. He kicked and stamped all over, some of the blows connecting, some just flying into the dirt. It was wild, he was wild, but Frosty wasn't enjoying it one bit, whimpering with every connecting kick or stamp.

"Your own sister, you dirty, horrible, scumbag!"

It was only as he paused momentarily to catch his breath, panting with exertion, that Charlie realised what he he'd been shouting. But before he could begin to worry whether anyone might have made sense of his unintentional revelations, a blood-curdling scream tore through the air behind him. He turned from the still moaning and tightly curled-up Frosty, as Billy used the now unconscious Tommy's face to push himself to his feet. Beyond him, Che stumbled around gripping the side of his face, blood streaming through his fingers and beard. A huge open wound ran red from his forehead, across his eye and down to his chin. Mickey Dunn stood there proudly holding a 5-inch kitchen knife. Just as he pulled his arm back to plunge the weapon into the stricken Che's stomach, police sirens filled the air as four patrol cars and two unmarked vehicles roared into the yard,

"Run!" Billy screamed.

"What about them?" Charlie pointed to the screaming Che and Knighty, who was still pinned down by

Freddy.

"They'll be okay, you won't. Now fucking run!"

Charlie did as he was told. He and Billy headed for the seven-foot back wall, scaling it easily with miraculous, adrenalin-fired speed. Billy jumped down first, but as Charlie landed his leg twisted; the left leg, the one with the tale of woe. The old football injury had reared its ugly head and he screamed out in pain.

"Billy, my knee!"

Billy turned around and without a second thought picked his friend up into the fireman's carry and then turned and ran, as fast as he could. He could see a taxi dropping someone off on the road to his left and he used every ounce of energy he had to propel himself and Charlie along. He reached the taxi just as the previous customer had finished paying their fare and looked up in shock at what was pounding towards him. Billy quickly opened the back door and threw Charlie in, as he then jumped in the front. The taxi driver's face was a picture of utter surprise and confusion.

"Afternoon pal. Wormwood Drive, ASAP please." Billy's tone was as breezy as he could make it.

He quickly pulled the door shut and glanced over his shoulder to the rear wall of the yard. Two policemen had clambered up and were looking around, judging the jump. Billy didn't think they'd seen them yet.

"Errr, I dunno mate... errr, I gotta another call come in." The taxi driver tried his best to dissuade Billy.

Billy didn't even have to say another word though; he just looked, long and hard into the driver's worried eyes, who promptly rethought his approach and pulled off. The policemen managed to get down from the wall and run in completely the wrong direction.

Billy smiled confidently to himself.

"We fucking done 'em, Charlie boy! Yes!"

He jabbed the ceiling of the taxi, before calming the now shaking driver and apologising profusely.

Charlie on the other hand wasn't so happy. He'd had his revenge, yes, but at what cost? Two of his closest friends had been left behind, one of them probably scarred for life and possibly blind, both of them definitely in police custody. And then there were the words he'd screamed at Frosty, breaking his promise not to tell. His stomach sank into his groin, as he felt the full weight of his actions.

CHAPTER 10

16th November 12:50pm.

Jack stepped out of the driver's side of his silver Vauxhall, Jenny out the passenger side. The uniformed police officers had already run into the derelict builder's yard to do the dirty work, and now the detectives strolled in and surveyed the scene.

"Call that one an ambulance, for God's sake," Jack instructed one of the uniforms pointed at Che, who was he still clutching his bleeding face.

"Yes, guv."

"Then arrest the other three. Get a van down here. I want them all down the nick and in the cells quicker than you can say 'yes, guv'."

"Yes, guv."

Jack walked around the site, looking for Charlie. "Where's Paccadillo?" He roared.

One of the other uniforms replied, "Two of them got away over that wall, sir. They're being pursued on foot. Another two went over that wall, who we lost immediately; must have had a car waiting."

"Bastards!" Jack growled as he looked to Jenny, furious with disappointment..

"Don't worry," she reassured him, "this morning we were a day behind him. Then we get a friendly little visit and now we're just minutes behind and we've got these four little charmers."

He smiled back at her confidence and gave her a secret, loving wink.

The friendly little visit had been made by a certain skinny blonde lady of the night, the girl who'd been 'visiting' Billy's flat two days earlier. She'd recognised Charlie's photo in the paper and come in to try to secure the reward; explaining truthfully, how she hadn't remembered the address as she had a driver and was also 'a bit out of it', but did have the number Billy had called from. Jack and Jenny had placed a trace on the phone. They'd heard the meet being arranged, but Billy and Tommy had cleverly disguised its whereabouts in code. Jack and Jenny's recourse had been to gain access to Billy's GPS signal from the phone's service provider. It had taken a nail-biting length of time, but they'd received the permissions and details just in time to lock in on his signal and trace it to the abandoned building site.

05:33pm

Knighty, a battered and bruised Frosty and a now conscious Tommy Dunn had been quietly processed and led to individual holding cells. Frosty and Tommy had refused any medical attention for their cuts, bumps and scrapes, whereas Che had gladly accepted the free trip to the hospital; his face and eye were badly cut and would require immediate surgery. Jack had sent an officer with Che under strict instructions to keep as close as possible at all times and a keen eye open for Charlie, on the off-chance he might foolishly turn up to visit his injured friend.

Tommy and Frosty had both been interviewed first. DCI Brent and Jack stood outside interview room number 2, where a shaken, but cool as ever Knighty waited his turn.

"So, which one of the terrors is in here, Jack?" Brent asked, his air of aristocracy bordering upon the ridiculous.

"We have one Paul Knight. He hasn't been interviewed yet, but we know from the discussion with Vole and the prostitute that he's friends with the suspect."

"Okay, what about the other two?"

"Both from the Aleister estate, sir. One's Tommy Dunn, who you know, the other a Lee Frost. They're both rivals of the suspects, so we are told, and both seemed to have taken quite a beating. But they're also claiming they were attacked and they don't know who by."

"So what do we have on them in connection with the murder?"

"Nothing, sir, as of yet. They've both got alibis for the night in question, which we're checking on as we speak."

"And they're claiming they were attacked and you have no evidence to the contrary?"

"Yes, sir."

"Well, then you have to let them go, Jack, but

check up on the alibis for the night, obviously. And what about the one with the facial injury, in A&E?"

"He is friends with the suspect. Again, we know this through the informants, but again, he's saying he doesn't know who attacked him or why."

"Bloody criminals and their ridiculous code of silence; it's pathetic!" DCI Brent hissed. "Well keep an officer at the hospital in case the suspect arrives to visit. You never know, eh?"

"Yes, sir, just what I thought."

"So, our only hope here today is the little bugger in here?"

"Yes, sir. I believe he knows where the suspect is hiding as they're all very close. There are four – two of whom we've got in custody, who work as the head of this unit distributing the drugs, so I'm going to scare the living daylights out of him until I get something. I'll keep him the whole twenty-four hours if need be. If you agree, of course?"

"Yes, definitely, the exact course of action I would take myself. I'll get on to the duty sergeant to get these others released and you do your best with this tacky little Herbert."

"Yes, sir."

DCI Brent turned about face and headed off down the hall like an army captain on parade, as Jenny came past him from the other direction, ready to join Jack in the interview.

Knighty sat on one side of the interview desk, trying his best to keep up the cool façade; his body slouched back in the chair, with a fabricated smirk plastered across his clammy face.

Jack and Jenny entered the room together, and Knighty immediately eyed up her good looks, even managing a cocky wink in her direction. The pair casually made their way over to the desk and took their seats opposite him. Jack placed a tape in the recorder and began the interview by introducing everyone in the room and stating the time and the date. Jenny kept her unruffled gaze firmly fixed upon Knighty, who tried to flirt with her in response: another brave wink and a kiss of his lips. Jenny laughed it off; it was the sort of bravado she had seen from men like Knighty a thousand times before, a transparent attempt to cover their nerves.

Jack got straight down to business. "Okay, Paul, what exactly where you doing at Savage Road at 12:45pm today, when our officers arrived and apprehended you?"

"What the fuck it look like I was doing, bruv? Baking a blad clat cake! Cha."

Knighty slammed his hands down on the table, kissed his teeth, and slouched even further back into his chair, shaking his head contemptuously..

"Oh, you were baking a cake, were you? Well, from what the first officers on the scene told me, you aren't very good at baking... Apparently you were pinned to the ground, so it's lucky for you we turned up and he legged it, really, wasn't it?"

"Whatever matey. Dat guy's a fucking pussy 'ole; he got lucky and dat's it bruv." He let out nervous giggle.

"Oh really? So you know him, do you, your attacker? What's his name?"

"He weren't fucking attacking me, man, I told you. And no, I don't know his name, never seen da man before."

"Do you know the names of anyone else who fled the scene?"

"Nah man, I was walking along the road, saw mans fighting in the yard, so I went in to see wha gwan, and before I knew, two of dem pricks started on me, yeah."

"Could you repeat that in English for the benefit of the tape, Paul, or should we get an interpreter in?" Jenny goaded him.

"What, you fucking racist or something, blondie? You want me press charges on you?"

Jenny just smiled back, doing her best at bad cop.

"Okay, Paul, so you didn't know anybody there?" Jack continued.

"No, as I said, bruv."

"What about Charlie Paccadillo?"

"Who?"

"You know who, Paul. Your good friend Charlie."

"I don't know any mans call Charlie, end of."

"Oh, I think you do, Paul. We've heard from many reliable sources that you two are very close and you also run a fairly sizeable drug ring in Stambro."

Knighty paused, the pressure beginning to get to him. "Oh yeah? What reliable sources? You got none, probably some bag rats."

"Now, that would be telling Paul, wouldn't it?" Jenny replied sarcastically.

Knighty glared at her, then back to Jack, who continued, "Okay, Paul, we know what you are and who you knock about with, fella, and at the minute you're also an accessory to murder, so stop pissing us about."

"Murder, are you crazy?"

"No, Paul, but you clearly are if you don't start talking now. Conspiracy to supply class A drugs, accessory to murder… you're going down for a long time, mate."

Knighty paused as the short but serious list of offences began spinning around his tired mind.

"Dat's bullshit and you know it!"

"Is it, Paul? Your prints were found all over your friend Charlie's flat, mate, on all sorts of things. And we have witnesses you've personally sold drugs to."

Knighty didn't reply, just looked down as he rubbed his sweating hands on his trouser legs to dry them. It was a futile effort; they were now leaking perspiration at an alarming, telling rate.

"Don't play games with us, Paul, we always win. It's our job, we do this day in, day out, and the Stambro taxpayers pay our wages, and I can tell you something for nothing: they don't like drug dealers as much as they don't like murderers." Jenny informed him, her tone raised to that of an angry head mistress.

Knighty stayed silent. He had no more bravado.

"Cat got your tongue, Paul?" Jenny continued.

He suddenly leapt forward from his seat. "Fuck you, sket!"

Jack, quick to react, was up and out of his seat and pushing him back down before he could finish his sentence. Knighty didn't resist. He just crumpled back into his chair, the panic eating away at his eyes like hungry maggots on rotting apples. No more coolness, no more fight.

"If you can't behave, Paul, you'll be charged with assaulting a police officer too. Do you want that?"

"Assault? Fuck dis, man, just take me back to my fucking cell. I wanna lawyer, now."

"We can do that, but you won't get one until tomorrow now, fella, and I'm sure they'll advise you to do the same thing: to talk to us, Paul. It's in your best interests. You could walk out of here now. Just tell us what we want to know: where's Charlie?" coaxed Jack.

But Knighty stayed defiantly silent, eyes fixed to the table. Jack ended the interview and got up, instructing Knighty to stay put. He and Jenny left the room.

"He's a mess, Jack," she excitedly announced.

"I know. We'll leave him in the cells to ponder and he'll tell us everything we wanna know after a cold tea and a slice of dry toast."

"Excellent!" she said, and reached up to his smiling lips with her own. He put an arm around her waist and pulled her close, the embrace electrifying their already buzzing souls to a new higher voltage until a door unexpectedly opened further down the hall and he quickly let go, their love still a dangerous secret.

"Right, I'll give him his Legal Aid crap and bang him back up. You tell the desk boys to keep him waiting whenever he buzzes in the night, really give him a hard time in there, heating as low as allowed, one blanket. Give him a taste of prison life. I know his type, and he ain't cut out for prison. We'll have this bastard's whereabouts before sunrise."

CHAPTER 11

16th November 08:00PM.

The gleaming black Lexus crept slowly down Hayley's road. Charlie and Billy kept their eyes peeled for any unwanted company, just as they had done the entire journey across town. It was a trip which Billy had pleaded they did not make, but which Charlie had insisted upon; he had to see Hayley. Arrangements needed to be made for the morning, for Spain, for their new life. Billy had finally given in to driving there after agreeing the use of phones were out of the question. They'd both come to the correct conclusion that phones were somehow to blame for the unwanted police presence at the builder's yard earlier that evening. They had also toyed with the idea of going to the hospital on the way across town, where they were sure Che would have been taken, but also correctly figured out it would be far too risky.

Billy pulled the car up in his usual spot outside Hayley's house.

"Charlie, please don't keep me waiting out here for a fucking hour again, not after today. I literally can't 'andle it, pal."

"Big old Billy Marine lost his nerve?" Charlie mocked, trying to keep a brave face on things and banter being the only way he knew how.

"Silly question, Charl and you know it, but I ain't in the mood for sitting about in the motor. We got Che all sliced up, Knighty banged up,"

"I won't keep you waiting, Billy, you got my word on that," Charlie informed his friend firmly, quickly dropping the banter.

"Keep your eye out for the OB and honk that fucking horn if they come. If I hear it I'll be off out the back and over the fence, and you drive round and get me from those playing fields round there."

"Yeah, okay, sounds like a good plan." Billy smiled instinctively, military-style tactics keeping him in the game. "Go get her pal."

Charlie smiled back and jumped out the car. He jogged up to the front door, hoodie pulled up and his knee still smarting. He slowed to a walk as he approached the front door; it seemed to be ajar. Manic thoughts raced through his head. Were the police inside? Had they found Hayley? There were no cars about. Could they be watching through the windows opposite? Paranoia slashed through his wounded consciousness as he slowly opened the door.

Something wasn't right as he entered the house; he could smell it in the air. He walked slowly toward the light coming from the front room, the only light that appeared to be on in the house. Each slow, quiet step towards the door intensified his fear, and then his worst imaginings became his actual reality. Hayley lay flat out on the sofa, her fluffy, pink dressing gown ripped open, her legs torn apart; one hanging loosely over the edge of the sofa, the other one bent up at the knee with her white knickers wrapped around its ankle. He scanned her limp, naked body up to her bruised and bloodied face horror and then ran to her. But his knee gave way and he fell to floor, words unable to get past the giant rock of sorrow building in his throat. He crawled the rest of the way, desperately searching and hoping for a sign of life. As he finally reached her head, which rested awkwardly on the arm of the sofa, he whispered her name, then took her face in his hands and called it a little louder. He awaited a response, but there was none. He grabbed her wrist and fumbled about with his fingers; checking for a pulse and noticing the purple bruising in a heavy band.

"Hayley!"

He shouted now, still looking for that pump of blood that could let him breathe. He was pushing down on the vein too hard; he wiped the cold sweat from his forehead and checked again, gentler this time, focusing desperately on what he was doing. And then he felt it, the slow pump of life-giving blood still flowing in her veins. He dragged in a huge gulp of air before he risked passing out himself, and pulled himself up to kiss her face, whispering her name with a quiver of unheard words as he did, caressing her blood-splattered body like a fallen flower.

Billy's heavy footsteps came stomping into the room and then stopped dead, as he took in the sickening sight.

"Charl, what the fuck?" he blurted out in confusion.

"Call an ambulance, mate." Charlie muttered back, still focussed on Hayley's closed eyes and cut lips.

Billy remained frozen and his jaw dropped like a huge block of solid ice.

"Call a fucking ambulance!"

Billy responded this time, pulling out his phone and leaving the room in a panic. Charlie managed to pull Hayley's dressing gown back around her in a vain attempt to save her dignity. He then continued to whisper her name, his face inches from hers. His only saviour from the week's madness now lay there in front of him, unconscious and violated. He thought, then knew, that it was Frosty's sickening work that lay before him. He thought back to her previous pain at the hands of this monster, and then, "Hitten!" he shouted, before struggling to get up off his wounded knee.

Billy came running back into the room upon hearing his cry.

"They're on their way mate."

"Hitten!" Charlie screamed again, ignoring his friend, who looked back at him dumbfounded. "The kid, Billy, the kid!"

"Shit, I'll go look upstairs. I'll find him, don't worry, mate. You stay here with her!"

And with that promise, Billy's heavy frame crashed up the flimsy wooden stairs, almost ripping the banister from its fixings as he gripped it to enable two steps at a time. Charlie looked back to his unconscious love. He tried wiping the blood from her bleeding nose and lips, but it just kept coming. It covered his hands, which he then tried to rub clean on his jean legs, but no amount of OCD-induced cleaning could clear it. He heard the hefty footsteps hammer back down the stairs, sure at any minute his friend would crash right through them.

"He's not up there mate," Billy panted.

Charlie reluctantly took his exhausted eyes from Hayley, then looked to the half cupboard in the middle of the room, before half-crawling, half-walking over to it, holding his knee up the best he could. He slowly opened the door and sure enough, there he was, his small body all curled up, face in shock, phone in hand.

"Come here, mate," Charlie instructed, trying to pull the boy out and towards him.

Hitten resisted. He refused, without words, to be moved from the sanctuary of that little space. All he could manage to do was pass Charlie the phone. Charlie smiled as softly as he could, accepting it with both trembling hands. He looked down at the image on the screen. It was the sofa, shot through the slats of the door, and Hitten's mum with a man on top of her. Feeling a wave of nausea, Charlie pressed play. There was screaming. It was Frosty and he was holding Hayley down by her throat with one hand and forcing her legs open with the other. Charlie quickly stopped the video; he'd seen enough and so had Hitten. He tried once more to usher the frightened child out of the cupboard, but was again denied.

"Okay, mate, you stay there. Try not to look at Mum, help's on the way."

He saw an action figure on top of the cupboard and passed it down to him. Hitten accepted it, gripping Charlie's hand as he did, but keeping his eyes firmly on his unconscious mother. Sirens blared in the distance.

"Charl, they're on the way, mate," Billy paused, pursing his lips together tightly. "I know you're not gonna like this mate, but we gotta go. I told the bird on the phone that, you know," he pointed uncomfortably to Hayley. "Anyway, there's gonna be old bill with 'em."

"I don't give a fuck, Billy. I'm not going anywhere!"

Billy looked back at Charlie, wanting to grab him and drag him out the door, but knowing he'd never manage it.

"Listen, you go back to the flat and wait there. Stash the money and wait for me."

"They're gonna fucking nick you, mate. Your face is everywhere."

"So what, Billy? I'm not gonna leave these two alone like this; what kind of man do you take me for?"

Billy knew the look in his friend's eyes and knew he wasn't changing his mind. The sirens quickly drew closer.

"Go, Billy, stash the money. I'll see you, go!"

The pair gave each other long hard stare, knowing it was farewell for now. Then Billy crashed through the hall and out the front door. Charlie looked back over to Hayley, still holding Hitten's shaking hand. His heart sank, his dreams crashed, but most of all, he hoped, prayed, and begged she would be okay. The sirens wailed again, closing in with every increasing decibel.

"Stay here, mate, don't move. I'll be back in two seconds."

Hitten glanced away from his mother for a quick,

begging look into Charlie's eyes.

"I'm not going anywhere, mate, you got my word. I just need a second."

Hitten nodded and then turned his attention back to Hayley.

Charlie limped his way to the kitchen, pulling the bag from his jean pocket containing his own personal cocaine as he did. He saw the lights flashing down the road through the kitchen window as he reached the sink. He ripped opened the bag and its contents flew into the sink. He reached for the tap to flush the evidence away, then paused, as the powder sat there invitingly in the basin. His hands shook on the tap as he contemplated one last line before his imminent arrest. The coke almost glowed white as it sat there. He knew a quick snort would help him through what was to come, and what was happening right now; it could ease his pain in an instant. The lights and sirens stopped outside the house, he had seconds to make a decision.

"Fuck it."

He turned on the tap, washing the entire contents of the bag down the sink,

"Not this time," he snarled through gritted teeth, washing his tear-stained cheeks with the water, before attempting to run back through to Hitten and Hayley. He made it to the hall with a disabled hop, as the paramedics rushed in and he pointed them to the lounge. His eyes searched for Hitten as he followed them through. He heard footsteps behind him and turned to limp out the way. It was two uniformed officers, who recognised his wanted face instantly.

"On the ground, now!"

CHAPTER 12

17th November 03:00am.

Charlie tried, with little success, to rest his tired head on the hard, blue plastic mattress. The bright fluorescent lighting that had cruelly lit his small cell since he had arrived there at 09.11pm that night, had not once gone off, and, he now guessed correctly, never would.

He felt like he'd been in there for hours, but without a phone or watch, he was clueless. In the same secure housing in which the light sat was a camera. A little red light blinked, just to let him know it was on. The only other things in the small clean cell was a metal toilet with no lid and an electronic push-button to flush, and a small shiny chrome sink above it, again with push-button soap and water. His belt and shoes had been taken away when he'd been signed over to the custody sergeant. He had then been rewarded with a blanket, which he didn't know whether to use as a pillow or as intended. He decided eventually upon his leather jacket as the pillow, and the blanket to keep his body warm, the cells heating had been set at its lowest and the chilly November sting was pinching at his tired bones. He had looked to the emergency call button on the wall and thought about asking for an extra blanket; but didn't want to show his perceived enemy any weaknesses at this early stage of the game. He looked to his hands and fingers, as he thought back to the earlier session of prints he had given them. He had washed his hands at least ten times since he'd been in the cell, yet still imagined the print ink to be on them. But he hadn't the energy to wash them again, instead letting the image of the ink torture his already hammered brain.

Throughout his entire criminal career, Charlie had never once been arrested; the threat was always clear and present, but until then never really tangible. Now the reality of it all hit him hard, harder than he ever imagined it could. But he wouldn't let it show, they wouldn't break him. He was too strong; his life, his ruined football career, had taught him to be strong. But inside a niggling feeling ate away at his gut: the tragic feeling of freedom slipping away. He had never been at another man's mercy as much as he had this night. He was locked in a tiny room with no way out and the law was against him one hundred and ten per cent. The law, a scary adversary to say the least. This wasn't ginger Blaze or even the Dunns, this was the British establishment, the biggest gang in the country and everyone was on their side, no one would feel sorry for him. He was a drug dealer, scum of the earth, who used violence to control his empire. An empire which kept feeling smaller and smaller compared to the one he was now up against. He was completely powerless in a way he'd never experienced before; no matter how big the cosh, the kick, the punch, the gun even, he didn't stand a chance against Her Majesty's government and was going to end up just another low life criminal with a number, a record, and a prison cell.

Then there were his parents; what would they make of their son, the criminal scumbag drug dealer? Feelings of guilt engulfed him, the reality of the crimes he had committed ripping through his stomach like a barbed wire worm. Everyone did it out there, in the 'real' world; he thought he'd done well to rise to the top, but he wasn't out there now, he was in here, in their hands and they were right, weren't they? They were the law, they even had God Almighty on their side. Then he wondered about God, if a god existed at all, or if Hayley was right when she had told him the only god was within him, that he could only punish or reward himself through natural laws; Karma she had called it.

His mind raced like a whirlwind. Hayley. How he hoped, prayed even - to whom he wasn't sure - but he prayed that she was okay, that part of his plan had to be right; she had done nothing wrong. He soon realised, though, with a harsh and grounding reality check, it was in fact because of him she had been raped and beaten again by the same sick sociopath as when she was fifteen. He knew full well it was his ego and hunger for revenge that had caused this girl he now loved so dearly, to be subjected to such extreme physical and mental abuse. He might as well have been the one to have raped her himself. Frosty had gone there to get his revenge for his bruised ego; they'd had a deal to keep things quiet, for everyone's sake, and he, Charlie, he had broken it. She had trusted him and he had shattered that trust, and the guilt tore him up more than breaking any written law, a guilt he feared would stay with him and haunt him forever.

The cell door's viewing plate slid open from outside and Jack peered in. He had his murderer, now he needed his confession.

The door clunked and clicked and flew open. Charlie gave him the same non-compliant look he'd given every other officer that night.

"Charlie, hello. I've been looking for you," he said, all enthusiasm and friendliness, upturned lips exposing teeth that gleamed in the bright fluorescent light. "Get up then, fella, you're coming with us."

Jenny stepped around the corner and leant against the cell door frame, an equally enthralled expression plastered across her pretty, tanned face.

The fox was in the hole with nowhere to go and the dogs were salivating from hungry jaws. Jenny and Jack had been tucked up warmly in bed at his mother's house when Jack got the sleepy call informing him Charlie was in custody. Already excitedly throwing on clothes, Jenny had then received the same call moments later, at which she'd had to act surprised

Charlie did as he was told and happily left the cell, welcoming a break from its cold isolation. He took note of Jenny and her good looks, but they had no impact on him; only one girl had space in his heart.

"How's Hayley?" he immediately asked Jack, trying to hold back his obvious distress and not beg for his help.

"Hayley?".

"The girl who was there when uniform got him, guv," Jenny enlightened him.

"Oh, that was some more of your handiwork was it?" Jack snarled at Charlie.

Charlie immediately went for Jacks neck with both arms, but Jack moved faster, stepped aside and let Charlie fly into the opposite wall, and then gripped him around the neck from behind and squeezed.

"Now calm down, fella, or you'll have to be restrained," he said, calmly.

Jenny called for backup and two uniformed officers came running down from one end of the bright corridor.

Charlie calmed down before they got there; again, not wanting to give them any advantage over him. Jack eased off his choke hold as Charlie relaxed. The officers stood menacingly to one side, waiting like trained pistols for Charlie to snap again, but he didn't. He shut his mouth and let them lead him up the corridor. He still had the sense to know when he was outnumbered.

Jenny led him into a room marked Interview room 1. It was about as basic as a room could get: one desk with cheap wooden veneer pushed up against the far wall, and four chairs, two either side. A simple tape deck was plugged into a socket above it.

"Take a seat, Charlie," Jack offered, pointing to one side of the table, as he closed the door. He sat down at the opposite side of the desk, Jenny taking her place next to him.

"Tea, Charlie?" Jenny offered, kindly, maybe falling into the good cop, bad cop routine a little too easily for Charlie.

"No thanks, love." He grimaced back.

Jack took a tape out of his pocket, unwrapped the plastic packaging, and then scribbled on it with a pen he took from the A4 folder he'd placed on the desk in front of him. He put the tape into the deck, pushed the mechanism shut and pressed the play and record buttons down simultaneously. A red light flashed up, as the wheels of the tape recorder began to roll silently. He flicked up the sleeve of his suit jacket to reveal a black wristwatch.

"The time is three thirty-three am, Thursday the seventeenth of November, two thousand and eleven. Interview started with Mr Charlie Paccadillo, interviewing detectives present: DI Jack Cloud and DC Jenny Pearce."

He flicked his jacket sleeve back down and leant his arms up on the table, leaning in towards Charlie, as Jenny leant back in her seat, folding her arms coolly.

"Hold on, don't I need a lawyer present?" Charlie interrupted hastily, before Jack could continue.

"I was just getting to that, Charlie. For the record, the suspect refused Legal Aid or any contact with a lawyer upon signing himself over to us at the custody desk at," he scrolled through his notes looking for a time.

"Yeah, yeah, whatever, just crack on then," Charlie

butted in, remembering his earlier comments when being booked in.

Jenny sat up slightly in her chair, laying her palms down on the desk. "We can suspend the interview for now, Charlie, and get you a lawyer in if that's what you'd like?"

"Nope, just get on with on it."

"Okay, Charlie," Jack continued. "Did you kill Harry Whittington on Friday the eleventh of November, that's last Friday night, Charlie?"

Jack had put it to him straight away, no messing around, and now he and Jenny watched carefully for the reaction.

Much to their clear disappointment, Charlie reacted the way an innocent man would: he sat up confidently in his chair and replied, firmly,

"No, I did not shoot Harry."

Jack snapped back in an instant. "Shoot? Who mentioned anything about a shooting, Charlie? I said did you kill Harry, not shoot him."

"Listen, my picture's in the paper as the suspect for a shooting. What you trying to do here, trip me up? It ain't gonna work, mate, I didn't do it."

"Oh, so you saw you were wanted in the paper, but decided not hand yourself in? Why was that, Charlie?" Jack continued to harass.

"Because I knew you raided my flat, and I knew what you found in there."

"Really, what did we find in there, Charlie?" Jack attempted at a simple direct confession for the drugs, and more importantly the firearm linking him to the case.

Charlie shook his head and before going any further with admitting his real crimes, demanded an answer. "I want to know how Hayley is, or you don't get another word out of me."

Jack leant back in his chair, annoyed at the stalling, as Jenny took his place. "Hayley's okay, Charlie, she's in the hospital and she's stable."

"So she'll live?"

"Yes, she'll live," Jenny comforted him, and he blew out the breath he'd been holding and smiled back at her with obvious relief and delight, completely unconcerned about whether she was playing good cop or not.

Jack quickly leant forward to the table, signalling Jenny to fall back, which she did like the trained professional she was.

"So what can you tell us about that Charlie? Anything you want to confess to there, while it's on the record?"

Charlie had deliberated with that question, as he knew he'd be asked, while waiting in his cell. He also knew the phone he had signed over when booked in contained Hitten's recording, and answered in an instant. He had worried about the unwritten code of criminals, about 'grassing', and how it wasn't acceptable to tell on a fellow criminal. But frankly that didn't apply to incestuous rape, he'd concluded, and as he wouldn't be getting his hands on Frosty anytime soon, he gave it up.

"Everything you need to know about that is on the phone I signed in when I was nicked. Check the videos, it's all on there, and for the record, you make sure that scumbag gets put away for good, this time."

Jack took his time and looked to Jenny, who kept a stern eye on Charlie. This wasn't the incident they were currently dealing with and intuition told Jack that

Charlie was indeed telling the truth, so he moved on.

"Okay, well talking of locking certain elements of society up for a long time, I deal with locking murderers up, so, I'll ask you again, did you kill Harry Whittington?"

"No, as I already said," Charlie huffed. "I had no reason to murder Harry."

"So you knew him?"

"Yes, I knew him."

"And will you at least admit you were there the night he got murdered?" Jack pushed.

Charlie paused; he knew what Jack was doing and didn't want to get trapped in a corner, but also knew he didn't murder Harry, so felt he had nothing to worry about. The truth was the truth.

"Charlie, your size footprints were at the scene, your tyre tracks, your texts, and phone calls to the victim, your blood-stained clothing; not to mention, and excuse the cliché, but the smoking gun, Charlie. The pistol we found in your flat, with your finger prints on it, fired the same bullet we found in the victim's body."

Jenny joined in. "Just tell us the truth, Charlie. Just look at the evidence. We know you didn't mean to kill him as you called 999 after you left the scene. We'll match your voice on this tape to the phone call, so just tell us what happened and we can help you."

Her gentler tone seemed to work better with Charlie, even though he knew what she was doing; Jack was rattling him and she was leading him into the safety of her light and while he knew they were one and the same, he also knew he was innocent of murder.

"Okay, I was there, but I found him like that. He

was dead when I got there. I panicked and left, I rung you lot from the phone box as soon as I got back into town and told them where he was and what had happened."

"And what had happened, Charlie?" Jack quickly snapped back at him.

"He'd been shot, obviously, he was dead. It doesn't take a brain surgeon, or a detective, to work that out."

"So how did the murder weapon end up in your flat, with your prints on it?" Jack pushed some more.

Charlie shook his head, biting his lip deep in thought, the nerves beginning to show now. He had not known hitherto the same gun had been used on Harry, it was all confusing news to him. How could it have been the same gun? His mind raged, that gun had been in his flat all along. He knew that for sure, didn't he?

"What you found is not the same gun that shot him. Okay, I admit, I had the drugs, I had a gun, but not that gun. The gun you found did not shoot him, and that's the god's honest truth." Charlie's voice raised in angst now, as the evidence against him sank in.

Jack paused to think. He knew there had been some irregularities with the murder weapon; it appeared clean when they had discovered it, not recently fired, but then Charlie could have cleaned it. Then there were the rifling marks on the bullet; they didn't match the marks of Charlie's gun when test-fired with the same size bullet from his gun. But this could be mechanical error. He was sure it was Charlie he was after, wasn't he?

"So if you didn't shoot him, who did?" Jack

quizzed.

Charlie knew who he thought it was: Frosty. But he drew the line at telling them anything about the shooting. This had all happened in his world and there were rules within his world.

"That's your job, mate, isn't it?" Charlie asked, not aggressively, but genuinely.

"It is, yes, you're right, and we work on evidence, and all the evidence we currently have points to you, so unless you can tell us otherwise, we're going to run with that Charlie, and let a jury of your peers decide the truth."

Panic began to rise in Charlie's gut and mind, and he struggled to keep it hidden. Hadn't they looked down any other avenues? Hadn't they looked into the Dunns or Frosty?

Jenny pulled herself up to the table, slowly.

"We know what you are, Charlie, who you are in Stambro. We had your friend Knighty in until a few hours ago, he told us a few things, you know, to help himself."

Charlie's mind yelled conflicting abuse at Knighty. He wouldn't do that, would he? And if he had, what would he say? He wouldn't have fingered him for the murder, surely; they were friends.

"Oh yeah, what things are they then?"

"Just how you run your little firm, and he works for you. Interestingly, in your defence, he also told us he thought the murderer was Lee Frost."

Jack looked at Jenny with a fierce glare to be quiet; he wanted a confession from Charlie and Knighty's opinions on the murder weren't going to help. His authority kicked in and their relationship left at the door. She sat back, put in her place, and he continued,

"What your friend said isn't entirely available to you at this time, but what you are allowed to know is, yes, he said you're the boss, you run the show."

"Hold on, she just said he pointed the finger at Frosty, so why haven't you got that sick fuck in here?"

"We had Frosty and Tommy Dunn in here after your little run-in yesterday, and they've got solid alibis, Charlie."

"Well get that piece of shit now and bring him back in!" Charlie screamed.

"Who? What piece of shit Charlie? What are you trying to tell us?"

Charlie paused. He could not believe they had had Frosty in custody before the rape, yet let him go; he was the murderer, not Charlie, after all.

"Nothing to do with the shooting, right, but that footage on the phone I handed in shows quite clearly Frosty raping Hayley. Again! He's done it before, you know, that's what he was inside for in the first place."

"We know all about Frosty, Charlie," Jack answered bitterly. "That's our job. What you're telling us now about what's on the phone, we didn't previously know. And we will look at that as soon as we're done here, and if it is what you say, he'll be coming down here with one of our colleagues."

"What, after he's been down here once already, and then done that? He'll be on a plane somewhere as we speak."

"Why would he, Charlie? We questioned him about a murder he had nothing to do with, he has a solid alibi for the night in question, so he's got nothing to worry about."

Charlie's mind raced. How could he have a solid alibi? If it wasn't him then who was it? It must have been one of the Dunns, but then Tommy had an alibi too, so the others probably would. He couldn't grasp at the truth of what was going on.

"Listen, Charlie," Jenny softly joined in again, at Jack's surreptitious signal to do so: leaning back in his chair. "Just do us all a favour, put your own mind at rest and tell us the truth. This is visibly getting to you."

Jack joined in again, briefly, "For the record, the suspect is sweating around the hairline and fidgeting with his hands."

Charlie had begun rubbing his hands on his jeans, the OCD taking over.

Jenny took her good cop stance again. "Listen to me, Charlie, we can help you. Admit to what you've done, you'll get a far more lenient sentence. If not, they'll throw the book at you."

"I didn't fucking shoot him!" Charlie burst out in anger as he slammed his frustratingly fidgety fists down on the table.

Jenny leaned back again as Jack stayed where he was. They both pondered on their next move; they had him where they wanted, but he wasn't giving them what they wanted.

Charlie knew what they wanted, but he wouldn't say it. How could he? He was innocent. He leant back into his chair and rubbed his hands furiously against his jeans, his thoughts scattering in a million directions. None of it made sense; if it wasn't Frosty or the Dunns, then who? Who had shot Harry?

CHAPTER 13

11th November 11:11am. – 6 days earlier

Charlie pulled the shiny black Mercedes up in his usual spot, in the fast food car park which sat on to Apex Corner roundabout, just outside London's busy din, and awaited Leon's arrival. He opened the hot burger wrapper and took a bite, the flavourless, salty meat filling his greedy, salivating gob. He was suddenly startled away from his junk food lust by a quick tap at the passenger window, accompanied by Leon's shady, gold toothed grin. He quickly swallowed his juicy mouthful, and threw the rest of the burger back into the brown paper bag it had come from. Leon opened the door and jumped in, his lanky frame filling the entire beige leather seat, squashed in further by his full-length black designer mac. He pushed his bright white trainers deep into the foot well as he made himself comfortable, rubbing a hand over his freshly shaved head with just a little left on top.

"How are ya, saan?"

His lips grinned from ear to ear. Leon was British-born, with Jamaican parents, but sounded like any other white cockney. There was no street slang about him, he was old school, and Charlie loved that about him. Not that he disliked anything about the new generation, such as his good friend Knighty, but for someone from a London overspill like Stambro, there was something thoroughly romantic about doing crime with a proper cockney. It also aided the fact he thought he was getting his drugs from what he assumed was the closest he could ever get to the source. Leon and Charlie had hit it off immediately when meeting at the football, and not just because of the world Leon had introduced him to. More than that, Charlie looked up to Leon; he was a proper London chap, the kind of chap most people in Stambro only wished they could be. Leon lived five minutes' walk from White Hart Lane and was born and bred there. But that wasn't the only thing that made him a face around the 'Yid Army' hooligan scene. He wouldn't back down from anyone or anything, and Charlie had witnessed this first-hand on several occasions. He wasn't necessarily the best fighter, but he was as game as they come. Charlie always guessed the tough streets of Tottenham had taught him to be who he now was, and admired him deeply for it; Tottenham made Stambro look like Disneyland.

"How comes you ain't been up the Lane lately? We proper 'ad it with those Chelsea mugs last week, you should'a been there sunshine," Leon asked him.

"Just been well busy mate, you know how it is, collecting all this paper in for you!" Charlie laughed.

"Speaking of which, you got it all, cock?"

"Course I have," Charlie declared, passing the two large brown envelopes in his direction.

"Never let me down, do ya, cock."

Leon grinned some more, as he shoved the envelopes inside his large mac. He then pulled out two large packages from the other side of the mac. One was the size of a house brick, wrapped tightly in black bin bags and duct tape. The other, more ominous looking package was wrapped in a dust cloth. He threw the brick shaped one in Charlie's lap, who immediately tucked it under his seat, knowing full well what it was: a kilo of London's finest cocaine, the kind of thing he didn't want any passers-by stealing a look at. Leon then went on to unwrap the dust cloth in his lap to reveal a black pistol.

"Fucking hell, keep it down, mate," Charlie begged him, as he scanned around the car park for anyone looking.

"Keep your hair on, saan, it's only a little shooter."

Leon was clearly much more comfortable around guns than Charlie, but wrapped it back up quickly all the same to keep his friend's nerves from shattering. Charlie took it quickly and tucked it under his seat with the cocaine.

"So you gonna tell me what you need that for, anyway, out there in the sticks?" Leon asked mockingly.

"Just these muppets from across town been trapping off a lot lately. We heard they got a gun, so, thought we better get one too," Charlie explained honestly.

"Fairy muff, me old china. You need any 'elp out there, you just gotta ask, you're one of my top earners, and more importantly a good pal, Charlie. Just say the word mate and I'll be down with a couple 'a lumps from the lane, we'll bring some propa' hardware with us too, freak these cunts right out," Leon offered, frankly.

"Okay, mate, I know," Charlie replied.

He'd always been offered help by Leon, but never took it, partly because of a weird macho pride and partly because he didn't want to stretch the good relationship he had with Leon. From where Charlie stood, Leon was kind of a boss figure. Charlie was self-employed, for sure, but without Leon, there were no decent drugs, and with no decent drugs, there was no decent money, and Charlie didn't want to upset that.

"Right, I gotta do one, cock. I gotta see my bloke, 'in I?" Leon explained.

"Okay mate, I'll see you here, with the dough for this, same time next week then?" Charlie asked, already knowing the answer.

"Sure thing, boss," Leon replied with a wink, cheekily pulling a small bag of cocaine from the top pocket of his mac.

"Wanna quick coin up?"

"Fucking right I do," Charlie replied, reaching into his coin tray under the stereo and passing one to Leon.

Leon dipped the coin into the bag and pulled a big lump of powder back out on the edge of it, which he snorted hard and fast up his wide nostril. He then did the same for Charlie, who accepted happily, and tried to snort with the same ferocity as Leon, but failed, as he did every time.

"Right, I'm off."

And with that Leon was out of the car as quickly as he got into it. Charlie started up the engine and reversed out of his space, and then headed back for the A1M to get his packages unloaded as soon as possible. The drive back from London was always an angst-filled half-hour which Charlie despised, but sweated out all the same, week after week, month after month, year after year.

Leon flicked back the sleeve of his black mac, revealing a large designer wristwatch which read 11:45. He cursed himself as he knew he'd be late, and the man he needed to see wasn't an easy man when it came to time keeping. He jumped into his large black Range Rover and sped out of the car park, cleaning his nostrils of cocaine with large snorts as he did.

He headed into London, pressing his foot to the floor with acceleration, weaving in and out of traffic, beeping the horn at anyone who got in the way and barely missing two collisions before eventually arriving at Brent Cross shopping centre. He worked his way around the tight car park in the cumbersome 4X4 until he reached the meeting spot for that week of the month. It was public, but perfectly out of view of any of the car park's security cameras, and about as far from the shopping centre as you could get. Yet there were still cars rammed solid, bumper to bumper, that far back.

He could see the silver Bentley waiting but couldn't get next to it, so he sped past without looking in the driver's direction and found a spot a few cars away. He reached into his glove box and pulled out another large brown envelope, to which he added to Charlie's two. Leon had made money from what Charlie had given him, of course, but was in the Bentley driver's debt for just over half a million pounds at present – about the value of the car the man he was meeting was driving - so everything he earned went straight back to him.

Leon and a friend had tried their hand at a bespoke kitchen business, which neither of them knew the first thing about, and ended up borrowing more than they put in to keep it afloat. But it sank all the same. Men like Leon couldn't just walk into a bank and ask for a loan, so there were people like the man in the brand new silver Bentley who more than willing to lend a hand. It came at a cost of course, a cost which was lower than the bank's rates, but would land you in slightly more trouble than bankruptcy if you didn't pay it back. You'd more likely find yourself at the bottom of the Thames, or underneath a new housing estate somewhere around London. Leon knew this when he had borrowed the money, of course, and the man in the Bentley knew Leon would struggle to pay it back, and end up forever in his pocket, doing favours here and there, and that he could use him for anything he needed to get done. The man in the Bentley always won; he wasn't some tough nut from a council estate, or a top boy football hooligan, he was a proper East London gangster.

His name was Carl Granger. He was from a time many people in the East End still romanticise even now. He had grown up around all the likely faces of the day in the 1960s and made a name for himself in the 70s doing armed robberies and specialising in big-money jewellery heists. He got into drugs and guns along with everyone else when the time came, and soon climbed up the ladders of the London underworld. He was a well-known face, a feared and respected face, but never in the spotlight. Mr Granger, as he was now extremely respectfully known, wasn't the kind of man you'd read about in a book of who's who in the criminal underworld, or that you'd see on a TV programme reeling off stories of long ago. He was still active, and you only knew about him if you needed to, and if you needed to you'd better be making him money, or running a hundred miles. He was into his late fifties now, but no less mean than the day his mother gave birth to him in their cramped East End mid-terrace. Some would say he was born bad, some a product of his environment. Whichever it was, he was not a man to be kept waiting.

Leon fumbled his gangly body out of the sparkling clean Range Rover, straightened his mac and headed for the Bentley. Upon reaching it, he tried for the passenger door handle; it was locked. He waited a minute, and then tried again, still locked. He knocked on the window; no reply. He hesitantly lowered his long neck down to look in through the window. Mr Granger sat there, looking straight ahead, his grey side parting the same as it had been since 1973, his black suit and tie immaculate, right down to the diamond cuff links resting on the leather steering wheel. His old, gnarled face held a scar running from his cheek to his nose, which spoke of a hands-on approach and hard-earned respect.

Leon knocked again, but to no avail. Mr Granger's steely gaze remained fixed straight ahead, his cold, glassy black eyes not moving an inch. Leon pulled his head back up and checked his watch; despite his best efforts and near-death misses; he was still four minutes late. He'd been late once before and knew exactly what Mr Granger was up to; he'd have to wait outside the car for the extra four minutes to pay his time back. He pulled a cigarette box from a crunched up packet in his jeans, then lit one up. He took a long, deep pull and blew the smoke back out into the cold November air, then he looked at his watch again. Three minutes left. He thought about getting the money out to check it over, but knew that would have landed him in an even bigger pile of mess, than the one he already stood in. Mr Granger was fanatical about the way he did business; there were rules and regulations to everything, and counting out undeclared, scruffy bank notes in public while standing next to his car, was not acceptable, not by a long shot. The rules and regulations, aided by greasing the right palms from time to time, had kept Mr Granger out of prison since 1979 and he intended on keeping it that way that. Although Mr Granger mixed with the likes of Leon, it was out of necessity rather than pleasure; it wasn't the kind of relationship Leon and Charlie had, or even Charlie and Blaze. Mr Granger could easily send one of his many henchmen out to collect the money, but he never did. He liked to show his face to all the main street dealers below him so they didn't forget who they owed it to. He would never personally drop off any product, but would always, come rain or shine, and bang on time, collect the money. Of course Mr Granger did mix in various circles for pleasure, none of which would include the likes of Leon or Charlie for that matter; he also had other legal business involving other so-called legitimate people. Most of the circles he mixed in involved funny handshakes and secret rituals, the kind of circles you were only introduced to when your bank account allowed it.

The car door softly unclicked from the inside. Leon took that as his cue to get in, and get in quickly. He flicked his cigarette into the bushes, opened the door and jumped in.

"You're late, Leon." It was a stern, East End voice, albeit with a meticulous regard for the importance of pronounced Ts. Mr Granger's face remained facing firmly forward, the cold black eyes not moving from their settled spot.

"Yeah, I know. Sorry about that, Mr Granger, the traffic, I couldn't get through, bleeding nightmare." Leon's head bowed down as he tried to explain.

"You got my paperwork, boy?"

"Yeah, it's all 'ere, Mr Granger."

Leon smiled at him, hoping to catch his gaze now and impress him with the huge envelopes of money. They amounted to a little under seventy thousand pounds.

"Stick it in the glove box then."

Leon did as he was told, adding his envelopes to several others already sitting there. He quickly closed the glove box back up, anxious not to seem like he was prying or wondering how much might be in there.

"Okay, same time next week, at next week's place," Mr Granger informed him, still looking straight ahead.

Leon had prearranged meets, car parks mostly, all

over north London, where he would meet Mr Granger each week, and god help him if he forgot.

"Okay, Mr Granger, I'll get out ya hair then. Oh, I need some more fire sticks later, I'm all out."

"Fire sticks?" Mr Granger hissed back.

"Shooters."

"Well why don't you say fucking shooters then? Don't give me all that old slang tripe!" He shook his head, keeping his eyes focused forward. "Tony will call you at three, be ready, in the right place."

"Okay. Thanks, Mr Granger."

Leon grabbed the Bentley's shiny wooden door handle, and awaited further instruction; there was none, and the gangster continued to look directly ahead. Leon opened the door, softly, as not to wake the sleeping lion from his gaze, and crept out of the car and back into the winter chill, as Mr Granger started the engine to a subtle growl. Just as he was about to close the door his name was called from inside. He froze for a moment, then leant back down and into the car. This time Mr Granger was looking directly at him, his cold black eyes locked onto his. An unnatural shiver ran down Leon's back, from his neck to his heels. He knew better than to look away, and kept the eye contact steady, remaining as visibly submissive as he could.

"Yes, Mr Granger?"

"Don't you dare be fucking late!"

He put his foot down on the automatic throttle and Leon just managed to pull his head out and close the door, before it got ripped it off.

"Old cunt," he whispered, ever so softly under his breath.

POISONED SAINTS

Mr Granger left the Brent Cross car park and headed southwest, towards Southall and his next meet, which he was now exactly four minutes late for. But, as it was to pick up another debt, he was in no hurry; they would wait for him, or they'd be sorry. He switched on the Bentley's attractive and expensive in-car sound system. Classic FM was his station of choice, it gave him a false air of aristocracy as he gently cruised about London, collecting his debts. He needed to know he was above the people below him at all times, as much as they needed to recognise their inferior station. He hummed along to the radio, as each speaker embraced the car in a 17th century composer's perfect musical prowess.

He pulled off the busy Southall high street onto a quieter side street, then immediately swung left behind the high street's bustling shops along a cramped road marked private in English, Punjabi and Arabic. He rolled the big rumbling beast of a motor along the messy alleyway, before pulling up behind a small travel agent. He honked his horn once. He looked at the car's inbuilt clock; he was exactly six minutes late but he wouldn't be made to wait as Leon had. The back door of the shop promptly swung open. A burly young Asian man exited, wearing a long white thobe under a thick, black, padded leather jacket. His bushy black beard was a good hand's length, while his moustache was shaven clean. On his shaven skull sat a black kufi. He stood a just few inches short of seven feet tall, and looked virtually the same in width, a man mountain of Allah. He tapped on the passenger window and Mr Granger wound it down.

"Mr Granger," he greeted the aging gangster in a thick, deep, Pakistani accent and then handed him another stuffed envelope to add to the collection.

"Good boy, Mohamed."

"Yes, Mr Granger, same time next week?" he smiled back.

"You got it Mohamed, and make sure you're on time."

"Ahh, I on time, Mr Granger. I believe it may be you who is late?" Mohamed dared to question back.

Mr Granger turned his head, and fixed the steely black eyes of death upon Mohamed, whose wide smile quickly dropped, and the gulp in his throat could be heard throughout the quiet Southall back streets.

"Whatever you say, Mr Granger, sir, see you then."

Mr Granger retained the stare as the window scrolled back up and then slowly pulled away up the filthy back street, crunching over a flattened pallet box and some rotten vegetables.

"Fucking kafir," Mohamed muttered into his hands, as he blew warm air into them. He turned and walked back into the travel agents, shutting and double locking the large security door behind him.

Mr Granger cruised west along the M4, eased his way into the M25 traffic, and skirted in a northerly direction around the city, on course and on time for his next destination, Chorleywood.

He hopped off the busy M25 after 40 minutes of Friday morning traffic, and twenty minutes late for his next meeting. This was of more concern to him now, as it was, in his mind, a peer and not a minion he was en route to. He glided through Chorleywood's un-

London like centre, passing a pristine cricket pitch on his right and a private girls' school on his left. Followed by a pretty, traditional red telephone box and a handful of old white ladies in expensive jackets walking small dogs. He took a sharp left down a small country lane hemmed in by thick woodland on either side, a huge contrast to Southall, which was a mere half-hour's drive away. He buzzed down his window and took a deep breath of the cold country air. *This* was England in his mind: green trees and fresh air. Although he had grown up in abject poverty, with grey concrete and black smog his daily scenery, this is what he aspired to as an old Englishman. He kept hugging the muddy edges of the country road in his half a million pound car, as it swept its way out into open fields. He put the window back up as a big horse stables came into view along with the smell it produced. He took a left onto a private gravelled road, and then passed three huge country houses on the right, before coming to the end of the road and a huge, black, metal gate. He put the window back down and pressed the entry buzzer. A thick, gravelly Russian accent answered.

"Carl? Is that you, Carl?"

"Yes, Drago, it's me. You going to open up or what?"

Mr Granger's accent affected an upper-middle class tone a million miles from his background when around his wealthy 'friends'. The words he used changed little, however.

The line went dead as the gates slowly creaked open. He drove on in, the huge white house engulfing his eyes with a sparkle as the Bentley crunched over the gravel before coming to a stop by the huge wooden main doors. The gates closed shut behind him with an aging shudder. He reached into the glove box and pulled out the last three envelopes, containing roughly £200,000. He knew exactly what should be in them, and quickly counted out ten grand, already wrapped in hundred pound stacks, and then slipped it back into the glove box. He slipped the envelopes into the satchel on his back seat and stepped out of the car, correcting his perfectly tailored suit as he did. The door of the huge mansion flew open to a crazed, smiling face, full of dark stubble, crudely complementing the slicked-back black hair. The 40-something white male at the door spread his arms out in a big welcoming gesture, revealing expensive gold jewellery under the colourful silk shirt, as he waded out onto the gravel in his black trousers and white socks.

"Carl, my friend! Good to see you again! Huh!"

"It's only been a week, Drago," Mr Granger replied, breaking into a smile for the first time that day and his arms spreading to receive Drago's hug.

He was led inside through the kitchen, where an old woman cooked, past the piano room, through the utility room, and down some stairs into a cluttered basement area, where Drago switched on the lights. He then tapped on what appeared to be a completely solid piece of concrete wall, but was infact a purpose-built hidden door which opened onto an underground bunker.

The huge mountain of a former KGB soldier, guarding the door from inside, greeted Mr Granger with a respectful nod and euro dance music seeped out from the room which had previously appeared to be concrete and earth. The guard closed the door behind them as they strolled inside.

The room was about 50 square metres in size, with a long corner, red leather couch and a huge and elaborate entertainment system which was delivering the questionable music. A small bar area sat in one corner of the room, behind which a pretty young girl stood. Another large Russian sat hunched over the bar, drinking. The walls were alternate black and solid mirror from floor to ceiling. There were two doors on each side of the room, one a bathroom, the other three bedrooms where the girls lived.

"Turn that down a bit, will you? I can't hear myself think," Mr Granger asked, as he pointed to the large stereo system.

Drago shouted something to the man at the bar in Russian, who begrudgingly did as he was told and got up to turn the music down, if only by a few notches.

"Getting old, Carl?" Drago mocked him.

"Not too old for you, sunshine," Mr Granger quipped back, as he lifted his fists up in a classic boxer's stance.

As the big Russian turned the stereo down the wall lights flickered on and off in the bunker. Mr Granger noticed one spark a little with loose electric current.

"Bit, dodgy, ain't it?" he mocked again, slamming his friend's £100,000 project.

"Fucking Polack electricians, what can I say?" the wild Russian laughed back.

The pair went and sat at the bar. The big Russian who'd previously been at the bar deferred to them and took the sofa. Mr Granger lay his brown leather satchel down on the bar and speaking his native tongue, Drago ordered the girl behind the bar to pour vodka. Her drugged eyes just about allowed her to aim the liquid into the glass. Mr Granger opened the satchel and passed Drago the envelope.

"I need more," he quickly added, before letting go of the envelope.

"Business so soon, my old friend?" Drago pulled at the envelope as he asked, passing Mr Granger his glass of vodka, in exchange for which he released the envelope.

"First we drink, then we fuck, and then we talk business, yes?" Drago insisted while raising his glass in toast.

Mr Granger gave a winked nod back in agreement, and then raised his glass. The old pair of hardened criminals downed the shots with no outward signs of distaste, and Drago signalled for them to be refilled.

"You wait to see what I have in today. Fresh to me first, before street, as always, young Albanian pussy, Carl, the finest in Eastern bloc!"

"I'll be the judge of that," Mr Granger replied as he downed his next shot with Drago.

Drago shouted at the big Russian on the couch again, who went to a button near the stereo system, and gave it a slap of his large thumb. The three bedroom doors slid open. Drago shouted some more in Russian, and then the big Russian shouted some more in Albanian, and then three, scared, underwear-clad young girls walked shakily out from their respective rooms, none of them above 18 years of age. Mr Granger immediately took a liking to a petite blonde from the far room. He stared at her with his strong black gaze. She looked down at the floor, clearly afraid, and with every reason.

"Ahh, I knew it! Always the blondes, and always the small ones!" Drago joked.

"Go ahead Carl; she's all yours. Drago's gift to you."

He pointed in her direction, as if this were his own personal possession that he'd just ordered from a catalogue, not a breathing, living, human being.

"She's clean I trust, Drago?" Mr Granger asked.

"One hundred per cent virgin, Carl. If not, your money back."

"Oh yeah? What, the whole envelope?"

The two of them burst out in laughter, knowing all four girls in the room together weren't worth a quarter of what was in the envelope.

Mr Granger downed another shot of vodka, before reaching into his jacket pocket for his mobile phone. He took it and speed dialled 4.

"Tony. Yeah, go see that darkie, Leon, will you? At three. Wants some more of the Russian dolls. Yeah, the usual place."

He quickly hung up and then immediately headed for the quivering young blonde. Her arms folded across her barely covered chest, as she tried in vain to protect her modesty.

"Carl, try not to damage this one please. She got to go on street Sunday," Drago asked of him in a semi-serious tone.

"I'm not making any promises," Mr Granger grinned, with the blackness of a thousand crows, and he pushed the small girl back into her red lamp-lit room. He hit the button by the door and it slid shut behind him.

Drago looked to the big Russian on the couch.

"Pizda," he snarled in Mr Granger's direction, using the Russian word for cunt to insult him, knowing he could not hear him from behind the soundproofed door of the young girl's temporary abode. More importantly, they could not now hear her, and her pointless screams.

3:33pm

Leon pulled up into the DIY superstore's car park just outside Edgware, where a fat, miserable Tony sat in wait. Leon spotted his small Porsche and headed over. He tapped on the window, and Tony hit the unlock button from within. Leon awkwardly manoeuvred his lanky body into the small car.

"Tell me, Tone, why a bloke as big as you has a car as small as this. It's facking ridiculass, saaan!"

Tony was an out of shape, middle-aged ex-bodybuilder who ate, drunk and sat too much. His muscle was still there, making him a huge lump of a man, but at only five foot, the extra weight he'd gained over the years of not training made him look at odds with himself. His bulky shape was somehow in direct proportion to his unhappiness and he was an even harder man to talk to than Mr Granger himself, albeit nowhere near as dangerous. A gentle giant, some might say. Mr Granger liked to keep men like Tony close to him though, as he was as loyal as a backyard dog.

"Yeah, funny, Leon. You're late. Now, how many do you want?"

Leon shook off the big man's miserable reply, as he was more than used to it. Tony was Granger's go-between for everything from pills to grass to guns.

"I need five."

"Well, I brought four."

The sombre Tony replied, without a hint of humour.

"But I need five."

"Did you tell Mr Granger you needed five?"

"No, but…"

"No buts Leon, he didn't tell me a figure. Last time you had four, so this time I brought four. Most other people of your level take twenty at a time," the moody Tony explained, trying to belittle the taller man as best he could.

"What ya want me to do, saan? Go down Brixton and set up a facking market stall or some'ing?"

Tony didn't reply; just used his fat thumb to point in the direction of the boot.

"They're the same ones I had Wednesday, yeah?" Leon asked, referring to the same batch Charlie had just that morning bought from.

Tony, again, said nothing, just gave a nod of his big head, which his four chins echoed.

"Right, I'm out. I'll see the boss next week."

With that Leon jumped, or rather, crawled out of the small car, shut the door with no goodbyes and headed for the boot. Tony popped it open from the inside; there was one carrier in the tiny boot, and Leon took a quick peek inside. Four black handguns, the same as before. He snatched up the bag and headed back to his still-running Range Rover with not a second glance back at fat Tony.

Leon headed east towards Hackney to deliver one of the guns. He made a call from his built-in hands-free kit as he did.

"Ooh dis?" the young voice answered the other end.

"It's me, Leon. I'm on the way, be at the spot, and be facking ready with the monkey."

He hung the phone up and carried on driving, trying to wedge the carrier bag full of guns under the passenger seat as he did. They wouldn't fit, so he left them in the foot well, with a worried glance. The bag contained at least a ten year sentence, and with his previous, well, it didn't bear thinking about.

He reached Hackney about half an hour later. The sun had begun to set on the autumnal evening, and he felt much safer. He pulled in behind a big high rise, where the garages were. Most were now privately owned storage or derelict. He could see the little crew of hoodies waiting in 'the spot' for him, and pulled up next to them.

Four young black males all jumped into the Range Rover at once. They all had short afro hair, loose fitting clothing, and expressions to match their bleak surroundings.

The leader of the small crew, Adrian, spoke up first.

"Dis a bad range, ya know."

"You got the monkey?" Leon asked, not wanting to waste any more time in Hackney than he had to.

"Do ya know what? I don't even know what dis manz on, wiv all dis monkey talk, is he calling one of yo'use monkey or some'ing?" Adrian laughed, fearlessly, to his friends in the back.

"A monkey, five 'undred, you little dimlow. Now

hand it over or fack off," Leon instructed.

"Oh, da dollar, blad."

The whole little crew cracked up with laughter, and Adrian reached into his baggy jeans pocket and pulled out a big ruffled-up bundle of money, which he passed to Leon.

Leon looked at the money with utter amazement.

"What the fack am I 'sposed to do with dat?"

"Whatever you want, blad. That's a fat stack though, yeah, so spend it wisely. Now where's the gat?" Adrian continued to laugh, accompanied his little cronies in the back.

Leon snatched the money from his hand, and began to count it. He pointed to the foot well as he did. Adrian saw one of the guns had rolled out of the bag in transit, and shouted to his friends. "Oh snap, blad! 'Ere it is!"

He picked up the weapon, and started pointing it sideways, American 'G' style, at his friends in the back, who all immediately rolled into balls, trying to cover their bodies any way they could, even using each other's spare limbs for protection.

Leon snapped, "What da fack you doing, ya little mug? This ain't a facking game, that's a gun, right! It kills people."

He tried his best to reassure his conscience that the boys only wanted it for interest and didn't intend on doing any harm with it, as he ruthlessly counted his money, working out what it would take off his large debt to Mr Granger.

Adrian put the gun in the lowered waist of his jeans.

"Chill, big manz, yeah? Just playing wid dese fools, ha! No one gonna get merced in ya Range, now where's da bulletz?"

"In the gun, you idiot. Like I said, it's dangerous. Now fack off, and next time you call me, have the facking money in order."

"Yeah, whatever, blad." Adrian completely disregarded what his elder had said and jumped out the 'Range'. The rest of his crew followed.

Leon shook his head, shoved the money inside his mac, and sped away as fast as he could; to eliminate any memory of what had just taken place. He was a businessman, and not a social worker, after all.

The four young black males headed off to their transport for the night, a stolen Vauxhall Vectra, all souped up with lowered suspension and an exaggerated exhaust pipe.

Adrian got in the passenger seat as he had no licence - not that it mattered in a stolen car, but he couldn't drive at all - and his friend took the wheel. The gang passed the gun around among themselves in excitement.

"That's a proper 'ting, blad!" One of the boys exclaimed from the back, as he posed for a photo on his mate's phone with it.

"Yeah, but before we start doin' what we gotta do, we need to test it works, get me?" Adrian asked from the front.

They were all in agreement, but not on a location were the 'feds' might catch them.

"Fuck it: we gotta a full tank of petrol, dat none of us paid for, a ride, dat none of us paid for, let's take a fucking road trip." Adrian figured.

"Where, blad?" The shout came impatiently from behind.

"I got a cousin, init, lives up dat motorway; I used

to go wid ma aunty. Wass the facking place called?"

He rubbed his hands through his short afro hair, and pulled his black hoodie down in frustration.

"Stambro, dat's it. Deres bare trees and woods and ting round dem parts, man, I'm telling ya."

The gang came to an agreement for a Friday night bit of fun, and as one in the back used the map app on his phone to direct them, the one in the driver's seat put his foot down and off they went.

11:00pm

After seven hours of wrong turns and service station stops, with a spot of shoplifting as they went, the gang of now highly bored youths took the junction to Stambro. Adrian tried directing the best he could but everyone was more than sick of his idea by now.

"Fack dis, blad, we been on road seven facking hours and still ain't fired dat piece," the driver announced impatiently.

He then took an impulsive and dangerous decision to turn right, with the aid of the handbrake, down a small country lane, before actually getting to Stambro. One of the rear passengers noted the small road's name,

"Facking Drivers End Lane blad, and dis manz 'andbrake turning into it! Drivers Facking End, blad!"

The whole car roared into a wave of laughter, excited again now, as the car sped up the dark, empty country road. After they'd driven for five minutes in the darkness, Adrian instructed the driver in no uncertain terms to turn 'da fack' back around, and his friend in the back to pass 'da gat'. They both did as they were told. With another dangerous handbrake turn, the driver sent them back the way they'd come. Adrian slid the top of the pistol back, loading a live round into its chamber without a care for safety. They'd all agreed on firing it out of the window while still moving, that way they stood less chance of getting caught. Adrian manually wound down his passenger side window, held the gun American gangsta style, sideways again, took aim at a road sign signalling a swerve in the road, and squeezed the trigger. The whole car roared with excitement as the gun exploded and a small plume of smoke erupted from its loading chamber, like a gunpowder firefly off into the wet night, ejecting the used casing with it, leaving it along the road somewhere.

"Dat was fucking looooud, bruv!" Adrian exclaimed with excited shock, as he looked at the clock on the dashboard and ,realised that at 11:11pm people nearby could still be up, awake, and in earshot of the blast.

"Get da fuck back to da yard, init!" someone screamed enthusiastically from the back, with the same concerns in mind.

The driver took his cue, and floored it, as the car sped off back to London.

The bullet had already missed the road sign, gone through the passing bushes, and hit the waiting Harry, as he stood relieving himself in the bushes. It had hit him square in the chest. At which point he'd manage to turn, take two steps towards his car, then fall backward, never even realising what had happened.

Death's icy grasp being quicker than his imagination for those final few seconds of his short life. Now all that was left was his limp body, as it lay there like a piece of slaughtered livestock, bleeding into the mud, awaiting Charlie's unsuspecting arrival.

CHAPTER 14

21st November 03:33pm.

Jenny had lovingly helped Jack to clear out the previously cluttered front room of his mother's house in the run-up to the funeral. Jack, unwilling at first, soon changed his mind upon delivering the first lamp and record player to a local charity shop; he felt the weight of old memories slowly lifting from his shoulders, and after that there was no stopping him.

They got rid of everything: the chairs, the record collection, the tables, the tablecloths, everything except the piano. That didn't move an inch, or the pictures that sat atop it. He wasn't trying to erase the memory of his mother or father, of course not, just to move on and into the future. He wanted only the pictures to be left after the clearout, as they brought back the happy memories, as did the piano, which he of course could never let go of; it was his soul's outlet to the universe, his means of emotional expression.

Jenny had become a much-needed rock for Jack. After getting Charlie safely locked away at the holding prison in Bedford, and then in the days leading up to his mother's funeral, she had helped him with everything, and he'd welcomed her presence and assistance. He could be as strong as an ox in an interview room, or breaking through a suspect's front door and slapping the handcuffs on, but the thought of his own mother's funeral and dealing with all the arrangements and guests, alone, had scared him to death. They had both been taking time off after the case was finished with Charlie, time to get to know each other personally, and time for him to prepare to bury his mother.

Frosty's case had been dealt with by others in the department, and he too was now awaiting trial while on remand in Bedford prison, albeit in a separate wing to Charlie; one reserved for the rapists and child molesters.

The pair had wasted no time in discussing her moving in with Jack, and how it would go down with the rest of the department. He was willing to take a transfer elsewhere if need be, and so was she. He was happy within himself for having locked Charlie up; the man they still believed was fully responsible for the murder of Harry Whittington. They had discussed the fact that some of the evidence did not slot together as perfectly as they would have liked, and how his statement and constant not guilty plea had been particularly convincing, but with no other leads on a shooter it had all pointed to him. The truth would come out in court, the jury would find him guilty or not. They had done their jobs, for now, and the satisfaction of concluding his biggest case to date was awesome.

So his immediate concern had then become the send-off of his recently departed mother in the best way he could, especially after she had died in such an unseemly manner. He hoped all the people he'd invited would turn up to the funeral and the following wake. The wake, at Jenny's recommendation, was to be held at the house, hence the de-cluttering of the front room. She had helped him to get a small catering company to provide food and drinks for the guests, and with all the necessary funeral arrangements: the obituary, the church, the flowers, everything. As a solid-minded detective, it was no big deal for her, and Jack appreciated every nanosecond of her spare time more than she would ever know. Each moment had also let him fall deeper in love with her. She had spent every night at his home since that first magical night, with each one just as magical in the bedroom as the last. Theirs was a love that had steadily built up in secret from one another, and once it was unleashed, it was completely uncontrollable, and totally unstoppable.

The funeral had gone as perfectly as Jack could have ever imagined, with all the invited guests, from Stambro, Cambridge and even Canada managing to make the journey, even at such short notice. It was a true testament to his mother's previous character, before his father's death, and the one he remembered so well now she had passed. His speech in church had brought up the sad circumstances surrounding her death briefly, but he had chosen to lighten the cause of the suicide as a show of her undying love for his father. And how now, he thought and hoped, they would at last be at peace, together and forever more. He went back into her past from there, managing to raise a smile from every guest in the large church hall, even a collective chuckle, at one point.

As her coffin was lowered into the cold, wet ground next to his father's, underneath their now combined headstone, he wondered if she had known what she was doing; if she had in fact, done exactly the right thing. She had found it impossible to move on after his father's tragic and long drawn out battle against cancer, and now she finally could. And so could he, with Jenny; so was it such a bad decision she had made after all? He still missed her dreadfully, after all it was only the previous week she had been there, but relief had gushed over him in that week. He hadn't felt quite so light as this since before his father fell ill. He pondered on this feeling and whether it was a selfish one or not, but then excused himself with suicide being equally selfish. Whichever way he added it up, he felt happy, and now remembered his mother as she had been for most of his life: a happy, caring, loving woman. Her inability to let go and move on had ruined her remaining year on the earth, and he didn't intend on doing the same, as he had many years still left in front of him with the beautiful Jenny and all that came with her: marriage, a family, a home.

They were both in the force, so he knew that the job would never be an issue as it had been before, in his earlier marriage. The future was definitely looking up for Jack. He would stick with it, and go wherever it took him, utterly convinced that wherever it was it would be good. He had been good in his mind, he had fought on the right side of the law, unlike Charlie or Frosty or the Dunns, or the now scarred for life Che or the still missing Billy. And so had Jenny. They deserved each other and their happiness together, as a reward. They both fully believed this with no doubt in their minds whatsoever, and that was where their power lay: they believed they now deserved happiness and would do everything they could to achieve it.

The wake was crowded, with extra guests turning up after the funeral. Most of the teachers from the school his father had taught at, all knowing his mother well, were there in proud attendance. DCI Brent had come, along with DC Barry Trump and others from the Beds & Herts Major Crime Unit. Jack was overwhelmed by the support and fought hard to hold back the tears. He was kept strong by Jenny the whole time. The rest of their department hadn't batted an eyelid at their now obvious relationship, as if they had all already known, and moreover, seemed happy for the pair.

Jack, at Jenny's prompting, decided to perform a song on the piano for the unsuspecting guests. The suggestion was well received, and various guests encouraged him with pats on the back and warm words in his ear as he made his way to the old piano and friend.

As he pulled the stool up and sat in his classically trained position, the room seemed impressed; especially those from his department. Jack had always kept his piano playing a great secret, as if it somehow signified weakness within him. But now he focused on what he was doing and forgot the room was watching. He looked to the untouched sheet music which lay in front of him. *Chopin's, Piano Sonata No.2 In B Flat*

Minor, Op. 35, "Funeral March" - 3. Marche Funèbre.

The instant memory of the last time, and previous times that year, he had played it to his mother hit him hard and suddenly, like a clenched fist to the gut. Yet he didn't bother to look for something else; it was a funeral after all. Noticing his suddenly more sombre appearance, DC Barry Trump brought him over a glass of iced whiskey and whispered in his ear, "Take this Jack. For the nerves, mate."

His kind, flabby, bald head was tilted as he looked down at Jack, welcoming glass in hand, and smiled. Jack debated necking the mind-numbing drink in one swift move, for a short moment, but then politely refused. He hadn't touched a drink all day, or the past few days in fact and had even thrown his cigarettes out; partly at Jenny's gentle request and partly at his sudden awareness of the cancer wrapped up in each and every one, and of how his father had perished at the cruel disease's spiteful hands. He could do it alone; he would do it alone. DC Trump backed off, as Jack laid his fingers gently on the keys, straightened his back and prepared to play. The whole house now buzzed with anticipation.

His eyes scanned the first few notes needlessly as he'd played them a hundred times before. His eyes then connected with his brain; his brain ignited his soul; which then sent waves down his arms, through his hands and into his fingers, as they gently stroked the awaiting keys. The first lonely and forlorn notes swept throughout the quiet house, like his mother's depressed ghost sweeping past each and every one of its guests, clutching at their quiet throats with her icy, firm grip. He continued, with fervour, as his fingers lashed down like black rain upon the pure white keys.

The sonata built and rose with a distressed grey depth, and the intensity of the opening piece was strewn across his face like a splattering of dark grey clouds, as it covered the room, the house, in a thick plume of glacial fog. He looked up to the pictures as he played, sitting neatly on the piano top; then suddenly was overcome by a reassuring warmth which flooded inwards through his eyes, as his mother and father smiled back at him. The piece suddenly lifted; the clouds, the fog, the ice, the ghosts, the despair along with it, the melody rose to an audacious high! But then, violently back down for a short, dark while, back into the murky depths of depression once more. Voices stayed silent, eyes affixed on the pianist, as the composition swiftly lifted again. And then he dared to rearrange Chopin's masterpiece, as he wandered boldly straight into the second third of the song, prancing past any more darkness with the lightness of air at his fingertips, and retaining the lucidity of a single, unbroken piece. The darkness had gone, and now the sun rose, as the piano's tired old strings produced a shimmering beauty of ice-melting light. The guests stood in awe as the pianist shed a tear of pure joy. His mother's ghost released her grip and pronounced her blazing smile to the room, to the world, to the universe, as one, and so did he. So did he.

CHAPTER 15

21st December 2012 12:11pm.

Charlie sat at the small desk, in his cramped, shared cell inside HM Prison Woodhill, a category A prison in Buckinghamshire only one county over from his own. He was working his way happily through a return letter. His roommate Sohan, lay idly up on the top bunk reading, with great concentration, a daily tabloid. As it was a Friday, association was from 1:05pm-5:30pm. So he was madly scribbling his reply down to get it finished in time so he could then get the letter sent off as soon as he was let out of his cell, where he'd been locked since 6:45pm the night before. He fidgeted about on his metal-framed wooden seat as he scribbled, moving from one buttock to another, as each one in turn went numb. The rank smells of old urine wafted up his nostrils from the slightly sectioned-off shared toilet next to the desk. Other than that, there was a TV, which the pair rented for a pound a week, a small FM/AM radio, and also a small white wooden shelf lined with a few old books. There were a couple borrowed from the prison library that Charlie had started, but not finished, fiction mainly. Sohan had an old copy of *The Guru Granth Sahib*, as he was a Sikh and away from his home in the Punjab, northern India, this was a prized possession worth dying for. The newest addition to the shelf though, was a book Charlie had received yesterday morning with the letter he was now replying to: *Teachings of The Buddha.*

Dear Hayley,

I was so glad when I received your letter yesterday morning, not sure who gave you my address in here, but thank them for me. I'm doing okay, the sentence you heard was right, 10 years, 5 for a gun they found and 5 for the drugs, to run consecutively. But, with good behaviour, I could be out in 4, as I already spent a year on remand, which isn't too bad, compared to some of the others in here. I'll probably be on licence for 5 years when I get out, which means no leaving the country, which is a shame, cos as you know, I wanted to get out with my Mum and Dad in Spain ASAP. They are doing okay though yeah, thanks for asking, they managed to find the money for the bar, although I haven't got a clue where from...

Charlie paused; he knew all the letters would be checked before being sent off.

He had found out from an illegal phone call that Billy had kept to his word and given Charlie's share of the money to his parents in Spain, and then kept on running somewhere else. He was now on the run because his flat had been raided on Jack's instruction the day after Charlie was arrested. All the obvious paraphernalia had been found, which would have landed him a good few years within the same walls Charlie currently stared at every day, especially with all his previous convictions. But luckily he wasn't there when they came, and neither was the money.

Charlie had guessed, correctly, the raid was made on the strength of Knighty's information, which Knighty had later backed out of giving in court, but he had no real way of knowing. But what he did know was that Billy was free, and running somewhere, with enough money to keep him happy for a long, long time. He'd also made sure Che's money had got to his mother before he left, again a sizeable amount. Sizeable enough that Che had opened a small shop in Stambro town centre selling all sorts of weird and wonderful hippy exotics, from crystals to rolling machines, and still had enough left over. Che was one of the few who still came to visit Charlie regularly, and he was continually grateful for this, Knighty on the other hand had vanished and had not been seen or heard of for some time. A rumour flew about Stambro that he was living in Birmingham, working with a dirty little gang doing smash and grab jobs on cash machines, but again it was all hearsay. Billy had divided Knighty's share of the money between the remaining three when he had vanished.

...But yeah, they're making good over there. You could go and visit if you'd like? With Hitten, they could pay; I've told them all about you.

I'm so glad you found it in your heart to forgive me Hayley. As you say, I was very confused at the time and not really aware of the repercussions of what I was doing, but, I'm glad you also see, I did what I did, out of love for you, wrong or right. Yes, I did hear about Lee, and yes I was happy to hear he got life, apparently he was gonna be in here, but got moved when he heard I was here, but I don't know if that's true or not. I heard he was in Bellmarsh now, I also heard his kind don't have a great time of it in there. That may please you, but then again I don't know, from what I've been reading in the book I got from you yesterday, which I've read a lot of in the past 24hrs. I've found it very interesting, and I am sure willing to try this way of life, it does make sense to me, it didn't when we first met, but my situation is very different now, I have nothing material surrounding me that's really mine, only my thoughts, and that book did seem to ease a lot of my thoughts. I hope I can learn a lot more from it. Hopefully I am serving my Karma in here now, and will not come back as a cockroach in my next life? Haha. What I do know is I'm done with that old life, for good, and no, I'm not writing this for the benefit of the prison officer vetting this (hello by the way, hope you're enjoying the read), that's the truth, I'm done with crime.

Charlie wasn't being one hundred per cent truthful there, as he planned to break the conditions of his licence and leave for Spain as soon as he was released, but the old life he was referring to - drug dealing, violence - was now done with for good. That much he now knew for sure.

Yes it was good, by the way, to get off the murder charge, of course. But deep down I knew I would, as I knew I was innocent, I was never in any doubt I would go free of that, that may sound weird with all the evidence stacked heavily in my odds, but I just knew. Luckily the jury did too. The Judge did his best with this sentence though, that I'm currently serving, they could have ran concurrently, my two different offences, which would have meant 5 years in total, but he chose against that. I'm fairly sure at the prompting of that detective, Cloud, he was there throughout the whole trial, never missed a day, him and his girlfriend, the blonde one, dunno if you read about any of it in the papers, they were mentioned, and even pictured, a lot, good for them, bad for me. You should have seen his face when I got off the murder charge though; it was a picture, I can tell you.

The thing that still bothers me about the whole thing though; Harry's killer is still running around out there somewhere, free as a bird. I heard a shell casing, which matched the bullet that killed Harry, was found by some bloke walking his dog, along the road behind the field, and Cloud has said he would find the killer, in an interview, but as far as I know, he hasn't yet. This was only in the last couple of weeks though, so who knows, surely there was fingerprints on the casing?? I'll leave that to the professionals though! I hope I'm not waffling on too much about me and my own problems here? Just trying to answer all the questions you asked.

This prison is okay, it's category A, which is maximum security, as apparently I'm high risk at the minute, but I haven't been here long since my sentencing, so hopefully next year I can get downgraded to category B. You get a lot more in cat B. There's some right loonies in here though. There's even a special wing which is called the close supervision centre, it holds some of the worst prisoners in the country, nice, I know. But yeah, I'm safe and well; I just keep my head down, go to the gym, have a kick about sometimes in the yard, and read. I'm hoping to get a job in here, they don't pay much, but it gets you out of your cell for a bit, you can also do courses and that, but I don't know if I'll bother with any of them, although there is a cookery class, could be good for when I eventually get to Spain, so I may do that. Yes, I do have a cell mate, his name is Sohan Singh, he got 20 years for trying to smuggle 2 kilos of heroin into the country from Pakistan.

I feel for him, he's a lovely bloke, not your typical criminal. He's from a little village in northern India, in the Punjab, that's where this Pakistani mob got a hold of him, and took him over to their side, promising him a good job; he did it to help his father get an operation on his cataracts, apparently quite expensive treatment where he's from. Everyone in here has a sob story, and most of them aren't actually guilty, apparently, but Sohan's is quite genuine, I don't think he really had any idea of what he was getting involved in. His family in India have now all disowned him, although he was trying to help them. But yeah, he has no one, no visits, no letters, nothing. He keeps his chin up though, somehow, he's a Sikh, and I know it's not the same as Buddhism as they have a god and stuff, but is quite similar; he doesn't eat any meat, a right pain for the canteen staff! There are a few vegetarians in here though weirdly. But yeah, I think his religion helps him a lot, he's got a book on the shelf he reads a lot, it's not in English, so I haven't got a clue what it's about, but he has explained a few things, and it sounds quite cool. It helps him as I say, so that can't be bad, can it?

There's a few Islamic fundamentalists in here too, on terrorism charges, all serving life at the minute with no chance of parole, I had a chat with one of them the other week, but they're on another level all together, he told me I would go to hell or something like that, if I didn't follow the Quran, I've tried to avoid him since, as interesting as he was.

Your book definitely makes the most sense to me so far, I have to say, but I guess that's a personal choice isn't it? And we should all be allowed that choice? Everyone needs something to get them through in here though I know that; there was a suicide, two weeks before I got here! Some eastern European bloke, they found him hanging one morning, stunk apparently, again, nice, I know. That road certainly ain't for me.

Apparently he was serving life again though, with no chance of parole, I don't know what for.

The hardest thing in here for me, is not being able to do what I want, when I want, being at another man's command, I struggle with that a lot, but I'm slowly coming round to it, I have to. We have a TV in here, but Sohan doesn't understand a lot of it, and most of its crap anyway, I pay his half for it, as he has nothing like I say, and it keeps us amused for an hour or so at night, that Big Brother rubbish just finished. Did you watch any of it? They're celebrities, apparently? And they wonder why we have so many problems in this country! I help him with other things when I can too, although he doesn't want much, just a paper every day, he likes practicing his English with them. He's almost cute! Don't worry, I'm not turning. He doesn't smoke either, luckily, as I've given that up too...

Charlie paused again. At that moment, he wanted to tell Hayley all about the fact you could get any drug you liked in prison, and how he had declined every offer, and was now as clean as a whistle. It was something which he was very proud of, but he knew the letter censor wouldn't be too happy with that information being sent out, and might just toss his letter in the bin because of it. He couldn't risk it not getting to Hayley; he'd waited over a year to hear anything from her and didn't want a silly mistake like that ruining his chance to reply.

...So that's good, our cell is nice and clean. I'm free from any unnatural substances, and intend on keeping it that way. I feel, honestly, so embarrassed, about the mess I was in when we met, but I guess, as your letter said, you saw the good in me,. I'm so glad about that Hayley, I really am. And I really hope you believe me when I tell you I'm done with all that old life

now. I don't know if there's any future for me and you, as you didn't really say anything on this issue in your letter, but I'd love it if there was, even just as friends, but again, I completely understand if that was your one and only letter to me, but I hope not. Your letter made my whole year, and that's no exaggeration.

I constantly think about that week and the time we spent together, and not for all the madness that went on, but the special times I had with you, although there wasn't many, they equal much more than anything else I've ever had before. I hope I'm not sounding like a crazy stalker! But I've been waiting to tell you this for so long. I didn't want to try and get in contact with you, because of what happened that night, I know you said you forgave me, and don't blame me, but I felt so guilty, for such a long time.

I'm so glad Hitten is doing okay too, and he got all that free help from the NHS, at least that's one thing this country is good for! I'm glad you still have that job you love, too, it's important to be happy in your work and it doesn't matter how much you earn either, you shouldn't worry about that, as long as you're happy, and Hitten is taken care of, that's the most important thing. I'm sure you know all that anyway, and was just letting off steam about your wages, which is fine; you can send as many letters to me, letting off as much steam as you want. I read your letter about 12 times yesterday! Sohan thought I was losing the plot.

So how is everything else out there? If you ever needed any help with money, my parents could help you, they have plenty, and I know they would do that for me...

Charlie obviously couldn't mention in the letter that the money was his, and that it amounted to thousands of pounds, not least because the crown prosecution had seized everything else he owned when he had pled guilty to supplying class A drugs: his flat, everything in it, and his car. He didn't want them getting his hands on what was in Spain, as he was sure they could if they found out.

...so don't be afraid to ask. I hope that doesn't sound too patronising, as I don't mean it to, but the offers there. I knew you were special the night I met you Alice Liddell (LOL), and haven't stopped thinking about you since. Even when I was sure there was no future for you and me, and you'd never forgive my part in what happened, I still got this warm feeling inside when I thought of you, and it's no less warm now, writing this letter. I'm not saying there is a future now, as I said before, I'm easy with whatever you want, and as much time as you want, that's one thing I have plenty of at the minute. But, obviously, I would like, more than anything in the world, even my freedom from here, to be a part of your life, and Hittens.

I think it's safe to say, I love you, Hayley, and always will,

I look forward to hearing back from you,

All my Love,

Charlie xxxxx

He folded the letter in half, then in half again, and slipped it inside the return addressed envelope Hayley had included with her letter. He gave it a quick sniff to see if he could smell any of her scent on it: his heart told him he could, but his brain disagreed.

"Vat you do, Charlie, All finish?" Sohan asked happily, in his high-pitched, broken English, full of optimism from up on his top bunk.

"Yeah, all done, mate," Charlie smiled up to him, screeching the metal chair around on the concrete floor to face him. "What time is it?"

Sohan looked to the cheap watch hanging off of his skinny wrist; another treat Charlie had managed to obtain for him, as he didn't like to wear watches himself, what with the germs they might transmit to his hands.

"Five to vun o clock."

Sohan grinned back down at him, knowing it was nearly time to get a fresh paper for the day.

He was a short, amazingly thin man in his late thirties, who had the innocence of a small child about him. He had a neat black haircut and rotten teeth, with pockmarks in his dark skin from acne as a young Indian teenager who had masturbated over too much Bollywood and drank too much fizzy cola, all by his own admission. That was another daily treat Charlie liked to help him with: a can of sugary, cold Coca Cola. It was something he always avoided himself, as it didn't fit in with his fitness regime down the gym. He felt the regime kept his body in shape and, more importantly, his mind. Sohan, on the other hand, never worked out and drank Coke every day, but was still as a skinny as a daisy's stem. Charlie often teased him about his size, especially as he had bulked up quite a bit himself since being incarcerated. Sohan always blamed his meagre size on his digestion problems, which he suffered with badly. The prison gave him all the help they could with this, and he took full advantage of the doctor's visits, once every two weeks, but to no avail. He constantly had pieces of tissue paper stuffed into his ears, as his stomach acid affected them too apparently, and was also going to the prison dentist once a week with complaints about his rotten teeth, which he also blamed on the acid. He had claimed to Charlie, on various occasions, that he never had these digestion problems in his village in India, where the air was cleaner, and so was the food. Charlie had no evidence to prove him otherwise, and while he had natural doubt about his claims, having never ventured further than Spain he had to take him at his word. He had horrible visions of poverty and malnutrition in India, and blamed all Sohan's problems on that in his mind, but kept them there and never let on what he thought to Sohan. He just let him complain whenever he wanted and agreed with him every time. Sohan would do the same for him, as his previous cell mate in Bedford had also; they became each other's own personal agony aunts.

"Vou know, vou read this, Charlie?"

Sohan pointed to a headline about midway through his daily paper.

"No, what is it, mate?" Charlie replied, not bothering to look properly as he knew Sohan would read it aloud to him anyway as practice, even if he had read it previously himself.

"They find a burnt-out... bunker complex... in north London!" Sohan informed him excitedly, pausing periodically to be sure he was pronouncing the words correctly.."Apparently, every vun dead inside, some kind of Ru, Ru, Russian mafia," Sohan always struggled to roll the Rs off his tongue when speaking in English. "They vere, it says here, keeping voman from all across east Europe.. locked in small dungeons. Very, very bad men, no?"

"Pure evil, Sohan. Scum of the earth."

Sohan looked down at him, a little bemused, as he

was a lot of the time, this time trying to work out what scum of the earth meant, but then continued on, "They keep tree voman there, at vun time!"

Sohan helped what he was saying with the aid of his free hand's pinched fingers, flying around in objection. "All these voman now dead, of course, but, they say, many more out on street, vorking!"

He looked at Charlie in disgust. "Big problem for beautiful England, is it no?

"Yes, mate. No good at all," Charlie replied, not really paying attention, just wanting to go and post his letter as the cells had now been unlocked for association.

"But, vun good ting, Charlie: the Mafia men, they die inside also."

"Oh well, at least that's something, but I'm sure someone will fill their boots soon enough," Charlie replied pessimistically.

"Boots? Vat you say boots? Someone steal their boots? Why, Charlie, why?" Sohan relied, completely confused now.

"No, not steal, fill," Charlie tried to explain, but quickly gave up, and just urged Sohan to continue on.

He then made his way to the sink to wash his hands before leaving the cell, putting the letter down on the side as he did.

"Also, they find vun English man, dead also, from thee burnings. Some rich business mans, and millionaire they say, with ties to tha London… underworld. Bloody bastards, Charlie."

"So, apart from the dead girls, it's no bad thing then really?" Charlie replied, as he turned on the taps.

"Dead girls always bad thing, Charlie!" Sohan replied, from the moral high ground of the upper bunk, once again misunderstanding him.

Charlie rinsed his hands with clean water and soap, noticing as he did how he hadn't scrubbed at them like a mad man. For the first time in years, he felt able to simply wash his hands like a normal person. He smiled with private joy up to Sohan.

"Listen, I didn't mean that, Look, never mind, I gotta go get your paper and send my letter, 'in I? I'll be back in a bit."

"Okay Charlie, vould you mind get me a coke also?"

"Don't I every day?" Charlie questioned him back, smiling warmly, as he headed for the cell door, picking up the letter tightly in his dry hands as he did.

Sohan thanked him with sincere and humbling gratitude, as he did every day, and Charlie brushed it off, as he did every day. Just as he was almost out the cell door, a scrawny young man in his mid-twenties, about five foot in height, with greasy brown hair and a face full of blackheads, stepped into his path.

"You're Charlie, init?"

The white male asked of him, twitching his eyes as he did, clearly clucking for a fix of either heroin or crack cocaine. A lot of the other young men with long sentences were; it was their only means of escaping what lay ahead of them.

"Yeah, I'm Charlie. Who are you, and what do you want?" he replied, impatiently. "I'm in a bit of a rush." He looked down to his letter as he replied.

"Don't worry bruv, nuff association time today, init," the weary young addict replied, the spittle gathering at each side of his mouth now.

"Yeah, I guess so." Charlie sighed in reply, used to men like this by now; they'd heard Charlie was a drug dealer on the outside and tried their luck with him on the inside, to see if he'd taken his work in there with him.

"Listen, I don't have any gear, okay? Nothing, so you're wasting your time," Charlie tried to explain.

"Nah matey, dis ain't bout gear. I got plenty gear coming my way, truss," he replied, getting more and more agitated by the second.

"Well, what is it then?" Charlie asked, confused and becoming angry. He racked his brains at what the hollow-eyed fiend might want, and why he wasting his precious time and keeping him from his long awaited reconnection with Hayley.

"You know Blaze, init?"

"Blaze?" Charlie questioned back, as Sohan watched on curiously from his bunk.

A vision of the ginger steroid freak then popped up, unwanted, in Charlie's head.

He had heard, a while back, through the prison grapevine, how Blaze had got into bed with the Dunns, shortly after being attacked by him with the cosh, and was now running the Crowley estate's flow of drugs for them as they picked their way through Charlie's dismantled empire. Some say he even slotted into Frosty's place with the Dunns, and was now with them at all times, as he had been at the end, with his head buried firmly up their backsides.

"Listen, I don't give a fuck about Blaze and what he's up to, right? He can do what he wants in Crowley, I'm done with that bollocks," Charlie informed the young druggy, trying to push him out the way and get on with his day.

But he would not move. He just stood firm, jittering like a trapped cat up a tree now.

"Yeah, well listen to me, I don't give a fuck about Blaze either, init."

"So what d'you want then?"

Charlie gritted his teeth in frustration and impatience, as he looked across to the big mechanical clock on other side of the wing: 1:11pm.

"He paid me, blad, to give you a message."

Before Charlie could ask what the message was, he felt the sharp steel rip into his guts. He looked down, and saw the smack-head's muddy hands quickly pull a prison shank out of his body and plunge it back into another part of his bleeding stomach.

Charlie's first instinct was to grab his stomach and stop the blood pouring, but as he did, he dropped the letter. He bent down to grab it, and as he tried to pick it up, the shank found its way in and out of his neck. He fell immediately back onto the cold cell floor as the pain shot its way down his body, lighting fast and white hot. The clucking young addict laughed nonchalantly and ran back down the hallway to spend all his hard-earned money from Blaze on a few bags of repulsive brown heroin.

The blood gushed out of Charlie's neck and stomach and Sohan jumped down to help him, screaming at the top of his voice as he did, "Guard! Guard! Come quick!"

Charlie wriggled around on the cell floor, overtaken by complete pain and anguish, not knowing whether to hold his stomach or neck as the blood continued to flow swiftly from both. Sohan ripped his small jumper off and joined in Charlie's attempts to stop the flow, crying wildly now as he exposed his thin body to the cold December day and pushed the thick piece of prison wool hard against Charlie's stomach.

"The button," Charlie managed to instruct him, as the blood found its way out of his mouth through gritted teeth and hurriedly, as if in a panic to escape, down his trembling chin. He lifted his shaking arm from his soaking red stomach and pointed to the call button on the cell wall. Sohan, with a sudden realisation of what he should have already done, ran quickly to it, then begun banging at it, manically, over and over.

"Guard! Guard! he cried as he banged.

Charlie then noticed the crimson liquid all over his hands, which took his attention off the throbbing wounds, as they numbed in shock. He begun to rub his hands on his jeans, like back in the interview room, attempting to wipe the blood clean, his OCD kicking back in with a chilling vengeance. Yet the more he rubbed, the more the blood spread, in between his fingers, under his fingernails, through the lines in his palms, and down his wrists into his sweater's tight, itchy sleeves. He looked at them with an undiluted horror, the fury of a thousand vicious nightmares engulfing his quivering face with terror. The blood, the thick, sticky red blood, flowed from his body like a swelled river bursting its banks, and all over the clean cell floor. His haunted eyes followed its flow as his neck gave way with sheer weakness and his head hit the concrete. The river ran hurriedly, like a spilt glass of summer wine, towards the letter which still sat in the doorway. With all his remaining energy Charlie went for the letter. He managed to grab it in his blood-filled hand, but as he pulled it towards him, his body fell flat, as did his face, as did his arm, as did the letter, into the pool of warm goo. He lay face down, one eye engulfed in blood, one still twitching open, as he slowly pulled the letter through the thick spillage toward him.

But the more he pulled, the more the now soaked envelope fell apart, until he could see the paper and his words. He pulled them out and into his clenched fist, as the blood and ink mixed together, creating a haemorrhage of words that would never be told and feelings that would never be shared. A solitary, salty ball of tearing torture rolled from his open eye and down into the lake of gore beneath him. The lid of the eye that had released it slowly closed shut, then flicked open again; the light to his soul now dancing like a broken lamp. His final bit of strength escaped his body through his clenched fist, as it, and the claret-soaked paper fell mercifully into the swamp of his burgundy grave.

His eyelid remained the only moving part of him now, as it flicked shut, then open, then shut, then open.

The guards finally came rushing into the cell, one of them slipping over in the gooey mess, and crashing hard onto the solid concrete. Sohan's eyes streamed like a tear-gassed Palestinian innocent at the horror which unfolded in front of him.

Charlie's eye glassed over and his pupil dilated like a black flying saucer, ready to take off and leave his now shattered earth for good. Yet still, somehow, it managed to hold on a moment longer, fixing itself firmly upon the ruined words.

His entire failing being flowed through that one remaining eye as it reached out, hopelessly, for the muddled letters which dripped black ink down the sodden red page, and then, accompanied by one huge

gulp of air from his blood-curdled mouth, it closed.
☐

THE END

POISONED SAINTS

ABOUT THE AUTHOR

Ben Coulter was born in 1980 and raised in Letchworth Garden City, Hertfordshire. He has been writing 'as long as he can remember' in one form or another. His first book 'Poisoned Saints' was released in 2012 to a pleasing response. Poisoned Saints is the first part of a three part series, the follow up to Poisoned Saints, 'Keep on Running' and the final installment 'When The Saint Comes Marching Home' will both be available in 2013.

Printed in Great Britain
by Amazon.co.uk, Ltd.,
Marston Gate.